THE LEAPING SONG

THE
LEAPING
SONG

STEPHANIE
PLOWMAN

THE BODLEY HEAD
LONDON SYDNEY
TORONTO

For S and M,
who constantly assisted
according to the French meaning of
the word, if not always in
the English sense

© Stephanie Plowman 1976
Maps © The Bodley Head 1976
ISBN 0 370 11014 5
Printed in Great Britain for
The Bodley Head Ltd
9 Bow Street, London WC2E 7AL
by Redwood Burn Ltd
Trowbridge and Esher
Set in Monotype Imprint
by Gloucester Typesetting Co Ltd
First published 1976

ACKNOWLEDGMENTS

Thanks are due to the following for permission to quote copyright material: The Oxford University Press for poems on pages 145-147 from *The Oxford Book of Greek Verse in Translation* edited by T. F. Higham and C. M. Bowra; George Allen & Unwin Ltd. for two extracts from *The Persians* by Aeschylus, translated by Gilbert Murray, on pages 142-3 and 263, and two from *The Suppliant Women* by Aeschylus, translated by Gilbert Murray, on pages 90 and 75; Penguin Books Ltd. for two quotations from *The Histories* by Herodotus, translated by Aubrey de Selincourt, on pages 121 and 127.

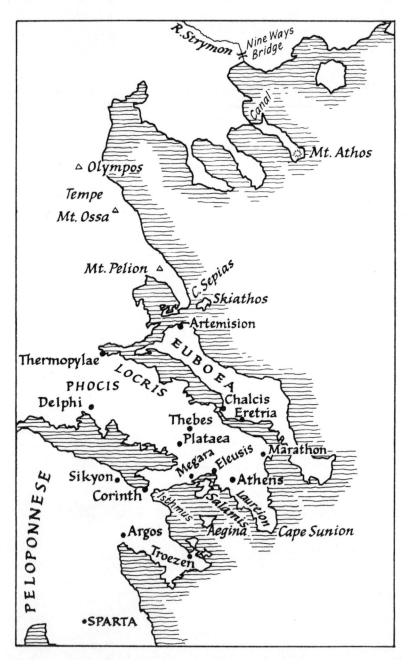

Greece at the time of Xerxes' invasion

THE LEAPING SONG

'. . . then was borne
A sound across the sea, a voice, a strong
Clamour exultant like a leaping song,
And Echo answering from the island rock
Cried battle.'

Aeschylus: *The Persians*
TRANSLATED BY GILBERT MURRAY

'. . . Persia, a nation that covered
as much territory as the United States –
attempted to conquer Greece,
a land smaller than New York State.'

Lionel Casson: *Ancient Mariners*

The Family of Theron

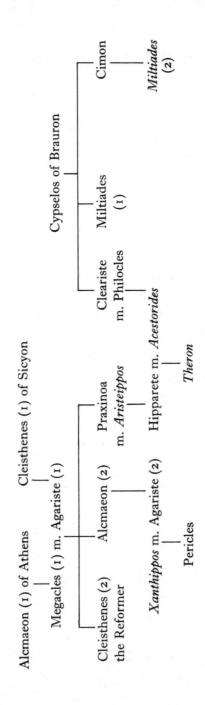

Alcmaeon (1) of Athens

Cleisthenes (1) of Sicyon

Megacles (1) m. Agariste (1)

Cleisthenes (2) the Reformer

Alcmaeon (2)

Praxinoa m. *Aristeippos*

Hipparete m. *Acestorides*

Theron

Xanthippos m. Agariste (2)

Pericles

Cypselos of Brauron

Cleariste m. Philocles

Miltiades (1)

Cimon

Miltiades (2)

Names in italics denote characters appearing in the story

Prologue

To be a living, walking symbol of failed alliance – two kinds of failed alliance – is not particularly pleasant.

My mother had died when I was still too small to remember much about her. My father never cared much for her. If he had, although at first it would have given him pain that I, by all accounts, resembled her so closely in face and manner, that resemblance would not have given him cause for increasing anger as I grew older – 'Sitting there saying never a word, but staring at me with her damned grey eyes!' he would shout. It had been a politically motivated marriage, as was common at the time, when the great families of Athens still made matrimonial alliances with the idea of ruling the state in the future; here a niece of Cleisthenes the Alcmaeonid had been married off to the nephew of the elder Miltiades, who had left Athens to rule the Thracian Chersonese,* but within months the two families had fallen out for good, and the only lasting result of that utterly unsuccessful power-bid was myself.

There is a pretty story concerning Great-Uncle Miltiades' departure for the Chersonese. He responded, it appears, to a call from the gods: a tribe of Thracians living in that area, having trouble with their neighbours, sent a delegation to Delphi to get advice from Apollo's oracle. They were told to offer the government of their people to the first person who offered them hospitality after leaving the temple. Leaving Delphi, they marched along the Sacred Road through Phocis and Boeotia to Athens. Not a single individual had made them welcome. (One can, of course, excuse the Phocian and Boeotian inhospitality; however kindly one's instincts, to take a band of armed Thracians into one's home also demanded a degree of foolhardiness.) When

* The European side of the Gallipoli Peninsula.

9

they reached Athens, they tramped by the house of Uncle Miltiades while he himself was sitting outside it. Seeing them, he invited them inside as his guests; they immediately acclaimed him as the man destined by the oracle to be their ruler.

It is a pretty story, as I said, but no more than that. In the first place, it is completely out of character so far as my great-uncle was concerned. Like other members of the family, he was a domineering aristocrat, not in the habit of sitting outside his house, offering passing strangers, particularly footsore and hungry Thracians, the freedom of his hearth and home. Bonhomie, particularly towards social inferiors, had never been one of his pronounced characteristics. In the unlikely eventuality of his inviting a band of barbarians into his home, he would have curtly directed them towards the stables, and, even there, they would have had to queue up for the straw not needed as bedding for his prize horses. (He had won the four-horse chariot race at Olympia. So, three times running, had his younger brother, Cimon, whose hippomania was matched only by his atrocious stupidity. In his will he said that if he predeceased the four mares who'd won him so much glory, they, when their time came, were to be buried in graves opposite his, and gave elaborate instructions as to their interment. He made no such careful arrangements for the bestowal of his wife.)

But to revert to the more intelligent of my two great-uncles, I have no doubt that the whole oracular business was another example of the rigging that goes on at Delphi. We were still being ruled by tyrants in Athens at the time and Peisistratos wanted to get rid of a recalcitrant aristocrat. And why should the leader of one of the chief aristocratic clans in Athens go off to the scarcely congenial society of brigands, whose religion is more Asiatic than Greek, with occasional human sacrifice, and who tattoo their bodies and those of their women? (Some Greek settlers in the area have actually taken wives from Thracian families, but scarcely, one would think, with real enthusiasm, particularly if their patterned brides had strong religious convictions. Raging Thracian women, after all, tore Orpheus to pieces.) Because Great-Uncle Miltiades, like so many of those who rail against tyranny, was only too keen to practise his own kind of tyranny if given the chance. So off he sailed for the Chersonese at the head of a band of Athenian colonists.

As the ability to maintain Olympic winning teams would indicate, Miltiades' family was wealthy as well as nobly born. It claimed descent from Aeacos of Aegina, son of Zeus, and, after his own decease, judge of the dead. No doubt such descent contributed to a degree of unscrupulousness exhibited pretty often by members of the clan; fortified by the knowledge that an ancestor is one of the judges of the dead, you feel there is less need for niceness of conduct on your part. My paternal grandfather, who married the sister of Miltiades and Cimon, wasn't badly off, but twenty acres of vineyard and seventy-five of cornland wouldn't come anywhere near providing the wherewithal for the upkeep of a four-horse chariot. He was, from all accounts, a quiet fellow, who died after enduring four years of matrimonial tyranny. After this my father, the only child of the marriage, was swept off by my grandmother to her old home, and encouraged to think of himself as the product of parthenogenesis.

In the Chersonese, Great-Uncle Miltiades ruled as despot; in Athens his namesake, the younger son of Cimon, established his more subtle form of tyranny over my father, Acestorides, so skilfully that the slave never comprehended his subjection. This was so profound that it survived even the tyrant's absence over a period of many years. For when Great-Uncle Miltiades died, his elder nephew and successor, Stesagoras, did not last for long. He was as stupid as his father had been; the only Thracians he had known before going to the Chersonese had been scullery-boys and so on; it never occurred to him that as free men in their own territory they might be more formidable propositions. So he was hit on the head with a chopper one day when he sat in the Council Chamber. One might expect the Thracians to have had enough of the family, but they were a superstitious set, and nervously recalled the oracle's bidding. They therefore invited the younger Miltiades to come to rule them.

A few months before, he would not have considered the invitation; a hatchet lodged in a predecessor's skull, is, after all, scarcely the best augury for a warm welcome. But his father had recently died, waylaid by a gang on his way home one night and left dead in the street. General opinion was that the gang had carried out orders given by Hippias and Hipparchos, Peisistratos' sons, who had succeeded their father as tyrants in Athens. Miltiades' position, in fact, neatly illustrated the proverb *In front the cliff edge, behind the wolf pack*. On the whole he felt he could handle the Thracians more easily, so to the Chersonese he went. And made himself master. He hired five hundred mercenaries, he married the daughter of a native king. Presumably she was one of the tattooed ladies of Thrace.

But he mistimed things badly by setting himself up as a tyrant, just at the moment that Athens, through the actions of Cleisthenes the Alcmaeonid, was becoming a democracy. Probably, of course, he did not think that democracy would last; he accepted the repeated assurances in my father's letters that this new government by the people was only a transient thing. 'Apes in purple don't last,' said Father. And even if Miltiades reflected that possibly his cousin's views were coloured by the fact that Cleisthenes, who had betrayed his class by breaking the privileged position of the nobles, was also the uncle of Acestorides' unprized wife, most of the other Athenian nobles echoed that the new state of things could not continue; unthinkable that power and privilege, instead of coming to you simply because you were born into the right family, should now depend on such vulgar qualities as merit. So Father, and other friends, kept assuring Miltiades that it was only a matter of time before the good old days returned, when the ordinary people were a lump of political inertia, meekly accepting as masters whichever aristocratic faction came out on top. 'The good old days,' that phrase often on the lips of Father and his cronies, was echoed from the Chersonese. But whether Miltiades meant by it a return to the free-for-all among the nobles, or that more recent development, tyranny, no one can say. Remember he himself was a tyrant in the Chersonese. And a man rarely grows more liberal with age.

And then, in the Chersonese, things went wrong for him. That they did is the only fact one can be sure of; why they did is a matter for debate. Miltiades was to arrive back in Athens in a hurry. He said he had been chased by Persian ships because of an incident twenty years previously, when he had been compelled, by reason of his geographical position, to take part in the Persian expedition against Scythia. The Persian army had marched across the Danube into the Scythian wilderness, leaving behind them to guard the all-important bridge Miltiades and a body of fellow-Greeks, tyrants of the Ionian cities in Asia, which the Persians had taken over when they came down to the sea. Miltiades said, on reaching Athens, that he had suggested to the Ionians that they should destroy the bridge, thus leaving the Persians to die in the wilderness, but the Ionians had refused.

The amazing feature of all this — if it is true — is that Miltiades stayed on at his post. And that the Ionians waited so long before telling the Great King. And that the Great King, not a man of a markedly forgiving nature, took such an uncommonly long time to deal with Miltiades' peccadillo.

Miltiades came back, a big man, vastly impressive physically, with black hair shining in the sunlight, when I was a boy of eleven.* He came back to an Athens where the democracy was not yet twenty years old, an Athens largely disregarded by the rest of Greece, who saw her still as an ancient but backward community out of the main stream of Greek life, an Athens where most of the nobles still regarded the majority of their fellow citizens as essentially passive spectators.

Can you imagine such meek neutrality among Athenians today? Democracy has made them active where they had been passive, positive where they had been negative. They would voluntarily fight and suffer and die for democracy as no other

* In 493 BC.

13

form of rule could make them do. They shouldered the obligations of freedom as willingly — no, as *joyfully* — as they accepted the rights and advantages.

I have been fortunate. I have lived in my dear City when her citizens have been in love with freedom — to say they have been attached to the idea is too cold a phrase, cannot convey the passionate intensity of our feeling. It is more than a matter of the mind, it is an affair of the heart, a mighty impulse, a strength, a glorious energy, a magnificent, beckoning future bringing a glow, a fervour to living. For Athens we would die, but if only we are permitted to live for her, what will we not do for her, what *can* we not do for her!

I

Before Miltiades returned to Athens, the Greeks of Ionia in Asia Minor had risen in revolt against Persia, and had been crushed.

Even to an imaginative child, mere talk of an event may make less impression than a picture. I only appreciated a little what had recently happened to these fellow Greeks in Ionia when I saw the tragedy *The Suppliant Women*. I suppose you always remember vividly a first experience, and *The Suppliant Women* was the first play I ever saw. But I do not think that was the chief reason why I recalled it so acutely, so agonisingly.

It scared me out of my wits when I saw it, I had nightmares about it that night, and for months afterwards.

It is the story of women fugitives coming to a Greek king and, on the grounds of kinship, begging for help against savage pursuers. There was a barbarian herald, a nightmare retinue, dragging screaming women by the hair. They talked in an animal language in which the only words you could understand were concerned with blood and torture and death. They yelled in triumph like animals.

I would have given a good deal to have covered my eyes, stopped my ears. But a boy old enough to go to the theatre could not do that.

As people began to crowd down the steps at the end, there was a great buzz of conversation. Everyone was saying the same thing – the author, Aeschylus, son of Euphorion, had taken a risk in writing the play. Why, I wondered (but did not like to ask). Because he'd frightened everyone? But no one seemed as frightened as I had been.

'After what happened to Phrynicos –' said someone.

Who was Phrynicos?

I should have liked to have touched my father's arm and asked him to explain things to me, above all, I wanted him to explain as we walked home together. I needed companionship as well as elucidation. But he had told me to make my own way home afterwards; he was going to a friend's house to discuss the best way of dealing with some 'swine of a demagogue', who was winning too much attention to his views in the Assembly.

I waited until most of the crowd had gone, then began to make my way disconsolately down the steep steps. But then I halted. I thought I would stay on in the theatre a while, and fight down my fears before I returned home. I didn't know why exactly I took such a decision, except from a vague feeling that since the theatre was the sunniest place in the City, the best defence against nightmare terrors was the calmness of Apollo's own strong sunlight.

So I sat down again. I rested my chin on my hands, my elbows on my knees. I found chin, arms, knees were all shaking. A hand touched my bare shoulder.

'Are you all right?'

Dark red hair, a square face, deep-set eyes, very bright, an unusual colour, grey-green, smouldering with energy. Is it harder to admit to a stranger that one has been afraid than to make the same confession to one's own father? I don't know. I only knew that, difficult as it was to make such an admission to this man, it was quite impossible to lie to him.

'The play scared me,' I said.

'I hope it scares many people,' he replied promptly, 'provided they're scared in the right way. Fear can paralyse. It can also make you do things you never thought yourself capable of. It just depends what kind of animal you are. What kind of animal are you going to be?'

'I hope I'd be like one of the animals that turns and fights,' I said, taking a deep breath. My hands were not shaking now.

He looked as if he loathed inactivity – even a child knows the look and mannerisms of such a man, the hands are usually restless, for a start. But although I had not tried to detain my father, I said suddenly to the stranger, 'Sir, why were people saying that the author took a risk in writing the play, and who is Phrynicos?'

'Phrynicos is a long-winded playwright whose plays contain so many metaphors the audience rarely get the hang of what he's saying. But last year the message came over clear enough. The play was called *The Capture of Miletos*, and it made the audience weep.'

'Because it was so good?'

'I don't think so; I believe men wept because of a feeling of guilt. But whatever the reason, the authorities didn't want another reaction like it – too dangerous; next the people might turn against a government that, by sending a little help to the Ionians had encouraged them to revolt, but, by sending too little help, had allowed them to be destroyed. So they fined Phrynicos a thousand drachmas – three years' pay for the ordinary working man. The reason they gave was that subjects for tragedy should be episodes from heroic legend, not events in recent history.'

I said, 'What would they have done if the recent event had been something to make everyone glow with self-satisfaction?'

He smiled suddenly, and his face was transformed. 'A good point! One raised, incidentally, by Phrynicos himself.'

'Poor Phrynicos.'

'Oh, he didn't do too badly out of it. He's won a little place for himself in literary history now – the poet who suffered for his convictions. And he didn't suffer all that much. Men who felt as he did helped pay the fine.'

'And *this* play –'

'Well, you can't scare a brave man who feels deep indignation. The characters may be taken from heroic legend, but the theme of the play is topical enough – whether war, and all that it entails, is not preferable to the betrayal of suppliant kinsfolk.'

'You think it is, don't you?'

He nodded. 'Even if one of my own family hadn't suffered at barbarian hands, I'd have felt the same.'

'Will you tell me about the Ionian Revolt?'

17

He looked at me, startled. 'Don't you know about it?'

'Only vaguely,' I explained, red-faced. 'When my father talks to me he talks more about things that happened long ago than those which are going on now.'

'What is your name?'

'Theron, son of Acestorides.'

'You're not much like him, are you?' he said thoughtfully. 'But, of course, you're like your mother – she was an Alcmaeonid, wasn't she?'

'Did you know my mother?'

'No, I didn't know her, I only knew of her.'

'Knew of her?' I was astounded. From all that I had heard of her, she was a silent, timid creature.

He said gently, 'I remember that when she died people in my own household told me they had rarely known slaves weep so bitterly for a mistress. That's not a bad thing to know about her, is it?'

She had grey eyes, my mother, and when she died, the slaves had wept bitterly. I said carefully, 'Thank you. And could you tell me of the Ionian Revolt?'

'Well, it was a hopeless business from the start. They waited too long – you know, don't you, that Darius seized the Persian throne? The Ionians should have risen while he was still fighting for power. But, although belatedly, they decided to rebel. They sent across to mainland Greece for help, went naturally to Sparta first as Greece's foremost military state. And they did it all the wrong way – they appeared before Spartans, Spartans of all people, in trailing purple robes, gold chains round their necks. 'We are fellow Hellenes!' they said to the Spartans, but to the simple Laconian mind they themselves looked uncommonly like Asiatics. And then they shocked the Spartans in another way. They were asked how many days it would take to get up from the coast to Susa, the Persian capital. Three months, said the Ionians. Uproar from the Spartans, scared as old-maid priestesses invited to leave the temple precincts for quarters in a port specialising in offering sailors what they want after a long cruise. "Get out of Sparta before nightfall!" howled the Spartans. "You have made us a highly improper proposal" – their very words.'

'Why improper?' I asked.

'To get the lords of creation to poke their noses an inch outside Holy Sparta's something of a miracle; to invite them to take three months' journey from the sea – '

'Do you think the Spartans might have fought the Persians if three months' journey upcountry wasn't involved?'

He considered. 'If the Persians came to Greece itself, yes. Not because of fellow Hellenic feeling – the Spartans don't give a damn for that. But they don't want anybody else playing the bully-boy in the Peloponnese – that's their own god-given rôle.'

'We sent ships, didn't we? I knew that much.'

'Twenty,' he said. He brought his hands sharply together. '*Twenty*! What in the hell was the use of that? Occasionally it may be useful to show half-heartedness in politics, although then, of course, you glorify it by the name of compromise. But in warfare you must never do things by halves. If we were going to help the Ionians, we should have done it wholeheartedly. But we sent twenty near-obsolete warships – my God, which of our warships *aren't* obsolete? – and a hell of a lot of good that did.'

'But we burned Sardis. That's the other thing I know.'

'Pure chance. All the houses in Sardis are thatched with reeds; most of 'em are made of nothing else. Set fire to one, and all Sardis goes up in smoke. And then our contingent beat it back down to the coast and out of the war. But Darius hasn't forgotten that we made even so feeble an effort. They say he'd never heard of us until Sardis was burned. He asked then who the Athenians might be, and was told they were men of a small state towards the setting sun. Then he ordered a servant to say to him three times a day, "Master, remember the Athenians." Considering the size of his royal establishment, I suppose that it must be gratifying to find new forms of employment.'

'And then he reconquered Ionia,' I said after a moment.

He looked suddenly furiously angry. 'They helped reconquer

19

themselves – through disunity. No unified command. The kind of divided counsels when defeatists can call themselves realists. And it's only a short step from defeatism to treachery. There was a sea-fight off Lade, where most Ionian vessels fought brilliantly, bravely – but the Samians deserted. After that Miletos fell, and the whole Ionian coast smoked with the funeral pyres of Greek lives and Greek freedom. Think of it! A coast of nightmare, flooded with refugees from the cities already taken, desperately seeking shelter, but not knowing where to turn.' After a minute's silence, he added in a low voice, 'The people of Troy were more fortunate. They slept happily and well the night before destruction. They didn't see it coming closer every day. The brutal degradation of humanity. The men killed. Good-looking boys like you castrated. The most beautiful girls disappearing into the harem.' Again he became furiously angry. 'They wept here in the theatre last year when they saw Phrynicos' play. They wept in guilty recollection of Ionia: creditable to their hearts, no doubt, but scarcely creditable to their heads. If they wept, they should have done so for a more selfish reason. For what has happened to Miletos may very well soon happen to Athens.' The grey-green eyes were looking at me intently. 'Isn't that why this morning's play scared you so much – *because it might happen here?*'

I nodded: on the stage we had been shown dreadful things happening about a Greek altar.

'The Persians would have marched against us in any case,' he said half absently. 'If you rule a great empire, you're either dreadfully logical, or mad. Darius belongs to the dreadfully logical variety. He would never have been content with rule over the Ionian Greeks alone, for he will have been told that beyond the existing frontier live members of the same race enjoying political liberties which the Ionians once enjoyed, and after which they are still traitorous enough to hanker. To such a potentially dangerous situation there is one obvious, simple and practical solution. The frontier must be pushed forward so that all Greeks are absorbed in the Persian Empire.

'Once Persia's had time to lick her wounds, she's going to launch on Greece the fleets and armies she's collected there in Western Asia to finish off the Ionians. Nothing is surer. Ionia's agony has bought time for us, who did so little to help her. It's taken Darius six years to crush her, and he's lost ships and armies in the process. But one day he's going to send his armies and his fleets westwards again – against us.'

Trying to keep my voice as gruff as possible, I asked, 'When do you think they will come?'

He gave his sudden smile. 'Do you know what I hope? What, indeed, I think is our only hope? That Darius, knowing he's an old man, and scared of dying before getting his revenge, will decide against the sure but slow approach, and send a smaller army on a sudden dash, aiming at a bridgehead in Greece, Athens, from which he can gobble up the mainland . . .'

'Well,' he went on briskly after a moment, 'I've depressed you enough. If any of my friends had been here, they'd have warned you against starting me off on the topic of the Ionian Revolt.'

He rose to go. I asked, 'Sir, why had *you* stayed behind all the others?'

'Because I, like you, could see all that happening in Athens. And I needed time before stepping back into today's Athens from what might be the Athens of the future. My apologies for having inflicted my apprehensions upon you!'

But the odd fact was that he had not depressed me. He had spoken of hideous dangers confronting us, but there had been about him as he spoke something almost like gaiety. There was in him such boldness that the horrors were driven away.

'What is your name, please?' I asked, rising too.

'Themistocles, son of Neocles,' he said, and then, very soberly, 'I don't think you should tell your father that you have been talking to me.'

I managed to get home before my father, luckily, for he came in raging. He had discussed with his friends – to no real purpose – how they might best clip the wings of the swine of a demagogue who kept demanding that Athens should entrust her safety to a fleet, instead of to the heavy armed infantry supplied by her gentry. The swine of a demagogue —Themistocles, son of Neocles.

2

Then everything began to happen in a rush. Miltiades returned
to Athens, and as far as I was concerned, the Persian threat
seemed less momentous than the fact that for weeks my father
was in a frantic rage. I kept edging into corners like a scared
puppy to avoid his notice; I myself had done nothing to offend
him – save physically to resemble my dead Alcmaeonid mother.
For the rest of Athens had not welcomed Miltiades' return with
the rapture shown by my father and his circle. A law known as
the anti-tyrant law was invoked against him; he was accused of
despotic behaviour in the Chersonese, and the Alcmaeonids
threw all their weight behind the prosecution. Hence my father's
fury at the sight of me. But eventually Miltiades was acquitted –
in triumph, my father declared. From what I gathered from
servants' gossip, however, this wasn't so. The acquittal was
more in the nature of a calculated risk. His military experience,
above all, the fact that this experience had been gained in
alliance with the Persian army, made him a man whose value to
Athens in the immediate future outweighed any more distant
threat. But my father did not see the matter in this way, and
when, after his acquittal Miltiades was elected to the ten-strong
Board of Generals, Father fairly glittered with pleasure –
glittered being a fairly apt term because, Miltiades having
decided the old family town house, long uninhabited, would not
do for him, lived with us while a mansion was being built for
him, and Father felt some of his cousin's glory reflected on him.

Certain of Miltiades' fellow generals came frequently to our
house. There was Aristeides, youngish then, but the kind of man
who changes little from sixteen to sixty, and always with a dry-
ness about him, so that you felt the hair of the tight curls
covering his narrow skull was so brittle it would snap if touched.

No, I did not like Aristeides. If it came to that, my father did not really care for him, since Aristeides watched Miltiades with too cool an appraisal. Yet Aristeides' other views were correctness itself — a close relationship with Sparta, and utter rejection of the blasphemous new theory that Athens' best defence lay, not in the heavy infantry (the gentlemen of Athens), but in a navy crewed by what was usually described as 'rabble'.

Other generals came to our house at intervals, notably Callimachos, the Commander-in-Chief, a man who seemed almost physically oppressed by the responsibility he carried. He was often accompanied by his close friend, Cynaigeiros, the kind of person any over-anxious, over-conscientious man might want beside him, since he was the personification of steady, sturdy optimism. Not, however, the kind of wild optimism that proclaimed that the Persians would not come; 'They'll invade all right,' I heard him rumbling to Callimachos one day, 'but you will do your duty, and so shall I, and I think you'll find that we'll surprise ourselves and the rest of Greece.' 'Although,' said Callimachos, 'you think we lost our best chance when we didn't do more to help Ionia.' 'We acted like Spartans then. Selfish, shortsighted — ' 'Well,' said Callimachos, smiling for once, 'don't set your feelings to verse like your brother.'

I asked the servants who Cynaigeiros' brother might be. To my astonishment, I was told that the most down-to-earth of men was the brother of the writer of *The Suppliant Women*. They were devoted to each other; Cynaigeiros' rage when some people had demanded that Aeschylus should be prosecuted, like Phrynicos, had been something to see.

Miltiades, I gathered, did not get on with Cynaigeiros. I was sorry about this, for I liked Aeschylus' brother. He used to talk to me about Homer as the basis of proper education.

And then the Persians came. Darius had indeed given up the idea of the slow, sure attack from the north in favour of a sudden dash across the sea. Word of their coming was first received from Naxos, a swift galley sent with the news of a great fleet of six hundred warships which had coasted the shores of Asia Minor until it was off Samos, then sailing due westwards, a force so great that the Naxians did not intend to put up any resistance. They fled to the hills. And within days we heard other news; the city with its temples burned to the ground, all humans within reach of the barbarian army remorselessly hunted down, shepherds butchered among their flocks, farmers cut down, then thrown back into their blazing olive groves, a dozen tiny shrines desecrated. Nothing was too small to escape the vengeance of the Great King.

Athenians had heard of dreadful things happening in Ionia, but Ionia was a distant country; mile after mile of sea lay between us. This was happening on our doorstep. A runner, Pheidippides, was sent to Sparta with an urgent appeal for help.

I began to get the horrors again, I recalled *The Suppliant Women*, remembered how it had been written in anguished recollection of the revolt of the Ionian Greeks against the very people coming against us now. I remembered the barbarian herald, and his horrible retinue, arriving to drag away the daughters of Danaus – nightmare figures, limbs dark against white robes, crawling like asps, darting like black spiders. And I remembered the hideous noises they had made – jeering yells of triumph as they had dragged the screaming women by the hair from the altar. They spoke in a barbaric gibberish in which you could understand only a few words of horror as the herald threatened the fugitives – 'irons your flesh to sear . . .' 'blood new-shed', 'trip-hook', 'severed head – '

It had happened to the Ionians.

It could happen to us.

Where would they land?

Callimachos came to talk to Miltiades; my father sent me in with wine for them. Callimachos aged daily, grew more pallid, but the approach of danger seemed to make Miltiades bloom, put a kind of gloss on him, his dark eyes had never been more

25

brilliant. I remember that contrast between the two men very clearly.

Miltiades was saying, 'They'll make for Marathon – shelving beach for them to draw up their ships, level ground so that they can use their cavalry – '

I finished serving the wine, and retreated in a state of utter depression. I knew Marathon well – hardly surprising when you consider my family background, for Marathon was one of the great places for horse breeding. Now the very features of the plain which had enchanted me possessed a sinister significance. The flat expanse over which I had galloped so joyously made it pre-eminently the spot for landing enemy cavalry. The gently sloping shore which had enabled me almost from babyhood to splash happily and safely into the sea was the shelving beach up which the enemy might safely draw his ships.

There are few things more shocking than suddenly seeing familiar and beloved territory through bleakly military eyes.

Pheidippides made good speed. He left Athens at dawn, and reached Sparta on the second evening, having covered a hundred and forty miles of rough road. Such a heroic effort deserved an infinitely greater reward than it received. The Spartans said they were ready to help us – but not immediately. They were celebrating a religious festival, the Carneia, sacred to Apollo. Once the festival was over, they would march.

We could therefore expect no Spartan help for ten days.

Within ten days everything might be over.

In the kitchen, the servants said that Pheidippides, the runner, swore that on his way back to Athens he had seen Pan, who had spoken to him, telling him that if the Athenians had forgotten him, he had not forgotten them. There was a great deal of argument. The older men believed the story; the younger men said, 'When did he sleep last? He was dog-tired. That's when you imagine things.'

Then they remembered it was time for the evening meal. I had to get out of the way, wandered out to the street door, stared into the dusk, wondering if the days of darkness falling on a free Athens were numbered. And then there were shouts, people were running, calling out breathlessly, gesticulating wildly with their arms.

'The beacon's alight! The beacon on Pentelicos! They've landed!'

At Marathon, then. Miltiades had been right.

With feelings of utter desolation I, with the old men and women and children, watched the army moving out at dawn, every able-bodied member of the gentry, ten thousand of them. They marched fast. Pack-animals carried the meal bags, slaves carried armour, Miltiades, my father, some other men, rode, but if it came to fighting, they would dismount to fight on foot in the modern manner. Spartans would have spat in contempt at the apparent lack of order of it all, but it was speedy enough.

They left Athens a city of empty, sunlit streets. The women had taken their grief and fear home with them. But on the following day, those who remained in the city came out into the open again – and so did treason. Treason masquerading as reason when it spoke to men, as something more brutal when it spoke to women.

For the women of Athens, wrenched from their quiet, contained lives, bereft of their husbands, left the usual shelter of their homes to cluster in the market place, or at the gate through which the army had marched, the gate through which news, good or catastrophic, must come. And the assault was made on their nerves.

I remember one undersized fellow. 'I've knocked about the world a bit,' he said. 'I've seen their armies. I've seen them storming a city that held out. They let their cavalry loose in the streets – horsemen and chariots. You see people running, screaming. Ever heard a woman scream when she's really scared? Then you hear other things – whips cracking, the rumble of the chariot wheels – like thunder, that is – and men howling, howling like dogs. Then they come rattling up the street, and at first all you can see is the horses plunging, and the men crouching down to make 'em go faster, and then you see the sun on the swords. Then, after the screams have got louder, it's all quiet. Nobody living in sight. Just piles of dead, and blood running in streams in the road and splashed over the walls high as your shoulder. Then you get clouds of flies, and the crows start dropping down out of the sky.'

Now, in furious hatred, I can appreciate the artistry of the effort. At the time all that I knew was that somehow I had to stop him. 'I don't think they've brought chariots with them,' I said in my rough, uncertain boy's voice, 'and if they had, they couldn't very well charge through our streets, could they? Too narrow and winding.' And then, with greater confidence and greater relevance, 'How did *you* manage to stay alive, then?'

It stopped him in full flow. He'd been having things too much his own way; being unused to interruptions, he didn't know how to deal with one when he met it. After a moment he recommenced, but he'd lost the thread. 'Wave after wave,' he said vaguely. 'Can't stop 'em coming – '

But now he encountered a far more formidable opponent. Behind me there was a growl, turning into a snarl – almost you could believe a giant watchdog was there. Then a big body sprang past me, and a sturdy, elderly man had the orator by the throat – was, indeed, shaking him as a dog might shake a rat.

'So what do we do, you scum? Go crawling to 'em as if Darius'll forget the past, as if he'd drunk Lethe water instead of his mother's milk?' He threw his victim against the gate, and he slid down, apparently unconscious. The newcomer turned to the frightened women – and now I was reminded of an old, grey-muzzled sheepdog with a threatened flock. 'Go home. Forget what he said. None of it's going to happen.' As they dispersed slowly, almost one expected him to nip at their heels to make them move faster.

He turned to me then. 'Look, lad, it's no use asking you to stick indoors, and if you're out in the streets, you're bound to hear more of this talk.' By mutual consent we turned to look at the man he'd sent crashing against the wall, but he'd taken himself off. The elderly man shrugged. 'Choking the life out of that one wouldn't have stopped it – that kind of scum's like mushrooms, finish off one lot today, and a second set'll spring up overnight. But don't listen, lad, and if you think it's getting dangerous, come and get me – down in the Cerameicos, I live, I'm Euphronios, the potter, I might be too old to go off with the gentry that marched out yesterday, but, by God, I'm not too old to defend the City in my own way, and I'm damned if I'll let these slimy devils creep out from under the stones now they think it's safe to do it.'

So in the extraordinary Athens of that late summer, with my father twenty odd miles away unable to control my wanderings and no mother to keep me or, indeed, need me at home, I found myself next morning making my way down to the Cerameicos. I had slept badly, dreaming of blood in the little sunlit streets of Athens, walls splashed shoulder high with it. I woke with the sickly smell of it in my nostrils, almost I could feel it sticky under my finger-nails. And throughout my dreams I had heard women screaming, and the raucous jabber of the barbarian herald in *The Suppliant Women* – 'To the galley, bloodily, back . . . Why should I pity a woman lost, without home, without honour, without city . . . Sob if you will and shriek and pray – Blood new-shed – Blood new-shed –'

They had caught the women by the hair, started to drag them from the altar. How they had screamed – but they had been actors playing parts, behind women's masks, not real women screaming in real mortal anguish.

Now that all the familiar faces had gone I went across Athens to find reassurance in one of the ordinary people (for so I put it then, arrogant – no, *ignorant* – brat that I was) who in defence of their new-found liberty were prepared to do as much as their betters who had marched away.

In normal times those little narrow streets would have been alive with industry, but now the animation was of a different sort. One or two very old men were still firing jars, blocking out scenes in the natural red colour of the clay against the black pigment, but mostly the potter's wheel lay still, and the kilns were cold – if men hurried in and out of Euphronios' shop, it was not to talk of trade. Most of them believed the army should never have left the City; most of them – and this came as an enormous shock to me – rated the patriotism of the nobles very poorly.

It may therefore seem extraordinary that they allowed a member of the class they so distrusted (even if so young a member) to hang about listening to their conversation. But, as my father remarked with a very different emotion, I was unmistakably a member of the one aristocratic family for whom my new friends felt trust and affection. Red hair or a thrusting jaw may run in some families; with the Alcmaeonids it's a marked bone formation about the eyes making for straight brows and high cheekbones, the eyes themselves being of a dark grey. It was the look of my mother, so detested by my father, and it was the look of her uncle Cleisthenes, instantly recognised by the men of the Cerameicos, and opening for me the door to their workshops, their confidences, their counsels.

The waiting would have been all the more intolerable if we had known at the beginning exactly how long it would be.

Only one good piece of news reached us during those days; one state had instantly marched to our assistance – unasked – even though Sparta, the great war-state of Greece, hesitated, and no other raised a finger to help us. Some years before, Plataea, tiny Plataea, had been threatened by her neighbour Thebes, and had asked us to help her. This we had done, and now, hearing how we in our turn were threatened, unasked she sent her entire manpower, the whole six hundred of them, over the mountain ridge from Boeotia into Attica and so to Marathon. If the entire Spartan army had turned up, it wouldn't have got a tenth of the cheers the Plataeans got, and, human nature – or perhaps I should say western human nature – being what it is, I don't think either that the coming of the Spartans would have given the same lift to the spirits.

Athens has never forgotten Plataean fidelity and courage. Ever after this, when prayers are offered up at the festivals, the herald, who once asked for 'all good things for the Athenians,' now adds, 'and for the Plataeans.'

As Odysseus said of his own birthplace, Ithaca, 'A small place, but a good place for breeding men.' May Athens and Plataea continue to stand shield to shield against whatever dangers may confront us in the future.

But this was the only piece of good news brought back to us from that plain a day's march away that had never seemed so distant. And if the optimists and the patriots took heart from the coming of six hundred Plataeans, you may imagine what the others made of the information coming back about Persian numbers. Each day of waiting, these numbers soared. And day by day, apart from furious activity in certain quarters like the Cerameicos, Athens seemed to die a little – indeed, parts of it seemed to be dead already, so few were the signs of life in some of the streets. The sun poured down on emptiness and silence, no rumbling carts or clopping mules, not a child playing in the street, or a veiled woman hurrying past. The only living thing was a green lizard flicking across a wall, the only sound the hum of flies, the chirping of a cricket – the emptiness and tiny noises seeming amazingly loud in the silence you might expect at noonday in the country, but never in a city.

And the sun beat down, scorchingly. I suppose mental oppression was responsible for the feeling of physical misery experienced by all of us who remained in Athens during those days. Even now, years later, I meet men of my own age who say, 'Do you remember how *hot* it was?' We all seemed to have blinding headaches, unquenchable thirsts. And to have been scared by the silence – and the shadows, the shadows that crept out like treachery as the day wore on, crept out and lengthened like living creatures intending to swallow up all Athens in darkness.

And then came the last day of waiting; in its way the worst period of all.

At about two hours before noon, an elderly man, standing in

31

the market place talking to a friend, suddenly cried out. He had seen, high up in the forests of Pentelicos, a flash like silver. Someone was signalling with a shield. But not to Athens. 'It was thin, like a knife-edge,' he said, 'as if I caught the flash sideways on, but they'd get the full effect at Marathon.'

Someone was signalling to the enemy.

For a moment all was panic and confusion. Then the stout-hearted men from the Cerameicos and their comrades took command; the elderly magistrate nominally in charge of the city stood mouth agape, afraid. The signal could mean only one thing – 'Now!' To attack Athens, deprived of her army. Which way would they come? Probably by sea, so any man who could carry a spear must get down to the harbour.

But some must watch at the gate through which the army had marched, to which the beaten army (for we had very little hope now) would retreat if it could.

I went back home, and found a hunting knife, stuck it in my belt, then returned to the gate.

Groups of women came there too. They were white-faced, but none of them wept. If it came to that, no one spoke. The strange silence that had fallen on the City after the army had marched away, temporarily banished in the uproar following the signal from Pentelicos, had made a triumphant return. It was not only that no one spoke – the hush was universal, the birds, even the crickets were silent, nothing moved, not a lizard, not a leaf in the plane trees beside the gate. Everything seemed frozen as if snow, and not sun, poured down on us.

And then, in the distance, we saw a little cloud of dust.

No one cried out or, indeed, said anything, but an indescribable sound came from us, the breath rasped in our throats as if we were choking in that dust coming remorselessly closer and closer to us.

One man bringing news.

We ran out to meet him. I, the youngest there, outran the rest. So I was the first to see he was not so much running as stumbling through the appalling heat, that he was blinded with sweat. I turned and shouted over my shoulder, 'Water! Get him water!' and ran on.

His face was caked with dust, drawn with fatigue, but as my hands went out to him, and touched him, and for the first time he knew someone was with him, I realised suddenly that he was trying to smile at me.

'It's all right,' he whispered through cracked lips.

'There's been fighting at Marathon?'

'Yes – but it's all right.'

He could scarcely remain upright, and I wasn't strong enough to keep him standing, although I had both arms about him. Thank God an elderly man came panting up, gave a shout of 'Pheidippides!' and lent his sturdy strength to mine.

The runner we had sent to Sparta to ask for help.

'It's all right,' Pheidippides said again. 'We fought them – beat them this morning . . .'

'*Beat* them!'

He nodded weakly, put his hand to his dry lips, said apologetically, 'Water –'

'It's coming. Thank God this boy had sense.' He turned and called to the people running to us. 'It's all right! *It's all right!*'

Pheidippides plucked at his arm. 'May not – be all right, though.'

'For God's sake, where's that water? Here, carry him to the shade of the plane trees –'

The leaves were fluttering slightly now. A little breeze had arisen. We managed to carry him over, and the light and shade dappled his face. Someone ran up with water. He drank some; I knelt beside him bathing his face. He clutched at the hand of the elderly man. 'You saw – the shield signal?'

'Yes.'

'We've beaten them – but some had already set sail before we attacked – and more of them got away. Then the shield signal –'

'An attack from the sea. We guessed that.'

'The army's marching back at once – but it will be a close thing. They'll be here – by the late afternoon –'

33

'Rest here. I'll take the news into the City, and send help to bring you in.'

'In a moment – I'll be able – '

'Rest here. Nothing's too good for you.'

I remained there, my arm under his head, still bathing his face. Women came to us, bringing more water, wine. They touched him humbly, gently. Some kissed his hand. I think we all knew he was dying. He kept trying to smile at us, to say again, 'It's all right,' but just before he died he was not seeing us, and he talked, partly in his own voice, and partly in a strange, rough accent I had never heard before, and which I did not identify until ten years later when I met men from all parts of Greece. 'Lord,' said Pheidippides in his own voice, 'I took them your message.' 'And I fulfilled my promise,' came the reply in the strange accent I did not know until a decade later was the harsh Arcadian speech. 'I fulfilled my promise.'

Only a few of us remained at the gate now – boys, one or two men, women and younger children. If the enemy landed in the harbour we were to take the women out of the city to the protection of the men returning from Marathon.

That afternoon was endless. Heat, dragging hours, eyes straining into the distance along the road, then staring out to sea. A day's march – twenty-four miles – and men who had fought a battle, men in heavy armour – say seven or eight hours. How long to sail from Marathon into the City harbour? Nine to ten hours with a favouring wind, someone had said, but he'd known the trip to take twelve. There was little wind that afternoon – but how long had the battle taken, how many of our men survived, how many of their fleet had set sail before the fighting started?

It was still almost impossible to believe that we had, indeed, won a victory, quite impossible to credit that we had not suffered dreadfully in doing so.

But in the late afternoon they came. They did not look like a conquering army, caked with dust and mud and dried blood, heads bent, eyes half closed – but they came on with grim determination, and they moved fast – and there were many of them,

34

many of them. And Miltiades at their head, smiling into the sun. He at least looked as a conqueror should look.

When the distant dust heralded their approach, we had sent boys running back into the City with the news, and most of those within the walls came pouring out to greet them, to run forward with the strangest sound I had ever heard, half sob, half cheer, to stare up into the strained, sweat-streaked faces, seeking one familiar face. Yet not one of them was really familiar, there was a fierceness, a wildness about them despite their weariness, matching the reddened tips of the spears they carried, their very hands were bloodstained – and I saw timid, gentle women running up to shower kisses again and again on those terrible murderous hands.

I ran along the grim ranks, but could not see my father. I raced back to the head of the tramping columns. Miltiades was shouting to the elderly archon, who had been more or less propelled out from the market place, 'We're making for the south of the City – Cynosarges, facing Phaleron and the sea.'

'Callimachos – ' croaked the archon.

'Dead.'

I shouted at the top of my voice, 'Is my father dead?'

He heard me. 'No – he's still at Marathon, with Aristeides and his regiment.'

I could not make out why my father should be with Aristeides, or what Aristeides was doing on the battlefield. But now women were calling out, in anguish, 'Where is my husband, in Aristeides' regiment?' and men were shouting back that Aristeides with his regiment had remained on the battlefield to guard the prisoners and the spoils, and wives sobbed in relief.

There were not many gaps, but faces other than Callimachos' were missing. I could not see Cynaigeiros. But I heard men saying, 'Wonderful – wonderful – *less than two hundred dead* – ' and embracing, sobbing and laughing in an ecstasy of relief.

They reached Cynosarges, in a precinct of Heracles, outside the walls, and drew up in line again. People ran out to them with water, wine, food, fed them, washed them, bandaged wounds.

35

And then – but not looking round at us, keeping their gaze fixed on the sea – slowly, almost unbelievingly, one after the other men began to talk of the battle, how they had taken up their position some two or three miles from the enemy by another precinct of Heracles, blocking any possible advance by road on the City, and waited – waited for the Spartans to come up, or for the Persians to make a false move, and then, at last, that morning, before dawn, some Ionians had slipped across to our lines in the darkness, to call out softly, 'Cavalry away!' So the Persians were dividing their forces, and the cavalry was being re-embarked to make a dash for the City itself. No choice now, but to attack, to attack to beat the enemy remaining at Marathon in time to make the march back to the City afterwards to deal with the cavalry transports.

There had been two problems. To cope with superior enemy numbers, and to get within spear-range before their famous archers could do much damage. It was Miltiades' plan which had been adopted – everyone agreed on this. If our men had been drawn up in the normal way, eight deep, the enemy line, their numbers being so much larger, would easily outflank us. So we sacrificed depth for an extended line, thinning out the centre especially, the idea being that this must hold the Persian centre as best as it could while the stronger wings dealt with the enemy opposite them, then swung round to deal with the enemy centre in its turn.

And they had dealt with the second problem simply enough. They had advanced fairly briskly until they got within arrow range – and then they broke into a run, getting through the hail of arrows before any real damage was done. After that everything had gone almost miraculously to plan. While the centre tackled the toughest enemy troops, Callimachos on the right, the Plataeans on the left, drove the enemy before them, into the Great Marsh – that was where most of the barbarians were killed, thousands of them – and then wheeled to attack the enemy centre, and, when that broke, chased them back to the ships. It was in the fight for the ships that Callimachos had been killed. We'd captured seven. The rest had got away, having embarked what soldiers they could, and –

'Here they come!' someone shouted.

And there they came, round Sunion Point, the squadrons whose quitting Marathon had brought about the battle, making for Phaleron, slowly, masterfully it seemed – and suddenly heaving to. They had seen the army drawn up facing them. The sight must have shocked them. Here, and drawn up in orderly line. Not a broken army. So their own people had been *beaten* at Marathon.

'What are they going to do now?'

'What would you do? Send a fast ship back to find out what the hell's happened. And they'll fall in with 'em in the state we left 'em in.'

'And then?'

'My God, that lot'll never fight again! And when these see what happened to them, they won't want to share the experience!'

The enemy ships rode at anchor for an hour, two, three. As the sun began to sink in the west we saw other vessels rounding Sunion, the vessels carrying those who had survived the battle. Some of the ships were blackened by fire. They, too, dropped anchor. Small boats passed between the newcomers and the earlier vessels, and then, as sunset swept into the western sky like a great flood of crimson and gold, the entire fleet set off slowly eastwards, through the fading light into purple dimness and then into darkness.

And as the enemy ships receded into the eastern blackness, admitting defeat, the entire city rose to Miltiades, those who had waited here in dreadful expectation, day after day – above all, those whom he had led to victory over the hordes of an enemy whose very name had hitherto struck such terror in men's minds that many had not even thought of resisting. It was as if Miltiades had made the men he led more than human. If those who had remained in the City felt – an understatement – gratitude, what emotion was felt by those whom he had made feel almost godlike?

He stood there before us, his back to the glare of the setting sun, so that you could not see his face. The sun itself had not yet sunk to the horizon; momentarily it seemed to hover, as if fixed by Apollo himself so that its dying rays composed a fiery wreath behind Miltiades' dark head.

In the gathering dimness a tall man came across to me, trailing his spear, shield slung over back. I heard what he said quite clearly, although he did not raise his voice against the joyful tumult. 'Are you the son of Acestorides? Did you know that your father was wounded?'

'Wounded!' I stammered. 'I asked Miltiades – he said he was with Aristeides. Then someone else said Aristeides was still on the battlefield guarding the prisoners and the spoils –'

'Also the wounded. Your father was wounded in the thigh when we were fighting for the ships. Will you be alone tonight? If you would like to come to my house –'

I thanked him, but said I should prefer to go to my own home.

'Very well,' he said. 'I'll see that your father is brought back tomorrow.'

I thanked him again, said his kindness was quite extraordinary. 'I should go in any case,' he said. 'They are burying our dead tomorrow, and my brother is one of them.'

'I am sorry,' I said awkwardly, and then, after a moment, 'Did I know him?'

'I think so; he came to your house. Cynaigeiros.'

'I am so sorry! He was very kind. He used to talk to me about Homer.'

'I am trying to take comfort from the thought that he would have chosen to die Homerically, in another battle of the ships,' said Aeschylus.

The Spartans, two thousand of them, came up the following night – an almost incredible feat of marching if they did not start until after the full moon. Not so incredible if they had been stationed on their frontier all the time waiting to hear how events turned out in Attica.

38

They went back almost immediately, after looking at the six thousand odd Persian dead, and muttering gruff technical comments to each other on arms and equipment. As far as our own performance was concerned, they seemed to be in a state of shock — partly because we, the despised Athenians, had won at all; secondly because of the way we had done it.

'You made that final charge *at the double?*' they said, in grating disbelief.

Aristeides, who always had a completely unrealistic admiration for them, said placatingly, 'We avoided the arrows, and gained impetus that way.'

'But the risk of it!' they said, with more emotion than one would expect any Spartan to show. 'No, give us a slow, steady advance. Better to be safe than sorry. *Cohesion.*'

Aristeides was left looking rather hangdog. According to the Spartans we shouldn't have won at all. We had broken all the rules of warfare.

We had close on a thousand wounded, mostly in arm or leg, these being unprotected. My father, in the frantic fighting about the enemy ships, had been severely wounded in the thigh, a bad wound that did not heal easily, and brought bouts of high fever. But when they first brought him home, although his face was the colour of tallow the pain was not too great, and he was smiling. 'Theron!' he whispered, grasping my hand. 'You see — I was always right. He's the greatest man Athens has ever known.'

'Yes, Father.'

'The eyes of the people have been opened,' he said rapidly. 'They couldn't save themselves —'

He was talking so quickly now the words were beginning to run into each other. I went to the door, called for help. He hadn't noticed me go. He was laughing as he stammered on incoherently. It reminded me horribly of the gibberish spoken by the barbarian herald in *The Suppliant Women*, when only one word in twenty was intelligible, words like 'My cousin', and 'right to rule'.

3

I should have turned against Miltiades in any case, because for months he did not visit my father. Father had, of course, outlived his usefulness. Miltiades' own splendid new town house was completed, to become the centre of political activity in Athens in that winter following Marathon. And Father, spending long days staring at the door waiting for a footfall that never sounded, a face that never smiled at him, always found excuses for that absence. It seemed that some kind of expedition was being prepared . . . If he hadn't found those excuses, if he had shared my resentment at the neglect, I think that resentment might have been less.

There were other visitors — ironically some of them men with whom Father had not had much contact, for with them he had had little in common. One was Aeschylus. He usually came in the evening, or at night. He would sit at the bedside not saying much, often going off into his own thoughts — those moods of abstraction, when you knew he was leagues and aeons of time away from you, should have been comfortless, almost repellent to a boy sharing the vigil, but they never were. It was not merely that he was silent; the stillness about him I knew was something far beyond mere unwillingness to talk. I have since thought of it as that strange hush and tranquillity that lies at the very heart of a raging storm; at the time I only knew that I blessed his every coming.

It was in the following spring that, coming away from a visit, Aeschylus said to me, 'Theron, you know, don't you, that your father will never recover physically from his wound?'

I nodded. 'They told me two months ago that nothing really could be done —'

Aeschylus said, 'Yes, that is true. But there's more to it than that. Nothing can be done about the physical injury, but your father's not letting himself recover from the mental wounding he's received. And we must take care that you don't suffer as a consequence.'

I had the idea then of asking him to approach Miltiades to ask him to visit my father; I did not have sufficient courage at the time, but three nights of broken sleep for my father, three days lying restlessly watching that damned door, brought me following Aeschylus into the street after his next visit, and after all the fine prepared requests, to burst out confusedly, *'Why* hasn't Miltiades visited my father? If he came –'

Aeschylus' dark eyes watched me thoughtfully. 'He's a busy man these days. An expedition is being planned.'

I said furiously, 'Is he trying to make use of other people now?'

Aeschylus said in a voice of extraordinary sadness, 'I don't look at it like that. I see him as a man who has been too fortunate. Now he has forgotten to walk humbly and to propitiate the gods. But I'm in the minority, and I'm not going to try to influence you.'

'Then I must make up my own mind, mustn't I?'

He smiled then. 'Yes, that's the right for which we fought at Marathon. There's an Assembly meeting tomorrow; I'll take you with me. You're too young to vote, but not too young to think.'

The Assembly at dawn next morning, no rose-coloured, gentle approach of day, but strong light suddenly in the sky, a blood-red sun, harsh, arrogant, burning in the sky above us. Scarcely a good omen.

We sat in partial shadow; that red light had not touched us yet. There was a man sitting just in front of us who seemed vaguely familiar, but before I could identify him, there was a wild burst of cheering. The fiery light shone full on the speaker's platform, and the steps above it. And there was Miltiades. Cheer after cheer, rousing every cock and dog in the City. Almost you might imagine they would rouse the dead at Marathon.

41

He looked different.

The big, loosely built figure had thickened in the months since Marathon.

It shouldn't — couldn't — have happened so quickly.

Someone said to me once, years later, that my shock of disillusionment must have left me feeling 'as if a light had gone out'. Nothing so pretty or poetic. There is nothing pretty or poetic in the sight of a coarsening body. And there is even less of anything pretty or poetic in the revelation of a coarsening mind.

The bulky, massive figure sat through the preliminaries with an air of — how shall I put it? — almost slothful assurance. He watched the crowd with a kind of gross possessiveness.

I said to Aeschylus, 'That isn't the Miltiades who won Marathon.'

I don't know what my voice sounded like. The man sitting in front of us turned. Dark, square face, deep-set eyes, very bright, an unusual colour, grey-green, smouldering with energy.

'This Miltiades,' Themistocles said, 'could never have won Marathon.' He swung back, resuming his old, vigilant posture.

Miltiades rose to speak. The cheering was a frantic ecstasy. What he said was quite incredible. He wanted command of our entire naval force, together with an adequate supply of troops, but gave no information as to where he would lead the expedition. All that he would say was that it would be a profitable business. And he was cheered to the echo.

I don't know which was the more intolerable, the infatuation of the crowd, or the attitude of Miltiades. Both were equally unnatural — the most quickwitted of Greeks, the most fanatically devoted to the idea of democracy, accepting this insane proposal with frenzied enthusiasm, while *he* —

What opposition there was to him didn't seem to anger him, you see. Xanthippos, my red-haired kinsman by marriage (his wife was my mother's cousin, Agariste) vehemently opposed the proposal, a predictable Alcmaeonid line, and Miltiades listened with an air of indolence, eyes half-closed.

But some of the indolence left him when the man sitting

ahead of us went up to the platform, took the speaker's wreath. 'This is a complete betrayal of the democracy Cleisthenes gave us less than twenty years ago. How can you, men of Athens, who defied the Persian King, be your own masters, when you are willing –'

He was shouted down. But if Miltiades still lounged, still listened with half-shut eyes, there was a tightening, a whitening about his mouth. He was enraged. He went on being enraged even though he got what he wanted, our entire fleet was to go sailing off into the unknown.

The actual vote was taken in a hurry; the storm threatened by the lurid sunrise broke over our heads before the count was finished. I splashed through puddles to take my place among the crowd of devotees about the great man. I think he noticed me because Xanthippos came across to say, 'Well, young Theron, I'm glad to see you out in the open for once!' and that he came down to talk to me simply to deprive my maternal kinsman of his audience.

I can't remember how he detached me from Xanthippos, I can't remember exactly how he replied when I stammered out my request for visiting my father, but I remember precisely how he stared down at me as I spoke.

And the change in him . . .

The words were the kind he'd always used; but the tone, the whole manner of speaking, was different. Not friendly. Blandly possessive. And it grated. God, how that tone grated.

But for a moment the blandness disappeared. So I'd been with Aeschylus – he hadn't noticed him, he must have been sitting in the shadow.

'He sat just behind Themistocles,' I said.

Only I saw that changed face, dark, flushed, convulsed with fury.

And then he had regained control, was turning away, saying casually over his shoulder, 'If I were you I shouldn't listen to Themistocles and his ideas.' He smiled as he spoke, and the tone was light, but the command was unmistakably there.

43

And it grated. God, how it grated!

I had not really expected that Miltiades would visit my father, but, amazingly, he came that very night. He did not talk much. And he said, more than once, 'I should have come before.'

He meant it too, but not for the reason imagined by my father, lying flushed, grateful, adoring. Hard-eyed, I knew the true reason. Selfishness. The easiness of manner which so long had cloaked a consuming ambition, was becoming increasingly difficult to sustain. With my father's eyes fixed on him like a dog's on his master, with my own homage as much taken for granted as that of a slave by the Persian King, there was no need to keep up the pretence in one house at least. And so I saw – and heard – naked arrogance.

Yes, he was glad to come to my father's house. That easiness of manner in the outside world was not a constant thing in those last spring days. In our house he would sit silent for long periods. No man has ever known exactly what he was planning then, but even I could tell that some desperate scheme was close to fruition, and even his self-assurance must have been less than perfect at times, nerves must have cried out under the strain of waiting . . .

So, I suppose, it must be with any man in his position who is not completely mad. He may have ambition enough, vanity enough, talents so great that others flatter him to the point that almost he might think himself a god. But unless he is a madman he cannot think himself a god all the time, and then the little snakes of panic creep hissing out of their holes.

Especially at night.

Nearly always he came to us at night – quite late.

Like the night before his expedition sailed for its unknown destination.

It had not been a good day. The wind had shrieked from the north-east, bringing rain mixed with sleet. As ever, Miltiades said little – it was Father who did most of the talking; he was like a schoolboy, excited, laughing at this tremendous prank,

Miltiades sailing off with every Athenian ship, and no one knew where. 'No – don't tell me, I'll know soon enough!' And then he said something unbelievable.

'I'm coming out tomorrow to watch you go.'

Miltiades himself was startled. 'Impossible. You haven't been out for months.'

'I wish to God I were coming with you. Since I can't, I'm going to cheer you on your way!'

Eventually Miltiades agreed. It would, of course, appeal to the crowd – a crippled hero of Marathon limping out to wish his old commander well. But he still had common sense enough to realise it would be as well if the crippled hero were not in too bad a physical shape, so he left earlier than usual, telling my father to get a good night's rest, and, as I escorted him out, he said to me, 'Tell him tomorrow he's to come out only if the weather's fine. If he came out in the wind and rain we've had today . . .'

. . . he would, of course, probably die, and that would not be a good omen.

There was another omen too, that night. We walked along the corridor into the outer hall; I was carrying a lamp so that I could go straight to my own room afterwards.

The doorkeeper fumbled with bolts and bars. The noises of the City at night flowed in from the opened door; somewhere an owl hooted, further off a dog howled eerily – and a sudden gust of wind came in with a rush, just as Miltiades bent to say again in a lowered voice that my father should come out only if the weather were good.

I felt a crawling of the flesh. God knows that for weeks I had been conscious enough of how he had coarsened, how his face had grown fleshy, but now, as the lamp flame dipped in the sudden draught, soared again, flickered wildly, the alternating light and shadow it cast upwards effected a fantastic transformation. Here the light rested on the line of the blurring jaw-bone with rare clarity, there a shadow stressed the hollow beneath the eye-socket. For one ghastly moment, he seemed a dead man, with

45

the urgent skull struggling to be free of the humanising confines of the flesh.

The next day the sun shone out strongly. We took my father out into the brightness to watch his cousin go, setting him on a marble seat where the life of Athens throbbed about him like heart's blood.

But there came a time when the only sound was an admiring murmur as Miltiades dismounted and came across and talked to Father. One word predominated in all the buzz of noise – kindness. But it wasn't kindness: the expression in the dark eyes was patronage, proprietorship, the feeling a master might show to a well-trained dog.

The sun shone down, and I looked at Miltiades over my father's head and beneath the burnished helmet I could still see only a skull.

The first news that came back to us was all triumph – he was sailing up and down, 'restoring to their duty', as he put it, those islands which had submitted to Persia. If necessary he used force – and always he imposed fines. Ceos, Cythnos, Seriphos, Siphnos, Melos – all fell to him. Every morning Father limped out on my arm to sit basking in the sun and his cousin's glory.

But in reality Miltiades stood on the razor's edge. Because of Marathon people expected him to make the impossible possible; only a triumph quite out of the ordinary would satisfy them now.

And then, on the island of Paros, his luck ran out. The Parians, hearing the fate of the other islands, had repaired and strengthened their walls. For twenty-six days, Miltiades besieged the town, to no effect. At last, in desperation, he planned to take it by treachery. A woman called Timo, an attendant of Demeter and Persephone, had been captured outside the town. She promised to disclose a secret which would place Paros in Miltiades' power if he came secretly by night to the temple of Demeter. This sounds desperately silly, crazy stuff – but imagine a man in a fever of desperation, his crews hungry and mutinous, his own thoughts circling as endlessly as the buzzing flies in the sweat and the sun of noonday — what were his enemies saying in Athens?

I have visited Paros, and have seen the temple. There is a little grove about it, with a sacred spring. I thought of Miltiades making his way through the dark trees, with the soft murmur of the water barely audible above the thudding of his heart, the racing of his blood.

And he panicked.

Whether it was fear of the gods, or — as is more likely — sudden realisation that he might be walking into a trap, he panicked. He had come to the gate of the sanctuary and, against expectation, found it locked and barred. So he had climbed the wall, and then made his way forward towards the temple, had come to the very door of it when his nerve broke. Did he suddenly fear that enemies stood waiting for him in the dark interior?

Whatever the cause, he was seized with sudden terror and ran like a man out of his senses. He was too blinded by fear to judge distances properly, he stumbled when leaping the wall, managed to drag himself over, but then lay prone, his thigh broken.

He had brought half a dozen men with him, but had told them to wait when he went into the little grove. He might have been rescued sooner if he had taken them into his confidence a little, but he had taken no one into his confidence for months now. He had told them, 'Wait until I return!' and so they waited for hour after hour, until dawn came, and one man rebelled against this passive acceptance of command, went among the trees and saw the helpless curve of great shoulders at the base of the wall.

Those soldiers have described what they found, venturing closer — a heap, no, a hulk of a man lying face downwards. When they lifted him up, they saw that his eyes were wide open, but he would say nothing to them, though he could not keep back the groans of pain as they raised him.

He was very thirsty, they said. All the way back to the camp his tongue kept licking the trickle of blood that was running down from the lip he had bitten through.

47

And his troops lost faith in him. He was no longer the fortunate, the invincible, the darling of the gods. He was a man who panicked in the dark, came running, and, having put on flesh, when he tried to get over a wall he came down too heavily for his own good. Hungry and mutinous, they sailed home.

He was still unable to walk when they brought him back to Athens. They had to carry him ashore. It was not easily done, though they meant no roughness; the huge bulk of him was so limp. He sagged like a half-filled sack of flour, his face was the colour of flour. His eyes were wide open, but I think – and hope – that he saw nothing.

I stood watching from the quay. Then I had to go back and somehow tell my father.

Before his injury was known, when the sole information was that the fleet was returning, unsuccessful, Xanthippos had said he intended to impeach Miltiades on a charge of deceiving the people.

He did nothing to defend himself. He lay on his stretcher in the courtroom, while his friends did their best to advance some kind of defence on his behalf – the best they could manage was to stress his earlier services to Athens.

He lay there, his eyes blind to everything about him. His mind, I think, was completely overthrown now. And from the body, defeated as was the mind, came the stench of gangrenous decay. There had been talk of demanding the death sentence, or banishment, but no one spoke of such punishments after that dreadful figure had been carried into the court. Sentence had already been passed; his mind was already in exile while his body rotted among us.

He was fined fifty talents – that was the loss incurred by the City over the expedition. They carried him back to his house, and he died there within days.

With him died any lingering hope of my father's eventual recovery. At times we feared for his reason – so wild were the

48

futile rages, so frenzied the bitter tirades against Athenian ingratitude. And if he hated all Athens in general, he hated one Athenian in particular – Themistocles, who, although disregarded at the time, had dared to oppose Miltiades in the weeks before the expedition put out to sea, Themistocles the nobody, the rabble-rouser.

There was some uncertainty about Themistocles' birth; some people even said that he was illegitimate; certainly his mother, long since dead, had once been a slave. She was not Athenian; she came from Ionia. Equally certainly Themistocles had loved her very much. When I knew him well, he told me once how she would tell him all that she could remember of her old home in Caria, and her home and family, gentleness and decency vanishing in blood and flames when the Persian armies first came down to the coast and a few – a very few – Ionian cities had resisted. And a small girl-child had survived to be sold in a slave market the very name of which she had been too young to know. But she had remembered the name of her city, and had begged her son to go one day to find if anything of it remained. So, years after her death, he had gone across the sea and landed near the headland in Caria he had heard so often described to him, climbed the height, and found nothing living. A few lines of wall, a shattered column or two, a narcissus pushing its way through the eye-socket of a skull, a crocus showing saffron among the bones of other unburied dead, the spring rain falling all about him. Such was his mother's home.

She had never known the name of the town where she had been sold into slavery, but she never forgot how she had crouched whimpering in the straw until someone bought her and led her off animal-like, a halter round her neck. And her son did not forget it either. In a way, her misfortune was fortunate for Athens. As he said to me one day, 'Slavery's just a word to every other politician in the Assembly. For me, it's something that happened to my mother.'

4

After the ruin of Miltiades, when my father once more became a very sick man indeed, my maternal grandfather, Aristeippos, took me to stay with him. I have not spoken of him before, for the adequate reason that, while my father was in good health, he let my grandfather have no access to me. But his long bouts of fever altered that; my grandfather was therefore able to have me under his roof for long periods at a time.

Among the many talents possessed by the Alcmaeonid clan, was a gift for annexing – no, more absolute than that, *absorbing* the men who married into it. (Its most conspicuous failure had been with my own father.) Grandfather had married the sister of Cleisthenes, who had given Athens its democratic constitution. Immediately Cleisthenes' ideas became his. And not only Cleisthenes' revolutionary ideas on politics. Cleisthenes followed ideas to their logical conclusion, another characteristic that made him unpopular with his fellow nobles, for it was he who started the dangerous notion that now that the people had the vote it would be as well to let them have education too, while to his own family he observed bleakly, 'I've no doubt that for a generation or so the people will be tentative in their attempts to exercise full power themselves, they'll be willing to delegate it to certain members of the former ruling class, but, by God, our children will need a new kind of education. Something beside and beyond knowledge of horseflesh and how to entertain dinner guests – in other words, intellectual as well as physical training.'

When this leaked out, there was about as much fury among the nobles as when Cleisthenes had worked out the new Athenian constitution. But the treacherous brute was past all caring. He was advising his relatives to import tutors from Ionia to instruct their children in philosophy, mathematics –

the gods knew where it would end. Ah, said the reactionaries hopefully, but what a set these Alcmaeonids will turn out to be – pallid, pimply, narrow-shouldered, pigeon-chested (inflating all the while their own powerful chests, squaring their own broad shoulders). But it didn't turn out like that. Alcmaeonids might be intellectuals; they were never physically soft, even though they did not spend all their spare time exercising thoroughbreds in the plain of Colonos, restrict their reading matter to treatises on horsemanship. I myself don't worship horses, yet I have owned as good as any – my black Melanippe, my shining chestnut Xanthippe. I could ride them as well as any one. Sometimes, putting a horse at a steep slope, or jumping a ditch, I outdid the other boys. But I also believed that having a good seat on a horse was not the most important thing in life.

But life under my grandfather's guardianship was not spent nose in book all the time. He told me that, since the estate would be mine one day, I had better get to know the people who worked on it. Startled, I said I knew them already. 'No, you don't,' he said. 'You've just scraped the surface of knowledge. You are going to *live* with them – spend days with the shepherds, the workers in the fields. How else can you know them?'

There was something of Themistocles in the way Grandfather thought. A man, any man, was an individual to Themistocles, not just a pair of arms to hold a spear, to grip an oar – or a hand to raise in voting or to write a name on a potsherd. Grandfather felt the same about every man who worked on the farm. It was an attitude very different from that of most other landowners. Hands to gather grapes, plough the land, tend the sheep, they thought. Grandfather thought of hands, and hearts, and minds – and the expressions on faces. Others might have riches; contentment came to him from a grove of olives, a field of ripening corn, trees bending under a weight of fruit, the bleating of newborn lambs, weathered farm buildings, the pleasant, homely farm itself – and the smiling faces of those who worked the farm with him, the frank, open speech with which they would greet him. They were all part of a whole.

51

I lived for months with the shepherds and ploughmen, getting up with them before dawn, setting out to work with them as they greeted the rising sun with a kiss of the hand, looking up to the mountain, if rain were needed, in the hope that it was cloud-capped, that Zeus, the cloud-gatherer, sat there. Townsfolk often laugh at the countryfolk as superstitious numbskulls, but this isn't so. You are superstitious only if you are terrified of the gods, and I have seen more hysterical fear in towns than ever in the countryside. For in the countryside you live with the gods, feel their presence all the while. That doesn't make for fear. They are kindly gods. To the city dweller Zeus is primarily the wielder of thunderbolts, an angry god demonstrating his presence with the roar of thunder, the flash of lightning that strikes down mountain tops, tall trees, man. The country dweller doesn't think of him in this way. Zeus to him is above all the cloud-gatherer, who brings the badly needed rain. And if he does cast the occasional thunderbolt, even that is always accompanied by the rain that feeds the grass, the crops, the fruit, fills the wells and dried-up river beds. Other peoples may worship the sun; a countryman in Attica kisses his hand to it at the beginning of his working day, but that is a gesture of affectionate familiarity, he does the same to the first returning swallow. And other gods are always with him – not the great Olympians, most of whom seem cold and remote to the countryman, but lesser deities at home with the beasts and woods, the fields and lonely places. In the town it is all too easy to set the god firmly in a marble shrine on a high place – and call on him only when in pain and fear; in the countryside the gods are your constant companions, you may talk with them as you go about your everyday tasks, feel their presence in a certain grove or cave or stream.

The two gods dearest to the country dweller are Demeter and Pan. No countryman would dream of grasping the handle of the plough when commencing the sowing without a prayer to Demeter; all agricultural toil – sowing, ploughing, harvesting – he calls her works. Nearly all agricultural festivals are devoted to the goddess whose gift of corn enabled men not to live like beasts; the happiest of festivals was the private holiday when the threshing was ended, and sacrifice was made to the smiling goddess whose arms were filled with sheaves and poppies.

And there is that other very different god of the countryside, Pan. He can be formidable enough; the windless calm, the heat of the sun at noon in summer can turn into nightmare if you needlessly disturb the god's rest. He can rouse in men the mindless terror you see in a herd of stampeding beasts, he is the avenger of wrongs done to animals, but usually he is a kindly god, well-disposed towards men, and should you hear his pipes (most likely at dawn or at evening, they say) in those places he loves, groves, pastures, rocky heights, caves, streams, springs, the lonely places that are the haunts of sheep and goats, you need have no fear, for the horned, goat-footed, dancing god smiles on countrymen, although it is said he dislikes foreigners — as any countryman might do. The wilder stretches of the countryside are his, but he is a friendly host, welcoming you to his home.

Nothing could better illustrate what I have said about the gulf separating the beliefs of town and country dwellers than the fact that until the year of Marathon, Pan, so ever-present to the countryman, had no shrine on the Acropolis. The story of how Pheidippides the runner saw Pan in Arcadia on his way to Sparta is now well known. There have always been those who have privately scoffed at Pheidippides' story; a tired man imagines things, they say — why, the poor fellow even said that Pan addressed him by name. But I have learnt that the man who died in my arms was a country dweller, from the wild Cithaeron region, a professional runner who would have trained alone in the lonely hills beloved by the god, and I believe that Pan knew him by name just as he knew Pan — because they had met before.

And then it was all over, my grandfather was dead, and I must return to the City, rarely left by my crippled father. And I began to forget the gods of the countryside a little, my chief devotion was given to the Maiden, the Lady of the City, Athene. She surely must be the goddess dearest to any Athenian in his youth, and she will always retain her place in his heart so long as that heart remains loyal to the City. But then, as he grows older, another goddess, previously disregarded, may take her place in his prayers. She is the least obtrusive of deities, Hestia, goddess of the hearth, that centre of the house, that symbol of the home, round which the newborn child is carried by its father as a sign that it is received into the family. For if a man should know the *Iliad* by heart, he should learn the *Odyssey* too, the *Iliad* because all life is a struggle, the *Odyssey* because life is a journey, at the end of which the traveller returns home, and a wife weeping with joy runs to meet him, for even as the sight of land is welcome to mariners, says Homer, so welcome to her was the sight of her husband. And equally welcome to the husband can be the sight of a beloved wife.

5

I came back to the city to be jeered at by my father for unEupatrid behaviour – a son of his to be able to plough, or tend a flock in the lambing season! But the real anger, utterly unforgiving, did not begin until I chose to set my hand, not to the plough, but to an oar, found myself more likely to be surrounded by the black beaks of dolphins than by the amiably silly faces of sheep – after I had sought out Themistocles, and accepted his belief that the Persians would return – and that this time they could only be beaten at sea.

With the easily acquired wisdom of hindsight, it now seems incredible that so many Athenian nobles were convinced that Marathon had ended the Persian danger for good. Granted, few of them were noted for powers of imagination, but how much imagination was needed to grasp that for a ruler like the Persian King, the knowledge that a minute, rather barren portion of territory had once successfully defied his god-ordained rule, was a running sore in his self-esteem?

Especially since a new Great King, Xerxes, now ruled in Persia. Darius died four years after Marathon, at about the time when I went back to the City. Now, Darius might have had a personal grudge against Athens, Darius might have the fixed idea that empires existed solely to expand by conquest, but Darius at least could grasp what was a realistic proposition and what was not. If Darius were arrogant, one might at least concede that he had something to be arrogant about, while if he claimed that he owed his position to divine favour, it might be argued that the gods had indeed favoured him in the fight for the throne. His son's claim to divine favour was less modest. He had been accorded it from the moment of his conception. A man with his inflated views on the majesty of monarchy would never forgive any denial of that monarchy's divinely ordained right to infinite conquests. A man of his nature might also secretly rejoice in any chance to succeed where his awesome father had failed.

I don't claim, of course, that to us in Greece it could possibly be immediately obvious what kind of man the new Great King was. I don't claim that every man should have had the foresight of a Themistocles. But I do say that to any sensible man not blinded by prejudice a Persian return in greater strength was inevitable. And any ignorance of Xerxes' personal character notwithstanding, his actions after his accession – his crushing of an Egyptian revolt, and then his reduction of that proud kingdom together with the ancient kingdom of Babylon to the utter subjection and degradation of the most barbaric of provinces – should have been enough to convince any thinking observer that Athens, which had successfully withstood the will of the gods and the Great King, was scarcely likely to merit any tenderer treatment.

Because I held such views, the break with my father began.

There were now frequent visitors to our house. They were nearly always old men. Sometimes they would seem no more than grey beards and splendid clothes – until, if they began to talk about Themistocles, you noticed their eyes. There was a strangeness about their eyes then, a blankness, yet a brightness, as in a viper's. And they often talked about Themistocles – that was the real reason they came to our house. My father had been ill so long that I noticed how few visitors bothered now to ask him how he was; his pallor, the blueness about eyes and lips, were taken for granted.

Not one of them seemed to realise that feeding his hatred and bitterness was no help to him.

I suppose that only one thing could have made my father forget my physical resemblance to my mother's family – a failure on my part to resemble them in mind. If mine had been the kind of mind that he could have moulded like wax . . .

So much easier if mentally I had been made of wax — or water. But there was something always stubborn, unmalleable that kept me from taking the easy way out.

My tutor having been dismissed, I was left pretty much to my own devices. I used to slip out early in the morning, before my father was up, to be alone for a time, to be myself for a time, in the grey streets of Athens before dawn. Being usually hungry, I would go into a bakery to eat hot toast dripping with honey, and on one such occasion I met a friend of pre-Marathon days, a boy of my own age, Cleandros. One of our reasons for being friendly then had been that both of us were motherless, although he was less lonely at home than I, having a younger sister. But now, he told me, his family circumstances had deteriorated further. His father had remarried. His second wife was the daughter of an immensely rich ex-Chief Magistrate called Hipparchos. Possibly her mother was even more important — she had been the sister of the tyrant Hippias, now living in exile in Persia. From the way his stepmother behaved, muttered Cleandros, you would think her uncle was still ruling Athens. He was especially bitter because he, unlike me, could remember his mother quite clearly.

Cleandros' father's remarriage, although his own family had been one of the noble clans most opposed to the tyrants, had caused little surprise, for he was a notorious spendthrift, and his bride brought a handsome dowry with her. But if through that remarriage he was enabled to buy back the ancestral vineyards and olive groves he had been compelled to sell, I don't imagine he ever enjoyed the repossession. Cleandros used to tell me, scarlet-faced, that his stepmother never let anyone forget for long where the money for the repurchase had come from.

Perhaps the chief fact anyone will remember of her father Hipparchos — a well-meaning dunderhead — was that he was the first victim of a further political device invented by my grand-uncle, Cleisthenes. If six thousand citizens voted that a man was a danger to the state, he was to go into exile for ten years, although with no loss of citizen rights on his return, or of property.* Now, no one in his senses could think of Hipparchos in himself as a threat to the state. But his very stupidity made him an excellent figurehead. He was, as it were, an eternal mouthpiece. He had been elected Chief Magistrate five or six years before Marathon as the candidate of the 'realists' – the peace at any price party who had been terrified since aid had been sent to the Ionian rebels. Hipparchos, they said, was the one man who could obtain forgiveness for what Athens had done to his brother-in-law Hippias, and to Hippias' patron the Persian King. Many people believed that he was in touch with Hippias in Marathon year. Since then, Hipparchos had been saying in his rather high-pitched voice that the tyrant's family was entirely reasonable in its demands; all it wanted was the restoration of its estates and 'proper position'.

As I had said, a dunderhead. The wonder is that he was allowed to go on talking like this for three years after Marathon, that he incurred no penalty worse than ten years' exile. But because he was the victim of Cleisthenes' device – as first put into practice on the suggestion of Themistocles – he became something of a hero to the aristocratic diehards, even though the old idiot, probably with no idea that such an action would justify every charge brought against him, went straight off on a visit to Persia.

So those who might have been prepared to collaborate with the Persians had lost their respectable figurehead. Cleandros told me his stepmother showed little grief but plenty of anger. Cleandros' father sought escape in drink. 'He can't go on much longer like this,' said Cleandros, who had long lost any filial respect or affection. 'I only hope nothing happens before I come of age.'

It was when he said this that I realised how much I, too, was longing for my own coming of age, even though the ceremony involved taking an oath that might involve a clash of loyalties –

* Citizens voted by writing the name of the man they wanted banished on *ostraka* – potsherds.

58

'to defend the City against all manner of enemies,' you said, and then, in the next breath, 'to be a faithful member of this the clan to which I was born.' But as far as I was concerned, there would be no conflict. Even then I knew where my priorities lay.

Nowadays coming of age also involves two years of intensive military training; before Xerxes' invasion the training was a much more casual affair, but even so it meant days down at the Peiraeos practising keeping your spears level, and yourself in line, although only battle itself could teach you the heave of it, the strain of it, till you felt your lungs would burst and your back would break.

It was after such an exercise that I met Themistocles again. We were sitting panting after a training session, taking off helmet and breastplate and greaves. My left greave pinched atrociously; I had begun to take it off and was rubbing my leg when our training instructor cursed, spat, and growled, 'I wonder the bastard doesn't come across and tell us it's all a waste of time.'

I straightened up, rubbed the sweat and dust out of my eyes. There was the big figure, not looking at us, gazing out to sea.

Suddenly I realised why, although I had been back in Athens for months, and had assiduously found out all that I could about the man, I had never tried to see him personally. I had been needlessly afraid that he, too, might have changed as Miltiades had changed. Success might toughen Themistocles; it never coarsened him.

'All right,' said the instructor. 'Dismiss.' Pathetically, he added, 'My heart wouldn't be in it now.' This met with no response from us. None of us believed he had ever possessed that particular organ.

'Are you coming?' Cleandros asked me, with a cracking yawn. 'We can —'

But I don't know what he went on to suggest. I sat there in the heat of the afternoon, feeling cold and sick. It was not the first time I had felt like this. Before I had become much good

as a swimmer, I had rashly run out into a furious sea. A wave
had caught me up, sucked me down. Eventually it had thrown
me back on the beach, unable to breathe, with a roaring noise
in my head, and a feeling of sickness and cold.

'Well,' I said to myself, 'I suppose this time it's politics. Are
you, inexperienced as you are, going to throw yourself into the
sea again — with no guarantee that this time there'll be a safe
outcome to it all?'

For if I went to speak to Themistocles, sooner or later my
father would know. Among my fellow trainees were half a dozen
whose fathers were his acquaintances. Within days, perhaps even
hours, someone would say, 'My boy's just told me a most
incredible thing, Acestorides. Your son went up to that swine,
Themistocles — '

And then there would be confrontation.

He hadn't taken any notice of us.

That gave me an excuse for doing nothing. It wasn't as if he'd
met me in the street, recognised me, spoken to me —

I needn't take any decision today.

One day that decision would have to be taken. Sooner or
later. But not today.

' — how do you feel about that?' said Cleandros.

I had no idea what he had been talking about, but I began
warmly, 'Yes, I think it's a good idea — '

But then the big figure turned, began to walk away.

'Don't wait for me,' I said rapidly. 'Go without me.'

And, trailing my spear, and with one flapping greave, puerile
travesty of a hero, I began to hurry after that retreating figure.
I did not hurry for long. Our instructor spat after me. However
passionate his obsession for a correct alignment of spear-tips
might be, he was, thank God, wildly inaccurate when it came to
expectoration. Yet the gesture slowed me down. So did the
babble of voices behind me — amazed, jeering. I plodded on
suddenly leaden feet. Why was I letting myself get drawn into —
But I wasn't getting drawn in, I was *advancing*. No one was
going to slam a door behind me; I was going to shut myself

in, away. Just because, accidentally, I had sat behind him during an Assembly meeting that had ended in a thunderstorm . . . And he had been kind when I was scared. What was I involving myself in? Prudence, all the natural inclination for a familiar way of life, told me to turn back. It would be stupid to pretend that I was happy, comfortable in mind at home; honesty had long since forced me to acknowledge that although I was sorry for my father, I also felt impatient with him, and could not feel the love for him that I should. But he was my father, it was my home. If I talked to Themistocles now, something told me it would not end there. I should be drawn into something that would end in –

In, possibly, a wave sucking me down and down and making an end of me.

He told me later he would never have turned if it had not been for that slapping noise of the loosened greave against my shin, an odd sound that he couldn't place. So he turned.

I thought, 'He won't know me – why should he? So I'll simply walk past him.' I congratulated myself on not having called after him.

But he recognised me, and he smiled, that smile of amazing charm. 'Why, Theron!' he said, putting out his hand.

Prudence said, 'Part of the old politician's trick of the trade, never to forget a face, always the ready hand – '

And I said, 'Themistocles, I am so glad to see you again!' and put my hand in his.

I was in such a state of confusion and excitement that for a time I scarcely noticed what he was saying. When I surfaced mentally, he was saying, 'Well, this *is* good luck – although perhaps not so lucky. I often come down to the Peiraeos.'

'Business?' I asked in a would-be man-of-the-world manner.

'Two kinds. Private in practice; pure wishful thinking where public's concerned. Do you know why I didn't notice the training going on under my nose? Partly because – and here you have a perfect right to take offence – I believe that what you've been doing, what you'll go on doing, is largely irrelevant. And

61

partly because when I'm here in Peiraeos I see, not so much the actual place, as what it could be. Do you know what my dream is, Theron? To make it the greatest port in Greece. A commercial harbour and a naval base.'

'Giving up Phaleron?' I asked in surprise.

'Yes.'

'But Phaleron's closer to the City – only three miles away. Peiraeos is a good five.'

'Agreed, but Phaleron's an open beach – think of the shelter you'd get here! Natural rock harbour to take care of bad weather, and look at nature's own fortifications to take care of attacks of the human kind! Fortify those rocks, build one continuous line of fortifications between here and the City, and we could snap our fingers at the rest of the world!'

'Provided,' I said, 'that we had a strong navy.'

He looked at me with amused eyes. 'Statement, question or challenge?' he asked.

I must have showed my surprise. 'Statement, I suppose, but I hadn't thought of it like that. It seemed the only logical – '

'Theron,' said Themistocles, 'you have made my day! If only others could accept a logical conclusion!' Then, in a lower voice, and more gravely, 'Your comrades are going. There is still time for you to join them. Too much damage hasn't been done so far – '

'Damage?' I asked, although of course I knew.

'Well,' he said, 'you've been out of Athens for about two years, so you mightn't know that to many of the well-born and well-to-do I represent pure poison.'

'I knew what I was letting myself in for before I came after you,' I said.

'I must go,' he said gravely, 'but, remember, my house is always open to you, and whatever assistance I can give is yours for the asking.'

He had gone. I turned to find that I was not completely alone, Cleandros was still there. He came across and said anxiously, 'They'll talk. It'll get to your father – '

'It'll get to *your* father that you stayed.'

'He won't take much notice. He doesn't take much notice of anything nowadays. It has its advantages. What will you do, Theron, if there's trouble?'

'If I'm thrown out, there's my grandfather's farm to go to, and a little house here in town.'

'Are you going home now?'

'Not yet. I want to think things out . . . Thank you for staying.'

'If I'd had more guts I'd have come across to talk to him. I've always wanted to.'

I rode out to the farm I still could not think of as my own. I did not approach the house itself, but sat in the orchard, my back to an old ruined wall, relic of fighting and destruction so far in the remote past that Grandfather himself had had no idea what had caused it. It would be self-flattering to say I sat and thought; I simply sat. The sun was still strong enough for the stone at my back to be warm; bees were furiously busy among the clumps of thyme clinging to the stones, and lizards lay panting on the rough weatherbeaten top. The only noise was the hum of the insects and the sound of my horse cropping grass.

And I simply sat.

It was a mental and emotional breathing space before I went back into the City and plunged into decisions and debate and bitterness. I realised dimly that in the future there would not be many opportunities simply to sit, unthinking, in the sun, and that I had better make the best of this one.

I went back with the evening, and straight into trouble. My judges were already there, sitting with my father. Unnecessary to repeat what was said; it was entirely predictable. The manner of its saying was entirely predictable too. My chief recollection, however, is not of voices, but of faces – sagging muscles, heavy jowls, slack mouths with the lines pulling down at the corners.

I was given a choice, and made my decision. I went off to pack my belongings. One by one every slave managed to creep in to

63

say good-bye. Many of them wept. I said I would try to buy them from my father, but, in his present mood, that could not be done for some time. The older ones talked a little of my mother.

Then it was finished, and I must go. I did not re-enter the room where my father and his friends had sat in judgment on me; I could hear angry voices still upraised. I crossed the dark hall; there was the hearth, there the altar, here the door to the street where the lamp had shown Miltiades' face like a skull — and here, beside the red-eyed doorkeeper, a strange slave with a note from Cleandros. 'If you have to leave home tonight you will need someone to escort you across the City.' I had forgotten the need for a torch; there was no moon that night — a fine fool I should have looked blundering about in the darkness after my ignominious exit.

It was only when we were crossing Athens that I realised that not only had I forgotten about getting to my grandfather's house, I had made no provision for myself when I got there. No fire, no food, no light. It was a primitive little house, in any case — heavy, clumsily-fluted pillars upholding the roof, no marble flooring in the entrance court as in my — my *father*'s home, but hard-pressed earth with a simple design in pebbles. I had been there only once two years ago; I didn't even know if there was any bedroom furniture.

But when we turned into the narrow street, Cleandros' slave stopped with a sudden exclamation. Outside the little porch laurel wreaths. Light shining beyond. And there in the entrance court, Themistocles, and fire on the old worn altar, and wine ready for a libation.

'Word gets around,' said Themistocles. 'Your father's slaves are fond of you; I get on well with mine. I'm not renowned for devotion to pious rituals, but I wasn't going to let the opposition crow over your entering into an unconsecrated house. And after the consecration, a meal.'

He stayed with me as I ate from a table that might have been old when Theseus as a boy sailed for Crete. I don't remember what the food was, or even what we talked about, but I know

64

that I realised even then that here was a man who could make me do more than I should ever have thought myself capable of, and this not by driving or exhortation, but simply by being himself.

Any sleep I got that night should have been wretched. The bedroom smelt musty and damp, there wasn't even the simplest reed mat on the floor, the leather straps of the mattress were so aged I didn't know whether before the morning they would break and deposit me on the floor. But in fact I slept so heavily I did not dream at all, and when I awoke in the morning it was in the knowledge that my little house, contemptible in the eyes of my father and his friends, at least was not haunted by bitterness and hatred, the ghost of an adored cousin who had died in misery and disgrace. It might be dark, and overlaid with dust and cobwebs, but you could live in it spiritually unshadowed, and you could breathe freely.

6

That was a marvellously exciting time to be living if you were young or if your mind was not shut fast to change; hellish, I suppose, if you belonged to the other persuasion. There were so many new ideas in government, philosophy – and warfare at sea.

Before I was born, our navy, such as it was, consisted of two kinds of craft. There was the thirty-oared galley, the triaconter, for lighter work, and, for the really serious business, the pentaconter, fifty oars, twenty-four a side in two banks (twelve along the gunwale, twelve along the lower thwarts) and two steering oars. This itself was a great improvement on the first pentaconters, which were one-bank affairs, making for an over-long vessel, the devil to manoeuvre and hideously unseaworthy. But no one was going to reduce the number of rowers. Oar-power, after all, has come to stay. From the moment some unknown genius invented the ram, the whole conception of a naval battle has been revolutionised. Hitherto the strategic idea had been to make a battle at sea as much like a battle on land as possible, you crammed as many archers and spearmen aboard as the ship would take, but after the invention of the ram, the oarsmen were the people who mattered, for only they could put the ship in the right spot from which it could strike with its bronze beak at the enemy's vital point. Then the naval architects between them had designed a new kind of hull, with two banks of oars, those on the upper bank placed over the space between two of the lower, so that everybody could be fitted in. It meant that the new craft, a third shorter than the old, offered as much less target to the enemy ram, and were immeasurably more manoeuvrable and seaworthy.

And then, some years before the Athenian tyranny was overthrown, another naval architect made the logical final step forward, adding a third bank of oars to give that clinching extra power and speed to any warship. To do this within the hull itself would have been self-defeating; a deeper ship would have been a heavier ship – slower, more sluggish in manoeuvre. So they added on each side an outrigger, above the gunwale, and projecting beyond it. At a stroke, all existing fighting vessels were made obsolete; all around the Mediterranean (for, whoever invented the trireme, the idea spread fast – they started building triremes in Egypt, Phoenicia, Greece, Sicily) you saw pente-conters rotting on the shores like beached sea monsters.

'If I could only get people to see,' Themistocles said to me, 'that the gods were fighting for us when they inspired that unknown architect! They argue that it's absurd for us to try to outbuild states who've always had strong navies. But the trireme makes all existing fleets obsolete! The newcomer to the race starts on equal terms! Here's our god-given chance to defend ourselves!'

But ships take money to build and to keep at sea; venomously Themistocles' opponents in the Assembly pointed out the difference between the insane expense of maintaining not only the totally unnecessary ships, but the 'sailor rabble' (a much-used phrase) that would man them, and the force of heavy-armed infantry who had saved Athens at Marathon, and would save her again *if* the unbelievable happened and, after such a beating, the barbarian returned, the point being that the heavy-armed infantry was composed solely of the better-to-do citizens who provided their own equipment.

The leader of the opposition to an increased navy was Aristeides. I believe he was quite sincere in his so frequently expressed belief that the hoplites plus 'our Spartan friends and allies' (a frequently but unwisely used expression which usually evoked some raucous comment such as, 'They'd be late for their own funerals!') could deal with any Persian invasion that might occur. And this, I think, shows the man's mental limitations.

I learned about warships on what warships we had. Themis-tocles' dream was of two hundred; at that point we never really thought the dream would become reality. At rare intervals I went back to my farm. But a great deal of my time I spent in anything but rural surroundings.

'We must find out all we can about what's going on in Persia,' said Themistocles. 'I want to talk to the foreign traders who come to Athens, and go on talking. It would help if you could learn something of their languages, for a start.'

I learned to speak Persian not too badly. My tutor was Sicinnos, the Ionian Greek who was the tutor to Themistocles' children: I practised my linguistic prowess amid far from scholarly surroundings. Ports are the noisiest places on earth, because they are usually the most crowded. To get to the shops of the merchants who were my chief contacts meant forcing my way through carts piled high with kegs of olive oil, goatskins filled with wine, baskets of pottery, sacks of vegetables, mules that brayed and kicked, men who cursed and swore. And then, amid the din, low-voiced conversations with swarthy captains of foreign trading vessels, money-changers, merchants. After a few months I had amassed an immense amount of useless information or rumours, but I had also learned much that was relevant. That to the east was a sanguinary, cruel, barbaric power so extravagant that one day it would choke to death on its own riches, but before that day it was the most formidable force humanity had ever seen. That this great barbaric power rested on incessant conquest. Athens had broken a link in that chain of conquest and servitude at Marathon; it would not be allowed to happen again.

And, little by little, I began to gather information as to the preparations for that return, this time to total conquest. Some of it passed on to me by men whose dark eyes were bright with gloating and malice, Phoenicians, usually, who did not like upstart Athens — if it came to that, they disliked all Greeks, but us they disliked more than most — and they took great pleasure in telling me of the hordes of soldiers, the squadron upon squadron of ships the Great King would undoubtedly soon send against us — and the hatred he had for us. And I couldn't comfort myself with the fact that they exaggerated. Malicious they might be, but, much as they wished to terrify us, there was no need for them to tell us anything but the plain truth. The greatest military power our earth had ever known was going to march against us in the near future, and the aim was our total destruction.

But at least the gods were giving us a chance to put up some kind of fight.

Hitherto, the forthcoming contest had been, to say the least, an unequal one so far as material resources were concerned. On the one hand, the Great King, with more than half a million men for fleets and armies – and the money to maintain them. Merchants told me stories of wealth that, much as I should have liked to doubt them, seemed well founded enough. In the treasury of Persepolis, one of the royal palaces, over a hundred thousand talents of silver, a large room called 'the King's cushion' with five thousand talents of gold at the head of the royal bed (over which was a golden vine with grape clusters of the most costly jewels), and a smaller room, 'the King's foot-stool', with three thousand talents at the foot. A thousand talents of silver annually from Babylon. Three hundred and sixty talents of gold dust from India – these two might have been the wealthiest of the Persian provinces, but there were also eighteen others. And against this we could put in the scales what we gained from the export of a little wine, a little olive oil, some marble. True, there was an increasing demand for our pottery, but the sale of a few thousand red and black pots was hardly likely to bring us anything like the fourteen thousand odd talents the Great King received annually.

We were up against the richest empire in the world, and we had always been beset by poverty. There had always been stories of lead and silver seams at Laureion, thirty miles from the City, but nothing much had ever been done about it. Even if you could get the labour (free men refused to work under-ground, and there weren't enough slaves), you couldn't get men to risk money in the disheartening business of sinking shafts – and probably losing all their investments.

69

The mines were state-owned, but leased out to small opera-
tors, who paid the City a royalty on their holdings. Although
perhaps 'speculator' would be a term apter than 'operator'.
Yields had been so low that royalties were practically non-
existent. Themistocles actually went off on a trip to the north,
to Thasos, to try to find out what techniques had proved
successful there. On his return he had a series of conversations
with hitherto reluctant investors. The talk was of a technical
nature – a second limestone crust to be pierced, the need for
more trial shafts, and so on. And then one evening as we sat
eating almonds and talking ships, the doorkeeper ushered in a
wild-eyed figure, Niceratos, a scrawny speculator whose face I
had never seen anything but sallow. But tonight it was so
flushed that I, seeing his unsteady walk, hearing his blurred
speech, thought Themistocles was perforce being host to a
drunkard. But the cause of Niceratos' excitement was not wine.
It was difficult at first to catch the drift of what he was saying,
there was so much technicality – crushing, milling, washing,
smelting – 'I thought it best to wait until I was absolutely sure,'
said Niceratos half a dozen times – and then, when I felt
inclined to expose him to some of the crushing and smelting
himself, he stopped babbling, and quite simply opened his right
hand which hitherto he had kept closed. Something glinted in
his palm.

'Good silver?' whispered Themistocles.

'Good?' shrieked Niceratos in sudden hysterics. 'Quality as
well as quantity!'

'*Quantity?*'

Niceratos' eyes rolled. 'Enough to produce at least two tons
of silver annually!'

Within the year the mine had yielded double that amount.
The discovery laid the foundation of Niceratos' family fortune –
and saved Athens.

But the salvation of Athens was a very near thing. The
royalties alone after that first year amounted to one hundred

talents, enough to pay all state expenditure for a year, and to build a hundred triremes, said Themistocles. But his opponents saw matters differently. One hundred talents breaks down into 600,000 drachmas. A drachma a day is a middle-class income. The opposition demanded that the royalties should be shared out among the citizens – ten drachmas apiece. God knows how much this was based on nothing more than the determination to prevent Themistocles from getting his ships, but it was perhaps the shrewdest move his enemies had hitherto made against him, for it seemed to cut the ground from under his feet. His chief supporters, the 'rabble', were having a bribe dangled temptingly before them. Ten drachmas. It meant considerably more to a poor man than it did to Aristeides and his colleagues.

You may imagine the hand-rubbing, the back-slapping, that went on in Eupatrid circles. The 'rabble' would win the game for the gentlemen. The surly dog had been thrown a bone; enough, assuredly, to win its loyalty. 'They're no more than animals; fill their bellies, that's all they want.' I heard that being said. But they might have remembered that curious creature, the dog, has an unshakeable fidelity to the man he has acknowledged as his master. Even so, at times I myself thought the opposition might win.

Themistocles remained his usual imperturbable self. 'Well,' he said equably, after I had poured out my doubts one evening, 'perhaps people don't believe the Persians are coming. That doesn't mean we don't need more ships. For a more credible enemy. To take on Aegina* again, for example. That would beat the opposition at their own game – if we trounced Aegina, we'd get the trade that used to go her way. More profitable in the long run than ten drachmas apiece.'

Certainly Athenians felt great jealousy for Aegina. The idea might work.

Yet when it came to the final debate, although Themistocles had talked about Aegina enough in the preliminaries, he now

---

* The island visible from Athens that had recently crushingly defeated Athens at sea.

spoke on an entirely higher plane. I suppose it might be said that he in his turn borrowed an enemy war-cry, and used it against them, but I will never accept this. I would even claim that, when he got to his feet, he meant to carry on the Aegina theme; he had been speaking along those lines until he left us to go and take the speaker's wreath. But then he stood silent, and in that silence, as he looked down on the upturned faces, his expression changed. The ironic, humorous look left it. I can only guess what he was thinking, but I have always imagined it to be a sudden revulsion against this pandering to greed and self-interest, an angry refusal to underestimate the people's willingness to sacrifice themselves for the City. So in one way he would not play the opposition's game. In another way, he played it better and with more conviction than Aristeides ever achieved —he raised the whole issue to the highest level of enlightened altruism and patriotism.

Although I don't think even he realised at that point what sacrifices the Athenians would make in the cause of freedom.

He did not speak at length, but he spoke with a kind of cold fire. He said that more ships were necessary if we were to remain free men. 'It all depends which you think more essential —ten drachmas, that's a twentieth of what you'd pay for ransom if you'd been taken prisoner, or the only means by which you can make sure you're not made prisoners for life. No hope of ransom then. Ask the Ionians.

'And, furthermore, you must make up your minds now and for all time as to what you believe is involved in being a citizen of a free city. Does it mean not only braving dangers, but sacrificing comfort, an easy life? What are we to be, fellow Athenians? Comrades in a high enterprise, with the constant vigilance, forgetfulness of self that's the essential part of being a good soldier, for the fight for freedom's a longer business than shoving with spears for a couple of hours on a battlefield? Or, as previous speakers have stated, are we partners of another kind, not even members of a commercial organisation, for there at least each man must first contribute something before he gets

72

his dividend, has earned his private gains! Shall it be said of us in the future that the much-vaunted but short-lived freedom of Athens was valued very precisely by her people at ten drachmas a head?'

As he stepped down, there was silence. I felt my clenched hands stiff, yet wet. And then there was a sudden storm of cheering.

The Athenians rated freedom higher than ten drachmas a head.

The opposition fought back savagely, but could not prevent the passing of a motion allocating the Laureion revenues for the year to shipbuilding.

That meant a hundred ships, and Themistocles had calculated that two hundred were essential for safety.

It was not surprising that more and more Themistocles won support from the younger men in Athens. His apparent humorous cynicism had an immediate attraction, but if you are young you want more than that – although you would die rather than say so. You want idealism. And on occasions like the Laureion debate, Themistocles shed the cloak of cynicism he usually wore for protection.

Cleandros was one of his followers, although he could not be as active as he would have liked. True, he met with no opposition from his father, who was so permanently fuddled with drink (he died a few months before the Persians returned) that half the time he seemed unaware of what was going on about him. At the same time it meant that Cleandros had to be out in the country running their very large farm. So I didn't see much of him; their estate was about as far from the City as possible, starting well past Eleusis and then going on up into the goat-haunted hills towards Eleutherae and Cithaeron and the pass going down towards Thebes.

I went out to the estate only once, and I met Cleandros' stepmother. After that encounter, I decided never again.

I didn't, of course, go out with the intention of meeting Hipparchos' daughter. I went out because I had good news for

73

Cleandros, the chance of serving in a new trireme under a good captain, Hormos, a man I knew Cleandros both liked and respected. There was no need for me to go; I could easily have written; Cleandros was not wanted immediately. But at the time I was glad of the chance to get out in the country, away from the sheer physical assault of the sound in the market place, and the bright glint of the malice in Phoenician eyes while a sing-song Phoenician voice talked endlessly of Persian strength – and it was spring.

I was glad it was spring. Much of the journey was across a shelterless plain where the goats and charcoal-burners between them had left a bare expanse which would be trying in the heat of summer. But the farm itself was well irrigated, there were clumps of trees, thickets of oleander and myrtle, and, behind the house, a green meadow.

Cleandros, I was told, was in that meadow, and I left my horse to go in search of him. The sun shone so strongly on my face that at first I could not see him, but when I did I saw he was not alone. A girl, presumably his sister, was with him. They were so deep in conversation that I was about to turn back, being unwilling to intrude, but Cleandros' dog, Augo, lying before him, barked a warning and Cleandros raised his head, recognised me and waved a greeting. So I went across, and sat down with them against a bank of wild parsley.

The girl said nothing, but sat looking straight ahead of her; I thought she was paying no attention to what was said. Even so, I felt it best not to start talking immediately of the business that brought me out here, so instead began to speak rather aimlessly of the last Festival. And suddenly the girl asked, still not turning her head, 'Did you see Aeschylus' *Suppliant Women* when it was performed?'

I looked at her averted profile with sudden interest. 'Yes,' I said. 'It was the first tragedy I ever saw, so I remember it very well indeed.'

Cleandros laughed. 'You can't know it as well as she does. She pestered me until I bought her a copy.'

She turned her head then and looked at me. 'Why do you remember it so well?' she asked.

I was unused to talking to women, but her directness made her seem like a pleasant boy. 'Because of the Ionian Revolt, of course,' I said in some surprise.

'What has that to do with it?' Her surprise seemed to match my own.

I replied to her carefully. Unusual for a girl to take such interest in the tragedies; not unusual for a girl to know nothing of politics and affairs of the world outside the home. 'The Ionians appealed to Athens for help against the Persians, Athens being the mother-city. But not enough help was sent, and the revolt was crushed four years before Marathon.'

She made an impatient gesture. 'Everyone knows about the Ionian Revolt. But what has it to do with the play?'

Cleandros was making helpless gestures and apologetic noises. Still carefully, I explained, 'It's not obvious, I suppose, for Aeschylus knew what had happened after Phrynicos wrote *The Capture of Miletos*, which openly protested against the abandonment of the Ionians. But the whole discussion's about whether war, with all its dangers, isn't preferable to the desertion of suppliant kindred.'

'It's a play called *The Suppliant WOMEN*,' she interrupted me. 'It's about women – and men. Women having to submit to men they don't love:

> From the arms of the defiler keep me free,
> Unwed, unbroken!'

'Cleisidice!' shouted Cleandros, scarlet-faced.

'Submit?' I echoed, staring. 'Are you talking about marriage? Granted, the men in this case were.'

'Isn't all marriage submission? Being handed over to someone you don't know, someone you may hate? You've no choice, and you've no chance. Because you can't fight – he's stronger than you are!'

The few girls I'd met – cousins at family gatherings in the

75

past – had been creatures of sidelong glances, whispering voices. Not this one.

'Cleisidice!' Cleandros shouted furiously again.

She was laughing with tears in her eyes. 'At last a poet understands how a woman feels – and the men all think he's just talking politics!' She sprang to her feet, looking as if she were about to hit me. It was all I could do to keep myself from doing what Cleandros should have done – get to my feet too, and give her a good shaking. But I went on sitting against that bank of wild parsley, and looked amused instead of angry. This brought her closer to furious tears than ever. She said, 'A poet at last understands how a woman feels and *you* think he's talking politics!!'

'You're repeating yourself, and you're repeating insults!' yelled Cleandros, jumping up. At that I got up too, and caught his arm just when he was about to slap her. 'No, she's not repeating herself,' I said. 'First it was all men who misunderstood Aeschylus, now it's only I.' I addressed her directly, 'What are you going to do about the sad state of literature? Rewrite Homer, for a start?'

'I could!' she said. 'Think of Penelope! Can't you grasp that there must have been times when she grew tired of waiting, waiting, growing older, only half alive, that she was sick and tired of *waiting*, thought sometimes that one of the suitors might be kinder to her than the man she was waiting for, the man she almost hated at times, the fool who'd left her to go off and fight at Troy – and perhaps that was all he was good for, raiding? Did *he* think she'd grow younger, waiting year after year for someone who might be dead? And did he ever care how she might feel? Does *any* man ever care how a woman feels?'

She whirled round and ran off across the soft grass.

'I'm sorry,' said Cleandros. 'I'm angry and ashamed. I've never seen her like this before.'

'It seems,' I said, 'that there is something about me she finds exceptionally detestable.'

'She almost hit you.'

'My God, I almost hit *her*, believe it or not.'

'I've never seen her blaze up like that before.'

'I must have come at the wrong moment.'

'Well — to be honest, she's unhappy. That's what we were talking about. There's some idea of marrying her to a cousin of my stepmother — just an idea, nothing more, we were at his daughter's wedding a month or so ago, and my stepmother said afterwards that now that the girl's married, her father, being a widower, will want a wife to run the house, and, of course, there isn't a son, and he might well ask my father for my sister.'

He spoke flatly. I said, 'You don't sound very enthusiastic about the idea yourself.'

He bit his lip. 'One marriage into *that* family's enough.'

'Yet I didn't get the impression that your sister thought politics important enough to explain *her* opposition.'

'Oh, she does know more about affairs than you'd expect from that outburst! After Mother died, we were very close, I'd let her read my books and talk to her about things. That's why her behaviour so astonished me. She doesn't like the idea of this marriage — we came out here to talk so that we couldn't be overheard — but she was discussing the business quite sensibly — she wasn't excitable at all, she was agreeing with what I said about not wanting, either of us, to marry into Hipparchos' family, and so on, and then — well, it was quite unbelievable the way she changed. Augo barked, and I looked up and saw you and waved, and as you came over she said, in this low, furious voice, "In any case, no matter what his family, I don't want to marry him. His body's flabby and his mouth slack —" and then she didn't say another word until — well, you know, the outburst!'

'Oh, for God's sake, let's forget it,' I said. 'I came at just the wrong moment, that's all.' I found the whole episode as embarrassing as he did; I had almost lost my temper with the girl.

We went back towards the house, talking now of the business that had brought me there. I meant to make straight for the stables, but a slave came running out, murmured to Cleandros. He went red, then said to me in a low voice, 'My stepmother's heard you're here. She says she'd like to see you. What shall I say?'

Having the idea that his stepmother ruled the household, and could and would make life unpleasant for a stepchild who opposed her wishes, 'Well,' I said, 'let's go in, shall we?'

All the dowry she'd brought with her obviously hadn't gone on redeeming vineyards and olive groves. Quite an amount had been spent on her person. I remember amber ear-rings and matching necklace, a dress of some brilliant fine stuff, a handsome face and arrogant eyes.

'Well!' she said. 'Acestorides of all people produced a boy like you! You're not at all like him, are you? The Alcmaeonids gave you those grey eyes, I suppose. Although I'm not so sure I like them. Too aloof. Taking in everything, giving nothing away.'

She went on talking with insolent assurance. I made my excuses as soon as I could, and escaped. It was only as I turned to go that I realised that Cleandros' sister was sitting in the corner of the room. Her head was bent over two piles of roses and violets, from which she was making wreaths for the feast that night. She did not look up. In contrast with her stepmother's self-possession she seemed forlorn, timid, melancholy. All the vividness had gone, as a candle flame loses its brightness at noonday.

7

In the following winter came the final, indeed the inevitable, struggle with Aristeides and his party. There had never been any real chance that Themistocles' opponents could be won over; they would never forgive him for being always right. One could only hope that the majority of Athenian voters would find it equally impossible to forgive Aristeides for being always righteous.

It was not the first attempt to get Themistocles ostracised; already Xanthippos, who also wanted a strong navy, had been sent into exile, and this time the opposition was taking no chances, they sent agents up into the hills to persuade or bribe the very shepherds and goatherds to leave their flocks for one day to come down to Athens. They bought up batches of spoiled black glazed cups for the manufacture of ready-made voting potsherds to be offered to bewildered peasants – Themistocles' name was already written on them.

One of the incidents on the brilliant but cold day when the votes were cast is well known – how the magnanimous Aristeides, coming upon a near-illiterate voter trying to write his own name on a potsherd ('Why do you hate him? What injury has he done you?' 'Never set eyes on him, but I'm sick and tired of hearing him called "the Just".') nobly playing the part of benefactor/victim, wrote the name himself. (Of course, the only person who could have related the incident was the modest Aristeides himself; the man didn't know him.)

There was also another episode, soon forgotten, I hope, by those who saw it, never to be forgotten by me.

In that crowded market place, I suddenly came face to face with my father, limping forward with difficulty, leaning heavily on his stick. 'Taking your last look at Athens before you follow that scum into exile?' he said. If he had been physically capable, he would have shouted the words.

'Father —' I began, but at that word he screamed, and lashed out at me furiously with his stick. I managed to catch it with one hand before it struck my face, tried with the other to catch him by the elbow as he lurched forward with the effort, nearly falling. He cursed me, tried to shake off my grasp as if he were a raging, trapped animal. One of the men accompanying him took him from me, another, taking the stick, said to me, not unkindly, 'Get out of his sight.' I could see from their faces that the scene had shocked them; I don't know what my face looked like.

And then, at Themistocles' house the long waiting, far into the evening. The sudden roar of the crowd in the distance, shouting a name, they were too far off for us to distinguish what they shouted, there was a hiss in the roar, after the second syllable, but this applied to both names, each of four syllables. But at last the trained, powerful, carrying voice of the herald, crying the name against which the requisite six thousand votes had been cast to ensure his banishment.

'Aristeides!'

But what he was really shouting was, 'Two hundred ships, timber, cordage, pitch-pine . . .'

There was no longer the slightest hope that my father would ever forgive me.

And now, day after day, I went down to the docks and talked to merchants, and often, in the evening, entertained foreigners in my home. Chiefly Macedonians. Because we had to get timber. Unlike the King of Persia, we had no forests of Lebanon to give us all that we wanted; we had to import, and from states not yet dominated by Xerxes. So we made diplomatic love to the King of Macedonia, whose timber was the best, smooth, straight, resinous. We obtained pitch from the pine forests of Macedonia too, though we also got some from Thrace. We damned Xerxes' eyes for having nearly all the resources. What we wouldn't have given to have had control of Egypt with hemp for ropes, flax for sailcloth, or of Cyprus with its forests!

Six to eight triremes to be launched every month. Timber to be obtained for the ships and a hundred oars apiece. Shipwrights to be brought in from abroad, if we did not have enough. And crews to be trained, many of them raw country boys down from the hills who had scarcely set eyes on the sea before. 'And when you're about it,' said Themistocles, 'teach 'em to swim.'

We were to have three years before the enemy finally came, but not full years, of course. Remember that from mid-autumn the sailing season ended, shipowners hauled their vessels out on to the beach or moored them at the quays, the foreign merchants and the ships bringing their goods had sailed for home. But our feeling of urgency was so great in those months of training that we chanced the kind of heavy north-easter you can get rounding Cape Sunion. Imagine a hundred and seventy oarsmen violently seasick – bad enough for the sixty-two at the highest of the three banks, worse for the fifty-four beneath them, worst of all for the fifty-four thalamites down in the depths, poor devils.

In that first summer after the ostracism of Aristeides news came that Xerxes had actually begun the construction of a canal to bypass Mount Athos. This terrifying piece of information at least had its uses; not even the most rabid of Themistocles' political enemies could claim that the Great King was dabbling in engineering as a harmless hobby.

Now we must set ourselves to learn every inch of the coast along which the barbarian fleet would come, each breath of wind, ripple of current, colour of water, movement of cloud. Our shipyards still continued to turn out raw, mass-produced ships, but the only rawness in the mass-produced crews manning them was in the palms of the hand after a long stint at the oars.

Raw, mass-produced ships need better crews than do superior vessels.

And even mass-produced ships have individuality: you

always get some that are bitches to handle, with vicious little tricks that somehow the crews must learn to recognise and cope with.

Sailing from early spring to late autumn; diplomacy all the year round. Spartan ambassadors appeared in Athens, long-haired, red-tunicked, harsh-featured, harsh-voiced. They spoke so infrequently, and then so briefly you might almost think they suffered from some chronic disease of the throat making speech a painful business. And the tone of voice was equally extra-ordinary. Questions, answers, comments – all sounded like brusque orders.

But at least the curt, harsh utterances expressed the right sentiments. Sparta believed the Persians would invade, and Sparta would fight to the death. 'All that we have to worry about is *where* they're prepared to fight to the death,' said Themistocles. 'It's the devil's own job to get them to set foot outside Holy Sparta. How in the hell did Paris manage to get Helen to elope with him? I wish he'd set down details of his technique for the benefit of posterity.'

But apart from Sparta – and ever-loyal little Plataea – we could count on no one.

Now more than ever I was down at the docks again, talking in their own languages to swarthy sea captains bringing cargoes of wines and dates from Syria, papyrus from Egypt, figs and nuts from Ionia, exchanging darics and staters at the tables of the money-changers. And they all told the same story – warships being assembled in every harbour controlled by Xerxes, tales of tens of thousands of soldiers converging on Sardis from every corner of the Empire. To do justice to the Great King, he was not being secretive. And then one day we had a secret message from Macedonia, from the King's eldest son, who hated the Persians. The Great King's heralds were on their way to the Greek states, to demand earth and water in token of submission. From Macedonia they would undoubtedly travel southwards.

It was the diffusion of this news that eventually brought about the Panhellenic Congress, summoned by Sparta to meet at Corinth to discuss the Persian threat.

8

It is fifty miles from Athens to Corinth, and not an easy road after you have passed Eleusis and Megara; here you come to the Bad Stairs, where Theseus, coming from Troezen to Athens, met and killed the robber Sciron. You will remember the story – how Sciron made travellers wash his feet, then kicked them over the cliff to feed the sea-tortoises, saying, 'It is good to feed the turtles,' but Theseus, after overcoming Sciron in fair fight, fed him to the tortoises in his turn.

The Megarans, of course, have a different story. According to them, Sciron was a virtuous road-engineer who, having constructed a good road over the dangerous rocks, justifiably levied a small toll on those who used it. Then along came that villain Theseus (all Athenians are villains if you live in Megara) who not only refused to pay his rightful due but killed public benefactor Sciron in the altercation that followed.

Whatever were the preliminaries to his abrupt descent into the sea, there can be no doubt that Sciron had a long way to fall. The road skirts the brink of a precipice for six miles; the sea washes the rocks some seven hundred feet below. Themistocles, although for a different reason, damned the Bad Stairs as roundly as any unfortunate traveller on his way to a rendezvous with Sciron – 'You know what some fool is bound to get on his hind legs and say – "The Persian Army'll never get through here." What we have to try to get into their thick heads is that they can turn any flank if they've beaten our fleet.'

The Bad Stairs ended, the road swung inland, there before us was the Isthmus, a long plain at the foot of the mountains.' Themistocles squared his shoulders. 'Remember,' he said. 'It will all depend on our getting Spartan co-operation. And remember something else – the uncommon nervousness of the

Spartan temperament when it comes to leaving the Peloponnese. Even if we coax them out, they'll scuttle back at the first opportunity.' He settled himself more firmly on his horse. 'In fact, the more I've studied this particular state and its people, the more I'm inclined to think that the general opinion of them is wrong—that in reality they're not tough, but timid, and it's because of their fearfulness that they're ready to accept this perpetual transformation of their state into one enormous barracks that no other people would put up with for a moment. They think it's their only way to salvation.'

Corinth's strategic position has for years made military men wax metaphorical. She is the 'hinge' or the 'keys' of Hellas. The same strategic position, of course, has made Corinth wealthy. She is the most opulent, and the most vulgar of all Greek towns. Also the most unlikeable. In this she stands in a category of her own. Sparta or Athens other states either love or hate. But they all *dislike* Corinth. This may be solely due to the showy ostentation of the place, but I think the antipathy really runs deeper. There is an unhellenic, oriental strain in the people, one feels— significantly the principal deity of the place is Aphrodite, and an Aphrodite more akin to the goddesses of Asia. Her great temple on the Acropolis of Corinth houses a thousand sacred prostitutes. It was the most incongruous place in Greece for the holding of a conference to discuss resistance to the barbarian from the East. The East was already there in Corinth.

We found the Corinthian delegates no more prepossessing than their city. The appearance of Adeimantos, the Corinthian admiral, gave a fair indication of his nature—a heavy face, arrogant eyes, pursed mouth, big jowls. He spoke with maddening deliberation. He hated our guts, and prided himself on never changing his mind. Sometimes we thought our best chance of success in the coming war lay in his deserting to Xerxes.

It was hot and depressing and frustrating sitting in the temple of Poseidon where the conference was held, and walking about the shops and warehouses. All that offered comic relief was the

84

Spartan contingent. Tramping about the streets of Corinth, they seemed like visitors from another world. Long hair, red tunics, harsh voices – those strange voices, strident as the sound of a rusty key turning in a lock – *were* they rusty through lack of use? They stalked about in pairs (presumably for security reasons) from temple to their lodgings, from lodgings to temple, and in no other direction whatsoever. They intimidated all who set eyes on them. No tavern-owner, no shopkeeper dared approach them offering wares. Neither, if it came to that, did a single woman of the town – brazen as that sisterhood might be, not even the most flaunting or adventurous ever hailed a Spartan.

But there was a more serious reason why I was glad to see the Spartans. They remained massively immune from the panic and pessimism infecting so many other delegates. For this reason, although no man could be more unlike them in character, although he represented the newfangled Athenian democracy so suspect to diehard Spartan eyes, Themistocles impressed the Spartan delegates favourably. They were grimly resolved to fight to the death, even if for purely selfish reasons. Persian domination meant the end of Spartan domination – it was as simple as that. And in Themistocles they recognised the one other delegate at that conference who was as uncompromising in his resistance to Persia as they were themselves. But whether they could ever be brought to accept his ideas as to the best way of carrying out that resistance was a different matter. He preached that success would depend on ships, not armies, and that the main effort must be made at sea. He also declared that the Persians must be met and defeated as far north as possible.

But if Themistocles' paramount task was to coax the Spartans north of Corinth, there were others. Strictly speaking, the most important of these, since he had gained Spartan support, should have been a joint affair – I mean the formation of a common front among the Greek states against the common enemy. But the whole negotiation fell to Themistocles, for the simple reason that the Spartans had no conception where to begin. It was inevitable, of course. Hitherto their rôle had been to issue orders, not to cajole. A master-race that has never stooped to trade has no idea how to drive a bargain. So Themistocles had to fight the battle alone. The Spartans told him they could guarantee (by main force, it was tacitly understood) the adherence of every state in the Peloponnese except Argos, whose loathing for Sparta was well known. But the Persians would be coming down from the north, Themistocles' whole strategy rested on stopping them as far north as possible. In the south the Spartan army was the blunt instrument to end all arguments; it was still very doubtful whether the Spartans could be persuaded to send that army north of Corinth.

So all depended on Themistocles to rouse the other states to some conception of the fate of Hellas as a whole.

He had one great obstacle to overcome, of course. Men from other states pointed out that there was no virtue in Athens' determination to resist. She had no choice. Hers was the heroism of the cornered rat. The Great King had condemned her out of hand. He would answer to that, 'But we *had* the choice years ago. And we chose to resist. And we beat them. They *can* be beaten.'

At other times the argument ran along these lines – 'Very well, you Athenians will fight because you have no choice. And you beat them at Marathon. But this time the entire Persian army is coming down on us. You're not saying you can tackle that single-handed!'

'No,' said Themistocles, 'but the Spartans are with us.'

'How can you be sure of the Spartans?'

Themistocles talked to the Spartans privately as to the best way of answering this. They said they would consult their government. A few sessions later, in the midst of a prolonged and pointless argument as to whether an appeal should be made to Crete to send help in the shape of a contingent of archers, a messenger came in and whispered to the chief Spartan delegate. He listened, his face quite unrevealing, then stood up. 'I have a statement to make,' he said abruptly.

The Corinthian delegate, whose speech he had so rudely interrupted, reddened, but sat down. The Spartan said, 'My government has this to say. The Persian is sending heralds again, demanding submission.We shall kill the herald who is sent to us. This should convince all Greeks that we expect no quarter, and will resist to the end.'

There was a hush throughout the room.

Seeming slightly puzzled at the shocked reaction, he went on, stolidly, 'Now let us get on with the business we were discussing.'

But if after this no one doubted the determination of the Spartans to fight, there were those who kept saying we had neither sufficient ships nor men to withstand the invader, and unspoken in the council itself, but voiced now and again in the evenings after a cup or two of wine, was the thought in many minds that accepting Persian rule would involve a less unpleasant disruption of a man's life than would war. Indeed, from some remarks that were dropped from time to time, there were still those who by the process of wishful thinking did not believe the Persians would really come at all. Persia was bluffing, and Themistocles for reasons of his own had seized on the opportunity to start a war scare.

But then another council meeting was abruptly interrupted. If, after that first interrupted meeting, no one could doubt the intentions of Sparta, after the second no one could doubt the intentions of Persia.

That afternoon it was Themistocles' turn to be interrupted. 'To make a mistake twice isn't allowed in war,' he was saying. 'We made our first mistake nearly a generation ago, when the Ionians revolted, and what help we sent was too little and too late. Now –'

And again a messenger hurried in. This time he whispered to Themistocles himself, and Themistocles' face was far more expressive than the face of his Spartan opposite number. With a gleam in his eye, he announced, 'Xerxes himself is at Sardis with his army. Now does anyone doubt his intentions?'

That day my direct involvement with the Panhellenic Congress at Corinth ended. One of the first reactions of the delegates was predictable; information as to the size and make-up of the Persian army must be obtained as soon as possible. Agents must be sent to Sardis.

Three men were chosen – a senior Spartan officer named Pantites, a man from Sikyon, Deinomenes, who had travelled in Asia, and I, who knew something of the languages. Themistocles was very solemn when I said good-bye to him. As diplomatically as he could he had tried to prevent a Spartan being chosen as one of our trio – 'He may be the best man to evaluate military matters, but no Spartan exactly sinks into the background, even in Greece. In Asia he'll stand out like a sore thumb,' as he remarked to me afterwards. He might as well have saved his breath. To the Spartans co-operation involved over-representation in all forms of military activity.

9

At the Corinth conference, the limitations of the Spartan character had been amusing when not exasperating. They were so used to rasping commands that were instantly obeyed, that dealing with others on equal terms – even, incredibly, having to compromise, to make concessions – left them scarlet-faced, eyes almost starting from their heads with indignation, but at least at the conference Spartan rigidity, that terrifying single-mindedness, lack of imagination, hadn't immediately threatened our necks: in Asia it did.

Because Pantites never really looked like anything but what he was – a Spartan who would never set foot out of Sparta save for a purely military reason. He rode, eyes glaring resentfully ahead – always fixed straight ahead – never turning to left or right to gaze about him at the people, the countryside, through which we were passing. He was completely uninterested in everything and anything outside military matters. His only emotion when we first set eyes on that strange and monstrously ugly beast, the camel, was exasperation, because it slowed us down, care and cajolery being needed to coax our horses past it, and his sole reaction when the valley widened into a plain covered with vines and olives, and criss-crossed with poplars and suddenly, in the distance, we saw a high outline that must be Sardis, was to mutter that he had calculated we should have reached our goal a day earlier.

Lack of imagination has its advantages. He really seemed to be quite lacking in fear. I can still remember — and my stomach churns again at the thought of it – every moment of the last stage of our journey, the River Pactolus flowing fast beneath high banks, the smell of chamomile as we sat at the roadside to eat, to try to eat, our last meal before coming to the city, the sight of the great mounds that marked the burials of the Lydian kings – and, then, every other spectacle seeming irrelevant after our first sighting of the army encampments, and, for the time being, every other emotion being swallowed up by black hopelessness as we began to comprehend the numbers that were being mustered against us.

But when we came to the gate of Sardis itself we found there can be feeling worse than the blackest hopelessness. There in the gate was pinioned a faceless, ravaged thing that once had been human, and was still, incredibly, alive. The Great King, being in Sardis, was executing his own royal justice on the spot. One of his kinsmen, laughing, was supervising the last refinements.

I will not describe in detail the other barbaric cruelties we were to see in the camp and in Sardis itself. They sicken the soul. I have spoken of them only to Aeschylus. Later he put these words into the mouth of Apollo:

> 'Are there not realms where Law upon her seat
>   Smites living head from trunk? Where
>   prisoners bleed
> From gouged eyes? Children with manhood's seed
>   Blasted are there; maimed foot and
>   severed hand,
> And stoning, and a moan through all the land
>   Of men impaled to die.'

Let us leave it there. Such was the rule of the East, as we saw it in Sardis.

We had come to Sardis to see the Persian army, and at Sardis it was impossible not to see the Persian army – Persians and Medians in gaudy tunics, baggy trousers; Assyrians in brass helmets, with wooden clubs knotted with iron; Indians in cotton robes with cane bows and arrows; Moschians with wooden helmets, Chalybeans with purple puttees round their legs and helmets topped with the ears and horns of oxen; black-skinned, woolly-haired Ethiopians, their bodies painted with stripes of white and vermilion, some wearing horses' heads as helmets, manes waving, ears pricked. But if there were variety enough in savage costume and weaponry, there was a dreadful uniformity in expression. It was stupid, incurious, animal. When I later saw some of them in action, again I thought of animals, for they came howling forward in a roar of sound that was scarcely human. This was the reason for their existence – killing. It was for this that they were part of what the subject peoples themselves called the Persian tax in blood. It was for this that they were trained – like animals, with whips. But when they were not being loosed on their prey they showed the other animal characteristics, the characteristics, that is, of the least intelligent kind of animal.

I tell you, beside *their* look of mindlessness, Pantites' face seemed a torrent of vivid and rapidly changing expression.

It was, inevitably, Pantites who gave us away. I think Deinomenes and I had known it would happen from the moment we set foot in Asia and realised that he would go on looking and talking like a Spartan not so much because he wouldn't do otherwise, but because he couldn't. We never knew who it was who reported us to the authorities, but I believe it was the inn-keeper, mixed among whose motives was insulted professional pride. It wasn't a bad inn, the food could have been infinitely worse, but at every meal Pantites' mouth turned down omin-ously at the corners, and he would begin to express longings for the Spartan national dish, black broth. If my guess were right, it was fitting that the arrest came when on our fifth day we were in the middle of supper – I can remember every detail of that meal, meat seasoned with onions, dumplings in some bitter sauce or other. There were shouts outside, and in came half a dozen Median soldiers armed with scimitars. They made straight for us; the other guests scrambled to the far end of the room and flattened themselves against the wall, frantically trying to put as much distance as possible between themselves and the doomed wretches. The gust of their terrified passage

91

made the brazier flare dangerously. The three of us had sprung up; covered by Deinomenes and Pantites, I managed to slip into the flame the last notes I had made, thanking God all the while I had been able to send off a previous batch; and then it was all over, even Pantites realised there wasn't any point in trying to put up a fight.

Out of the smoke-blackened room, smelling of cooking oils and onions, into the dark street, urged on by kicks and blows and curses, and then thrown down steps into an underground prison. An official gave orders, and we were hustled into three cells, evil little holes so low-roofed that only inside the door could you stand upright, nowhere could you lie at full length. This made shackling us to the walls a slow and painful matter, but eventually we were left alone in complete darkness and complete isolation. The walls were so thick that no voice could penetrate; if it came to that, the very darkness seemed thick.

I crouched in that thick darkness, no other position being possible to me because of the way I was tethered by both hands and feet to staples in the wall. It was so cold that soon my fingers had lost all feeling, were too numb even to distinguish between the chill of the iron and the stone of the wall running wet. But even more oppressive than the cold was the rank smell of stale sweat, the sweat of terror, of generations of terrified men. I wondered if the thing we had seen at the gate when we rode into Sardis had once been a man crouched in this very cell where I crouched now, and if, though he sweated with terror as he thought of the morning, it had been in the sure knowledge that in the morning the agony of pain would be even worse than he had feared.

Almost one could imagine in that cell that the very walls sweated with terror – or blood.

We ourselves should have been dealt with out of hand next morning but for the fact that the weather turned bad, and was likely to go on being bad for days. The Great King was therefore in some danger of being bored. He could not hunt, he could not inspect the army. It was suggested to him that examining the three suspected spies might be amusing. He agreed. But leave them for a time, he said, and in the interval let them be frightened as much as possible.

Since our cells were underground, there were no windows. Light came only if a lamp were brought. It was difficult to tell how time was passing, whether in the outside world it were day or night. I don't know how long we were held in those holes underground, foul with the stink of fear; suffice it to say that it seemed a very long time.

Not that we lacked visitors. No one ever brought us food, or water; but twice I was beaten, quite badly, no doubt in order to reduce me to the proper state of contrition before I was brought before the Great King. For the beating-up a lamp was necessary. For what might be termed the mental beating-up, light was unnecessary — indeed, light was a disadvantage. What happened was that someone came into the cell and squatted down in the darkness quite close to me and in a low, almost gentle voice gave me an extremely lengthy and detailed account of the various ways in which the Great King dealt with traitors — the Great Kings of Persia, in fact, took pride in the various forms of treatment they devised, the present monarch's father having caused examples of his kind of justice to be carved high up on a distant rock face to last for all time. I had portions quoted to me: 'Fravartish was captured — I cut off his nose and ears and tongue, and put out his eyes. In my gates he was kept bound, all the people saw him. After that I impaled him . . . his chief associates I flayed . . .' And so on.

(I found out later the others had the beatings-up but not this bedtime story treatment. Since I was by far the youngest of the trio, it had been decided that I was the likeliest to crack.)

They made one mistake. The lack of any light was effective enough in one respect; in the darkness one saw appalling pictures. But the same darkness meant that whoever was with me could not see me. If he could have seen my face . . . But he

93

couldn't, and except for a few carefully contrived yawns I said nothing.

So eventually I was left alone, to the darkness my eyes could not pierce and the cold that pierced me, and the dripping walls and mud floor without even a shred of filthy straw to lie on – if one could lie down – and the stench of fear and my thoughts. Death would soon be the end of it all. I found I was whispering to myself (it was difficult to speak aloud for my mouth was so dry), 'Try to die like a human being, not a trapped animal' – only to reflect that trapped animals usually died with much greater courage than human beings. And that the Great King probably showed more mercy – a quick death – to a trapped animal than to a human being.

It would be slow.

It would involve more pain than I could imagine until I felt it.

It would also involve humiliation. Being left some dignity might help to give a little courage. The indignity of an Oriental execution would be excelled only by the pain of it.

I wished to God I were a trapped animal.

Torches flared outside, voices shouted. Huddled there, half dead with cold and thirst and starvation, I prayed that hours, days might pass before the door was opened. My cell was suddenly a refuge, for here I was still only half, three-quarters dead. Once they dragged me outside . . . I drew myself as far back against the dripping wall as I could, inch by inch as if each inch were an inch closer to salvation.

I heard them dragging out first one, then the other of my companions. Now they were at my door. I pressed myself against the wall. The torchlight hurt my eyes – that, I told myself, was why I kept them shut for some moments after the door was flung open.

Although the chains were struck off, it was still difficult for me to move, but eventually I was prodded with spear points out into the passage, to rejoin two filthy, bloodstained, almost unrecognisable spectres of those who had been my companions (did *I* look like that?) and, with more blows and curses up steps, into the street, along the street, out of the gate where another tortured thing made an endless crying noise (or was it the same thing? One could not tell. This too had been tortured into facelessness) into the camp, towards a great pavilion. The Great King was roughing it; he had left the palace to share the hardships of his brave troops.

I was nearly finished by the time we reached that pavilion. The moment they let me go, I fell down. And even at that moment I was capable of finding some comfort in the fact that Pantites wasn't much better, he collapsed too. The conversation, a few feet above my head, seemed to come from miles away. I was too stupid to distinguish words; if it comes to that, I don't think I'd really been able to distinguish any words since they'd brought me out of my cell, but the method of communication chiefly used then had been that most international of all languages, blows and kicks. But someone was shouting in a great rage; and someone else was almost squealing with terror, and eventually I was kicked to my feet again, fell down again, was dragged off, a long way off, dumped on the ground, and left. I fainted.

The most extraordinary thing to me about my rousing was that it was not ungentle, someone was moistening my lips, bathing my forehead. The next was that a voice was speaking Greek to me. Thirdly, when I opened my eyes, a Greek face was looking down at me – although, as my eyes shifted past him, there were faces non-Greek enough in the background, three Nubians, extreme types of that stupid, incurious animal sort that had so oppressed me.

The Greek was very well dressed and clean. I, by this time, had acquired a black and buzzing coronet. Flies at least one had been spared in the underground cell, but the moment I had been brought into the open they had come swooping down to fix upon the stale sweat and stale blood on my face.

I said, 'Can you wipe the flies from my face?' In Persian; I was taking no chances.

He said rapidly, 'Good. Keep talking Persian – they know the sound of it, even if they haven't much mastery of it. And I'll do more than wipe the flies away. I've been given orders to clean you up generally and give you some decent clothing.'

'Given orders by whom?'

His face was impassive. 'By the Great King himself.' After another moment he added, 'He is always very much afraid of catching any kind of disease . . . you, in your filthy condition, straight from the worst prison in Sardis . . .'

So that was why there had been all the shouting. 'He didn't see me – us – himself, of course.'

'Oh, no. The guard wouldn't allow you to come anywhere near the presence.' After another moment's pause he said, 'Do you know what the name Xerxes means? Hero among Rulers.'

'When does the Hero among Rulers receive me?'

His eyes flickered momentarily towards the Nubians. 'Keep a more respectful tone. Be careful – you're forgetting your rôle. You'll be taken to him after he's seen the others. Individually.'

I made no reply. He stood there in that stifling tent, I slumped at his feet, and then he said rapidly, 'I've sent slaves for water, clothes. They won't be long. One of them is my own slave, the other not, so I cannot speak before him.'

I had learned my lesson. I sat on the ground and said nothing. We were an incongruous pair – he, fresh from the bath and the barber, a gold brooch fastening his scarlet cloak, gold rings on his hand, I haggard, unshaven, in filthy rags, face stiff, livid with bruises and crusted dried blood, lips swollen and blistered, both body and the rags covering it so rank that the clouds of flies still buzzed ecstatically about it. Yet *he* stared down at me with pity – there is no mistaking that expression – mixed with envy. And he, as if he could read my thoughts, said in a low, furious voice, 'There'd be a difference between us even if you weren't like this. When any of you – other Greeks look at us Ionians, what do you see? Men usually much better dressed than yourselves, prosperous, living in comfort. But most of us don't see ourselves that way. We feel spiritually dirty, despoiled. I feel dirtier than you look now.'

96

If I looked anything like Pantites and Deinomenes I was a battered, bloodstained piece of human misery and degradation, with an ending by ineluctable pain steadily approaching. My expression must have been eloquent. He said, 'I don't know, it may not happen, he's in a good mood, they say. He's like a child – one never knows how he'll react. What I can do I will.'

'If it comes to – that thing at the gate –'

He said, 'As soon as I can, a knife thrust straight through to the heart. I promise you.'

That was something.

He went on rapidly, 'But it's not certain. You never know which things will make him angry, what will amuse him. That's one of the things it means to live under a tyrant. There are worse things, of course. Like cursing the gods if you have a beautiful child – because she was not born ugly. Here are the slaves.'

Two slaves came in. One was Greek, carrying clothes; the other, dark-skinned, carried a silver bowl of steaming water, a towel. 'I'll do it!' said the Ionian abruptly, taking the water from him. 'You can go.' But, with an insolent look, he went only a few paces away. So all that was said to me as I was cleaned up, and shaved, was whispered hurriedly, and I could not catch everything. 'You're Athenian, aren't you – you babbled a bit when you were unconscious, and I know the accent – I visited Athens once in the old days. You think you are free now – I tell you, you don't know the meaning of freedom. It's only we Ionians who know that. Until you've lost it, you don't know what it means. (*Raise your chin.*) If you get away, and get back home, tell them it's better to die than to submit. Cleaner to rot on a battlefield if you've died fighting for freedom. (*Turn your face a little.*) I mean *die*. You know you're defeated, and you're stupid, deaf, blind with fear. But they don't kill you and you think you're saved. Saved for what? You're alive, but you're a slave. You go on feeling things like fear and pain, but your pride's gone, and soon your shame. Tell the Athenians this. If their land is in danger of being overrun by the barbarian, while there

97

is time venture everything in seeking a new world, anywhere, rather than live under the conqueror.'

I was shaved, clean, they put on me a rather splendid white tunic, a scarlet cloak. An official jangling with gold chains strutted in. 'Is he ready?'

'Just. But the others were to be seen first.'

'They have been dealt with.'

It sounded ominous. The Greek slave suddenly and meticulously began to adjust the clasp of the cloak they had given me. Momentarily his hand gripped my shoulder. His master took me by the elbow. I caught the faintest breath of, 'The gods go with you.' To me the most important thing in the world seemed to keep myself upright, erect, marching in a soldierly fashion to whatever Xerxes had in store for me.

Somehow I managed it. But I don't know whether I could have managed it without that grip on my elbow.

The Hero among Rulers sat on a couch covered with dark green shining stuff the colour of an emerald. The couch was set on a dais. Behind it a crimson silk curtain was looped back to show the brilliant sky and beneath it a plain suddenly drenched with spring sunlight. I advanced between two hedges of courtiers in long robes of glowing Indian stuffs, crimsons, purples. Rubies and sapphires winked from dark fingers, but above all there was gold everywhere, on bracelets, necklaces, embroideries, chains, stiff caps. And there, on the couch, Xerxes.

The odd thing is that I haven't the slightest recollection of what he was wearing, although it must have been the ceremonial purple. But I remember his face. A blue-black beard, a waterfall of a beard, very full, very red lips, so red that at first I wondered if they were painted like the rest of his face. (Even when he was in a rage, as I was to see for myself, he would never compress those lips into a line as other men do; always they remained very full, and very red, like plump cherries.) A soft face, soft yet heavy, dark eyes, slightly slanting.

Of course, I should not have been able to describe his face at all. I should have crawled towards him, lain prostrate. But I didn't. I marched towards him. I have since been told that although my face under the bruises was white and set, my eyes were furious. I think this must have been true enough, for the first words Xerxes said were, 'His eyes are not like the eyes of my condemned people.' (I was to see those, too. Their eyes were not like human eyes. Yet they were not like the eyes of animals. No animal lives for days on end in fear of death.)

It was scarcely a promising opening. I looked about me; there was no sign of Pantites or Deinomenes.

'His eyes, in fact, betray him whatever his tongue may say,' continued Xerxes. His comments, received with admiring murmurs by the entire flock of courtiers, were addressed directly to a pair of them at his left hand. They had the proper attitude to royalty — eyes lowered, hands before mouths to avoid breathing on their master. Behind him were two slaves, one carrying a golden umbrella, another an enormous and ornate fly-whisk. Since their hands were necessarily employed, their mouths were muffled by voluminous scarves.

'Tell him to come closer,' said Xerxes.

To show my knowledge of Persian, I started forward. After one pace I thought the torture was beginning immediately. I was surrounded, a smoking dish was thrust beneath my chin. But it was a dish of spices — additional precaution against disease.

So, made as harmless as was humanly possible, I advanced to my encounter with the Great King. Whether he would prove as harmless to me was a different matter.

Gems, gold, silks, perfume, musky perfume. Was it the strong smell of musk that made me think of a wild beast?

'At least,' said a voice, 'the carrion now lowers his eyes before His Majesty.'

I was shocked to discover that this was precisely what I was doing.

Because one watches a charging boar from beneath lowered lids.

99

I was nearly at the foot of the dais. I looked up again. And the dark eyes, slightly slanting, were smiling at me. I thought with incredulity, 'He wants to – to win me over.' No doubt he himself thought of it as another instance of annexation, the acquisition of another docile slave. He could never make up his mind whether he wished to conquer by fear, or by charm.

He turned to the courtier standing beside him, whispered instructions. The man bowed, retired backwards down the steps, bowing on each, disappeared into the crowd of courtiers, returned with an elderly man who stared at me, then prostrated himself before the King.

'He is, of course, too young for me to know, Lord of All Men,' he said, 'but I swear there is Alcmaeonid blood in him. The eyes are unmistakable.'

My mother's eyes, so often cursed by my father. Alcmaeonid eyes. Perhaps I myself should curse them now.

'It is, indeed, many years since any follower of our last tyrant set foot in Athens, long before my birth, in fact,' I said sardonically. (There was nothing to be gained now by trying to keep up the pretence.) But the moment I had spoken, and saw the look on his face, I was half sorry. He was an old man, and he had been out of Athens for thirty years. If he were eaten up by inner bitterness – well, I hoped I could understand a little.

But Xerxes now had his cue.

'So you admit you are an Athenian.'

'I am *proud* of being an Athenian.'

'Proud!' He laughed, and everyone else laughed, wave upon wave of sound. No one stopped laughing until he stopped laughing, and then the guffaws were cut off as by a knife. 'Athens!' he said. 'A squalid little town as insignificant as it is insolent. I know all about your Athens – what there is to know.' He thrust out a hand. A courtier who had been scribbling furiously on an ivory tablet fell on his knees and put the tablet in the royal palm. 'Less than twenty thousand able-bodied men,' said Xerxes, reading rapidly, 'a mere seven hundred square miles of rocks and marble quarries, goats and olives, a rabble wasting all their energy in bawling praises of their newly gained liberty, equality –'

I said, 'When it is necessary, we will do what we have to do.'

He burst out laughing. 'And I do what I *want* to do, and I know it is the eternal law of nature that the weak must do the bidding of the strong!' He lowered his voice. 'You Athenians interest me after a fashion. I rule from India to Egypt, Arabia sends me frankincense, Ethiopia sends me ivory, ebony, I have all the gold of Asia at my command, the world has never seen such armies as mine, I am lord of the East, soon I shall be lord of the West, and you – you contemptible tribe of madmen and rebels – think you can stand in my way!'

I said, 'When it is necessary, we will do what we are able to do.'

'What you are able to do!' He gestured widely. 'Athenian, did they send you here to kill me by laughter? You have made up my mind for me. When I had you brought here, I had not made up my mind what to do with you. Now I have hit on the worst possible torment for you –'

By the grace of the gods, not a muscle moved in my face, and my knees remained steady.

'You shall be shown every unit in my army, given muster-rolls, and allowed to return back to your miserable anarchical rabble to tell them what the Great King of Persia is able to do! And then wait for him to do it!'

It might have been a master-stroke, of course. He thought he could beat us not so much by sheer strength of numbers as by our knowledge of that sheer strength of numbers. There were Greek states that still wavered; definite information on the hundreds of thousands to be launched against them might well tilt the balance against resistance in favour of abject submission. I know that in the days I remained at Sardis, I was in the charge of a high Persian official who spoke good Greek, but whose vocabulary in the frequent harangues to which he subjected me was limited to a few repetitive sentences. 'You are an intelligent man. The King has no ill will to those who see the matter in the

101 of them stays.

correct light. And all that is needed to win his friendship is a little earth and water! But if that earth and water is not forthcoming all that the King will give is death!'

But for part of the time I was moving in even higher social circles. Xerxes announced that he himself would show off his army to me. But first Deinomenes and Pantites were produced. They had been examined before me, and had been treated to a long list of the possible fates awaiting them. But the Great King had not yet made up his mind. He had therefore had them bound and gagged and bundled away to the rear of the ranks of courtiers, having been informed that what happened to them would depend on the way I impressed Xerxes when I was brought in last. The strain on their nerves — and the strain on their ears — must have been considerable until I made that fortunate statement ending, 'what we are able to do,' which had given Xerxes his idea for the worst kind of punishment. They had been bound so savagely that even Pantites, toughest of Spartans, was incapable of walking for a time, and could only fall in at the very end of the lengthy procession that followed Xerxes as he showed off his army to me.

In one way it was laughable — the spoiled child showing off his toys.

In another way — which I had not foreseen — it was horrible.

And it was all very slow and ceremonious.

We processed out of the tent, Xerxes carrying a long gold-knobbed walking stick, behind him the attendant with the fly-whisk, the attendant carrying the golden umbrella, an attendant carrying a fan, an attendant carrying his handkerchief, an attendant carrying his scent bottle. An attendant carried an ornamental bow, another a large golden object I was eventually to identify as a mounting-stool.

At his side, by royal invitation, Theron of Athens, in borrowed clothes, and wishing the Lord of All Men had not chosen to soak his beard in oil with so sickly a perfume. (You will remember that I had had nothing to eat or drink for some considerable time, so my stomach was queasy.) I had just made the discovery that the Lord of All Men painted his eyelids. His hands were soft and flabby and smelled of roses.

We emerged from the pavilion. The royal parasol was brought forward to shade the royal head – and a kind of miniature hand-drawn chariot of gold and ivory was brought forward to save him the trouble of walking. He ascended via the golden mounting-stool.

Such was the laughable aspect.

The horrible aspect made itself apparent soon enough too.

As he was drawn before those long lines of soldiers, they were sweating – with fear. If he ordered a halt and stopped to speak to one of them the man gave little whimpering cries of relief and pleasure. That frightened me more than anything else.

And so I gained that knowledge of the Persian army that was to equip me for a special service I have never forgotten. I was not only given writing tablets, to make my own records; scowling high-ranking officers and scared-looking clerks produced lists, muster-rolls – 2,000 chariots and camels, 80,000 cavalry, thirty generals commanding forty-six regional contingents, the 10,000 Immortals of the crack royal division in gold-woven robes, General Hydarnes, a bull of a man rigid at their head, a clerk hurriedly telling me that these had the privilege of taking their own servants and concubines on the campaign, in special wagons, had special food and drink. Medes, Elamites, Sarangians, Moschians –

We had never been able to do more than prowl about the outskirts of the camp. Now I got the full impact of the size and the noise – and the smell of it. God knows what most of them ate, but some of the cooking smells were stomach-turning, and the stench of the hundreds of camels made me realise why horses panicked and ran wild. And the noise – rather the noises – dozens of languages, dozens of peoples, all brought together by fear of the Great King.

At first I think I was stunned by the size of it all. Stunned almost into hopelessness. But then – how shall I put it? It is usually held to be a bad thing if one cannot see the wood for the trees. But this is not always the case. Xerxes wanted me to be so appalled by the sheer total size of his army that I had no eyes for anything else. But before long I was not seeing his army as the enormous whole he wanted it to appear, I was seeing it as a conglomerate of different races, different languages, *not* a whole, because with so many races and languages it could never *be* a whole. And I was noticing other things too. Wickerwork shields, leather jackets, felt caps – nothing like our defensive body armour.

And not one race carried spears like ours.

Suddenly I was back on the training-ground, heard the instructor shouting that it was important to know the man on your right, for it was he who would cover you with his shield. The importance extended beyond individuals. You must know who were the men on your right, not strangers, but fellow Greeks, speaking your language, worshipping your gods.

'Thirty generals,' said the Great King, 'commanding forty-six regional contingents – have you written that down, Athenian?'

Yes, I had, and drawn my conclusions.

'Six supreme marshals –'

'Many of the generals and all the marshals are His Majesty's kinsmen,' said a clerk with real awe. 'Ten are no less than his brothers and half-brothers.'

'Remarkable,' I said.

And reassuring, of course. Because ability simply did not come into it where appointment to a high command, or, indeed, any key position in the Persian army was concerned. You just had to be born in the right kind of bed.

'I believe,' said the Great King from his hand-drawn chariot, 'that you Athenians actually elect your generals every year.'

'Yes, we do,' I said. I did not add that when you were electing the general who would lead you yourself in battle in the coming year, unless you had suicidal tendencies you took damned good care to pick the best man for the job.

'Well!' said the Great King, God knows how many hours later, 'have you seen enough, Athenian?'

I said boldly that, Sardis being an inland place, it had been impossible for me to see his fleets —

Possibly a less than servile approach struck him as a delightfully abrasive novelty. He laughed. 'You shall have the lists before you go.'

I *must* have the lists. More and more I was beginning to see the future through Themistocles' eyes. After inspecting Xerxes' enormous army, I was more and more convinced that it was all going to depend on the fleets.

That evening we were invited to a banquet. This was held in the palace of Sardis. The pillars of the principal rooms were of solid silver, the walls were hung with curtains of purple silk embroidered with gold, and the lights were perfumed globes imitating the planets and constellations of the zodiac, taken by conquering Persian Cyrus from the palace of the captured, star-worshipping Babylonian king.

'Ah, Babylon!' sighed the official assigned to watch me, and for once departing from his earth-and-water theme. '*That* is where we should have spent this last autumn and winter!'

He explained that in normal times, in order that the Great King should think he lived in perpetual sunshine, he always spent the autumn and winter months at Babylon, where the weather remained warm and sunny, the three months of spring at Susa, two hundred miles to the east, and the summer itself at Ecbatana. He stared at me resentfully. The sacrifices Xerxes was making — and compelling his courtiers to make — on our account!

We were awaiting the King. We had been offered sherbet to drink, invited to wash our hands (and, if we possessed them, our beards) in rosewater. Once more the smoking dish of spices was held under our chins before Xerxes arrived.

It was an odd kind of banquet. They rigged a curtain across the hall, separating him from the majority of his guests, although many of them would be summoned later to drink with him. Heavy drinking, in fact, would be encouraged, as important affairs were to be discussed and intoxication would make the nobles say what they really felt. No one seemed to think there were easier and more direct ways of inducing frank speaking. I had a sudden vision of an Athenian Assembly where plain speech would be conceivable only after heavy drinking as an essential prologue.

In the King's presence you ate, eyes lowered, food passed by servants muffled as usual so that their breath might not contaminate. I was honoured by a Persian apple* from the King's own hand. Each time his golden goblet was filled a page had to taste the wine first for fear of poison. Absolutism is a time-consuming business. And then it was time for the heavy drinking and the discussion of important matters, and we had to go. Xerxes hesitated for a time before he gave the order for our dismissal. I swear that, such was the self-confidence of the man, he even considered letting us hear his plans of campaign.

'Farewell, Athenian,' he said to me. 'I think I will see you soon, bearing me the tribute of earth and water.'

That, I said, was as it pleased my fellow countrymen.

'If you are rational men —' he said, shrugging.

But we were men who were having a love affair with freedom, and no man conducting a love affair is ever rational.

'I have ordered lodgings for you tonight, tomorrow you will be given the naval lists, and when you choose to leave Sardis you will be provided with clothes, horses and supplies.'

I gave a stiff bow.

'I already have some Greeks about me. If you should wish to enter my service, it could be arranged.' He was smiling again. One of his failings was that he had to be admired, even by an enemy — or, as a few hours before, even by a poor wretch he was considering condemning to death.

'But that must wait until you return with the earth and water.'

He was also a man with fixed ideas. Possibly being a king does not make for mental flexibility.

* A peach.

10

It was interesting to see the reactions to the information we brought back from Sardis. The Spartans and the Corinthians demanded the army muster-rolls; Themistocles' hand shot out for the navy lists.

'My God!' he said a moment later. 'Overall, 1,207 warships, 3,000 transports. Could the figures be faked? You saw the army for yourself, but not the ships. And he's out to impress us to the point of submission.'

'I don't think they're faked. There wasn't time to fake them, files were handed over instantly. I hardly think they'd have laboriously prepared faked muster-rolls on the off-chance that they'd catch Greek spies prowling about. And I think anyone who's spoken to Xerxes, seen the – the massive self-confidence of the man, would say he doesn't need to bluff.'

I learned what had happened at Corinth after we had left for Sardis. The one positive action was the unanimous passing of a motion calling for the indefinite suspension of all hostilities between member-states. Oaths had been taken to wage concerted war against the invader, and not to forsake the common cause.

Embassies had been sent to those states in Greece itself which had not sent delegates to the conference (notably Argos, Thebes and the northern states), and to Crete, Corcyra* and Syracuse. Gelon, the tyrant of Syracuse, was powerful in wealth, troops and ships – above all, ships. No reply from Gelon could be expected yet, but the replies from within Greece itself had been disheartening.

The Argives had said they would join the league if they shared with Sparta the command of the army, a concession they must have known could never be made. On the other hand, one could

* Corfu.

appreciate how the Argives felt; so recently beaten and humiliated by Sparta, it was perhaps expecting too much to ask them to place their forces under the command of their victorious enemies. But the Argive attitude would not help when it came to tempting the Spartans north of the Isthmus, leaving an uncommitted enemy in their rear.

There had been no definite replies from Thebes and the states to the north. Plataea, of course, would fight and die with Athens, if need be. Themistocles was sure in his own mind that the majority of Thebans had already decided to collaborate with the enemy, but Thebes would not declare itself until the Persians were close at hand.

'And those were all the decisions that were taken?' I asked.

'There was one other,' Themistocles said. 'The question of the high command.'

'Well, that more or less settled itself, didn't it?' I asked, getting up to go. I had reached Athens late at night, and was tired. 'Command-in-chief to Sparta, command of the fleet to Athens.'

'Sparta is getting command of the fleet as well.'

'Sparta!' I had been turning towards the door; now I flung round in such a hurry that my cloak swung wildly and nearly knocked over the lamp.

'Are you going to forestall Xerxes and burn my house over my head?' asked Themistocles, barely managing to right the lamp in time.

'Sparta, which hasn't any ships worth talking of, to command a fleet in which our ships outnumber the entire contingent from the Peloponnese!' There were tears of rage in my eyes. 'And YOU—who are the brains and heart of the whole resistance to Persia, who created our navy—'

'Do you want all Athens to hear you?'

'For years you've studied the geography of the northern coast, talked strategy with your captains—will *they* accept a Spartan? Hardly! I know—'

'But it had to be accepted,' said Themistocles. 'Everything was in danger of falling apart ... My God, Theron, from the way you've just been acting it's as well you weren't there. Aegina said she would never put her ships under the command of so recent an enemy. Corinth said we couldn't be trusted not to give all the dangerous assignments to other ships, while keeping our own safe. And no one seemed to think much of our discipline. Discipline and democracy, it seems, don't go together. "You Athenians can't *obey*," said a Spartan. "You have to be *persuaded*!" You should have seen his face – no, judging from your own expression, it's just as well you didn't. If we hadn't swallowed our pride, the squabbling would still be going on with Xerxes knocking not too politely at the door of the temple.'

'We've the ships and the man – you. Without us, without you, they haven't a chance in hell –'

'Without *them*,' said Themistocles, '*we* haven't a chance in hell. You're letting the Marathon legend blind you as it's blinded too many others. Ten years ago we didn't take on and beat the entire Persian Empire. But we're taking it on now, and – well, let's get down to basic facts, simple arithmetic. Could we alone deal with the numbers on those lists you've given me? Not a chance. But with *double* the number of ships – ours and the rest – we have a chance.'

'*If* they're properly handled.'

'I'll see to it that they're properly handled,' said Themistocles.

If you should ask me what I chiefly remember of that late winter before the invasion, I should reply the smell of shipyards – wood, pitch, sawdust, pine. Six to eight triremes were being launched every month, by the spring we must reach our target of two hundred, and two hundred ships needed ropes, sails, 20,000 oars, cut from best pine or fir. Crews must be mustered and trained. The pressure was being fully applied now.

But attention was not confined to newly built ships; some forty ageing vessels were having a refit. The Plataeans (with a boldness that makes me catch my breath now – at the time, that extraordinary time, one accepted the abnormal as the normal) despite the fact that they knew nothing of ships and sailing,

109

insisted on playing their part. 'We realise,' they said, 'that you wouldn't entrust your best ships to us, but surely you have a few that are expendable?' We did, what we called the cemetery refit. Forty-seven of them. Volunteers from Chalcis crewed twenty, the Plataeans the rest. We supplied the officers.

They were good, those Plataeans. They never grumbled – and unless you've experienced it, the difference between fighting on land and sweating on a bench in a ship's stinking hold is unbelievable. They trained more rigorously than any other men I've ever known; I've never seen such appalling blisters, never winced so much in sympathy with sore muscles.

In the evenings we talked strategy. Themistocles discussed his ideas with us so thoroughly that we made them our own, began almost by instinct to think like him. It is impossible to describe the flavour of those talks – it takes one genius to describe another, even though Themistocles was that unusual form of genius – a brilliant brain with a simplicity of explanation and action.

And we studied that north-east coastline. From Mount Olympos to Cape Sepias an eighty miles wall of mountains, harbourless. But then comes the six-mile strait between Sepias and the northern tip of Euboea, called Artemision because of the temple of the goddess there, a temple justly rich in votive offerings from sailors. If the strait of Artemision were held in force, an enemy fleet coming south from the Gulf of Therma faced an unpleasant prospect. The distance was too great to be covered in a single day unless you drove your crews brutally hard. In any case, this would be pointless, for it would involve approaching the enemy with exhausted oarsmen. The alternatives were equally unpromising; you could bring your fleet south piecemeal, in squadrons – which would leave them liable to piecemeal destruction by the enemy – or you could ride out the night at anchor off that iron, harbourless coast, and pray to your barbarian gods that the weather remained fair.

'Let them come to us in the straits after a long voyage along a harbourless coast, and we'll beat them,' said Themistocles.

If the Spartans and the Corinthians and the rest played their part.

And in the morning, down to the shipyards, to talk with ship-wrights, then on to the harbour, to drill the ever-willing Plataeans, and explain to them the mysteries of ramming. 'It's now or never. You can afford to miss once, if you've a particu-larly tough crew you might get away with missing twice, but after that your rowers are too exhausted to repeat the gruelling business of backing water at full speed just far enough to get into proper position again before running forward for another try. And the speed's all-important. If you're too slow, he'll back water, get out of range. If you're too fast, the ram will go too deeply into his hull, and we can't back water and get clear before his marines can board. The Phoenicians carry thirty marines and archers to our eighteen, and they build higher ships than we do, so that their archers can shoot down into ours. But don't worry about that thirty/eighteen ratio; think of it like this. We use the entire ship as a weapon. *They* try to kill individual men; *we* aim at destroying their entire ship with one thrust, and doing for the entire crew at the same time. By the way, *they* don't seem to be able to swim.'

And then we put to sea to try to give them the elements of the two chief manoeuvres, the diecplus,* and the periplus.** The diecplus can be used when opponents are facing each other in two long lines, and involves dashing forward at a given signal so suddenly and at such a rate that you're through the enemy line before he can take counter-measures. Then you wheel round and ram his unprotected quarters or stern. It's a beautiful manoeuvre, but – my God, it requires a lot of you. You need fast ships, superb steering, and crews trained to perfection. And general co-ordination.

The periplus is a simpler stroke altogether; you turn the enemy flank to take him astern.

* 'Break through.'
** 'Sailing around.'

There was another manoeuvre we didn't practise with the Plataeans, a variant of the diecplus which needed oarsmanship of an order you couldn't acquire in a few months, lion-hearted as they might be. In the attack, you swerve so that your bulk-heads sweep away the oars on one side of an enemy ship – you yourself having drawn your own oars inwards just before the impact. That left the enemy crippled if not sunk, but was a manoeuvre you couldn't expect of the Plataeans.

One evening, Themistocles was more silent than usual. I was a little piqued. He'd seen the Plataeans drilling that afternoon – they'd even made a pretty good shot at the diecplus. As he was washing his hands at the end of the meal he said abruptly, 'The Phoenicians invented the diecplus, remember. Instead of practising it so much, we should be thinking about how we're to counter it if it's used against *us*. We'd better have an early night, and sleep on it.'

When I went to his house the following morning, he was exultant. 'Simple question, Theron. What's the best way of preventing an enemy from breaking your line?'

'I've had a sleepless night, and the only answer I could come up with was to have two lines of ships – the second could deal with the enemy that broke through. But that's no good for us, because it needs superiority in numbers.'

'I told you to sleep on it. I did. And I've found the answer, I think. Ask me the question.'

'How do you prevent the enemy from breaking your line?' I queried obediently.

'By having no line to break,' Themistocles said promptly. 'Draw up your ships in a circle, with prows pointing outward; and sterns towards the hub. He hasn't a line to break through then, has he? Let someone else drill your Plataeans today – we have to try out this idea.'

That time of waiting was dreadful, and nerve-racking, but – my God, it had its exciting moments!

I I

Themistocles was duly re-elected to the Board of Generals at the beginning of the year, but it was anything but a clear-cut victory. He just scraped home. The opposition remained as violent as ever. And if he could not get his own city behind him, what chance did he have of carrying the Congress at Corinth with him, the Congress whose morale sank steadily lower with the knowledge that no aid could come from Syracuse, even if Gelon wanted to help us — his belief that the Carthaginians were preparing an attack there in Sicily seemed only too well founded. And while the Corcyrans had made promises, they were vague to the point of being non-committal.

The reaction to all this in Corinth was predictable. Everything had seemed to play into the hands of the anti-naval school of thought. Almost one could see satisfaction in their faces when it became plain that we had no hope of aid from overseas. Without strong naval contingents from Corcyra and Syracuse, what chance had we of taking on the Persian fleet with any chance of success?

There was also plenty of unwelcome news reaching us from the east — and, eventually, from the north.

For Xerxes was coming. Not even the most muddle-headed wishful thinker could doubt it now. A month after Themistocles had just managed to get re-elected as one of the generals, the Great King's engineers and native forced labour completed both the ship-canal through the Athos peninsula and a bridge of boats over the Hellespont. The latter undertaking had not been without incident. A storm destroyed the first bridge; Xerxes promptly had the engineers executed and punished the Straits themselves by having them scourged (three hundred lashes), branded with red-hot irons, and fettered. While sentence was being executed, the workmen were ordered to shout at the water, 'Xerxes the King will cross you with or without your permission,' and add insultingly that no one sacrificed to the Hellespont because the waters were so acrid and muddy. The Hellespont took it pretty quietly. Xerxes was in towering good form at this point; when the canal cutting had begun, he had sent a letter to Mount Athos threatening to topple it into the sea if it caused trouble.

It was no wonder that we had found it almost impossible to get any flax from Egypt. There were really two bridges – 360 ships to the north-eastern, 314 to the other. On each of these bridges was laid two heavy cables of flax – each a hundred tons in weight – and four lighter cables made of papyrus. There was a continuous roadway of planks, and parapets, so that the thousands of animals that must cross would not be frightened by the sight of water. At the same time the River Strymon was bridged at its mouth, and all along the Thracian coast, well into Macedonian territory, great food dumps were set up, mountains of salt meat for the ordinary soldiers, since Persians are not grain eaters, great bales of paper for the lists and reports without which it seemed the Persian army could not function – and, of course, for the King and his nobles stacks of luxury tents, beds, table-utensils, and great piles of fodder, big as houses, for the beasts who would provide fresh meat for Xerxes and his court, and bushels of condiments so that his cooks might adequately practise their culinary strategy.

Xerxes' own departure from Sardis was marked by an act of barbarism completely in character. When he had come there in the previous autumn, an old Lydian named Pythius had not only entertained the King and his entire army in the most lavish manner, but had offered Xerxes his entire fortune as a contribution to the expenses of the campaign. Xerxes had been delighted. 'You are my personal friend,' he said. 'You will never regret your gesture.' (I remember that the Persian courtiers were still talking of the episode when I was briefly feasted in Sardis; enviously, they said that Pythius was made for life.) When the army finally left Sardis, Pythius approached Xerxes once more;

there had been an eclipse when the troops first began to move and he was a scared man. Reminding Xerxes of his age, he asked if the eldest of his five sons serving in the army might be allowed to remain at home to take care of his father and his father's property. Xerxes, enraged at such presumption, ordered the executioners to find Pythius' eldest son, cut him in half, and put the two halves one on each side of the road, so that the army might march between them. In such circumstances the barbarian invasion of Greece began.

It was to continue in the same manner. When the enemy reached Thrace, they crossed the Strymon at a bridging point called Nine Ways. When they discovered the name of the place the Persian priests, the Magi, took nine native boys and nine girls and buried them alive there.

'Two months?' said Themistocles. 'Do you think we still have two months in which to win over Athens to the right strategy, and then the Congress?'

Underneath his easy manner he was growing desperate. The Persians might be approaching Macedonia; not only was Greece still disunited, but so was Athens.

It was in this mood of desperation that he decided to seek the advice of the Delphic oracle – he was ready to try anything that would give him the slightest chance of beating down opposition. He chose, predictably, his best friend, Habronichos, for the mission – and, less predictably it seemed, me. But we were so desperate, as I said, that we were clutching at straws, one of which was the fact that the temple at Delphi had been rebuilt by the Alcmaeonid family. So an Alcmaeonid in the mission might help.

Two stories account for the choice of Delphi as the site of the oracle. According to one tale, a goatherd searching for a missing animal eventually found it, frenzied, in a chasm below the cliffs. Then the goatherd himself, possessed, began to utter prophecies, and so did others going to the same spot. So strange a manifestation, as powerful as it was mysterious, must be the work of the gods; this remote, earthquake-ridden spot was one of those holy places chosen by the Olympians where they would communicate their will to men.

The other story runs that Zeus, wishing to discover the centre of the earth, loosed two eagles from the ends of it, and they met at Delphi. Well, there are eagles enough at Delphi now, they wheel and circle endlessly above the crags, have done so from unrecorded time, will do so through the centuries of the future when Athens and her story will be as remote as the story of Troy. But may it be a happier tale!

Apollo took the shrine for his own later. Some say he came south from Olympos, others that he left his holy isle of Delos in a dolphin-guided ship, and leaped from the vessel disguised as a star. This would undoubtedly be the easiest way to reach Delphi; the god himself advises his devotees to visit his shrine in summer; in the winter it is freezingly cold and when the sun rises the mists pour off Parnassos. Even in the late spring, when we went, the going is not easy – had we been proper pilgrims, that is, had we walked, it would have taken five days, nine hours a day of heavy toil – Eleusis, Eleutherae, Plataea, Thebes; as it was, the journey was rough enough, difficult, precipitous mountain passes, still maintaining a chill in the shadows, the peaks themselves hidden in cloud in early morning and the evening. The sun itself seemed to bring little warmth, but at least it brightened the countryside through which we rode, showed us the silvery-blue waters of little mountain tarns, and the great splashes of colour of spring flowers among the grey crags and the dark green of forests, bright cyclamen and scarlet anemones, and the paler asphodel on its skeleton stems.

Most of the Delphians are shepherds – the very coins of the place bear the heads of rams or goats – but within the little town itself there is a small circle of families like the Labryadae, who traditionally supply the ranks of the priesthood, cosmopolitan, travelled men very different from the simple countryfolk. Each of these families has links with individual Greek states, offering hospitality to any official representatives who may come to Delphi. Habronichos and I were therefore entertained by Timon, the son of Androbulos, who entertained us in more than one sense; he was a sophisticated man, subtle, with a cynical sense of humour. When we thanked him for his hospitality, he said, 'My dear fellows, if only you could appreciate how delighted I am to play host to Athenians, and not Spartans! *That's* a trying job if you like – practically a full-time one, too. You'll always find Spartans in the queue for advice. Telecles, who has to look after them, poor devil, has a hell of a time of it. A couple of years ago – before they started the war with Argos – their ambassador turned up with his wife, an awful woman, who took over the hall so that she could do her exercises – naked – and told Telecles' oldest boy, only nineteen at the time, and a modest young fellow contemplating the priesthood, that she would like an affair with him.'

That, I think, was the only time we laughed in Delphi.

'The point about the Spartans,' Timon continued at the end of the meal, 'is that, not only are most of them as superstitious as any old granny in a remote village, but they're unhappy, ill at ease in the modern world. Put them on a battlefield, in the barrack square, and they're at home, more than adequate, but gradually it's being borne in on them that there's a world outside Sparta, where unSpartan activities like trade and art matter. And if you've been brought up to obey orders, your initiative paralysed almost from birth, you're not adaptable, you can't cope. So, bereft of any instinct to think for themselves, what do they do? Regimented into the acceptance of external commands, they look to the god for advice on every damned triviality you can think of, fairly lay siege to him. If I were an Olympian, I believe I'd find excess of religious zeal far more distressing than lack of it. And infinitely more tiresome.'

There was one of Delphi's famous thunderstorms that night. Thunder bellowed deafeningly about the towering cliffs and made sleep impossible, but the next morning was clear enough after the mists had evaporated. Timon went over the ritual with us since neither of us had previously visited Delphi as a suppliant. 'You drink from the Castalian Spring, you bathe in it. You wear festal dress, an olive garland. You will be led into the temple by the five sacred guardians, of whom I shall be one. There in the adyton you will put your question to the Pythia – it's incorrect to call her the priestess, she's a quite uneducated peasant woman. Elderly too – despite the beautiful young women you so often see on vase paintings and so on. She wears a girl's dress, but since a sacrilegious lout of a Thracian raped a young priestess once, older women have always been selected ...' And so on. He was very businesslike about it.

You come up from the little town, past the Castalian Spring, and up the steep zig-zag of the Sacred Way. There are five steps up to the main entrance, with two large basins of holy water from which we sprinkled ourselves. So, higher and higher, past dedications, trophies, inscriptions, treasuries, until we came to the temple, only recently completed, and built by my Alcmaeonid kinsmen during exile from Athens. Here, in the little level court before the temple, could be seen some of the more famous offerings.

As we entered the temple, I found I was drawing a deep breath. I glanced at Habronichos. He was one of the most intrepid men I knew, but he looked grim and pale.

We stood without speaking, awaiting the Pythia. Timon had told us that she too had bathed in the Castalian waters, she had put on the special robes of prophecy, and was approaching us now.

She came in, led by a priest. An elderly woman, bluntfeatured. Calm to the point of placidity. She looked at us incuriously as she passed by. Led by Timon, we followed at a respectful distance. A priest came to join us. This was the exegete, who would explain to us any obscurities in the answer we received. Something within me bristled at the sight of him. He had about him too much of the air of the courtier for me; he would, I thought – possibly blasphemously – have fitted in nicely at Sardis.

With the Pythia was the priest who would act as her interpreter.

I remember that as we followed them from the main hall there was a savage growl of thunder outside, and, when it died away, one could hear the first great drops of rain splashing down.

At the southern end of the temple we halted. We were in the adyton, a tiny quadrangular room about eight by twelve feet with limestone walls, a flat wooden ceiling, and only one door, through which we had entered. There was a very steep staircase plunging down into what seemed nothing more than a dark cavity. Here the sacred tripod stood; here the Pythia would be possessed by the god. She went down, with her attendants.

We were told to sit on a stone bench set against one of the walls, on which hung consecrated weapons. It was dark, only one lamp burned. It was smoking. In the centre there was a gilded statue of Apollo, glittering in the poor light; in one corner a tomb – the empty tomb where the mortal remains of Dionysus had been placed after the giants had torn him to pieces and before his father Zeus restored him to life. There was a little grating in the floor.

It was hot in the little room. The reek of the flickering oil lamp was strong. Below us, in that narrow cleft in the earth, they had seated the Pythia on the tripod straddling the channel through which the prophetic stream Cassotis ran. They had put our question to her. She would drink water from a silver bowl, and they would place in one of her hands a sprig of bay-laurel, in the other one of the sacred fillets of wool almost concealing the limestone omphalus* at her feet, marking the centre of the universe. Now, holding the god's emblem in one hand, with the other hand linked with the source of all creative power, she must speak as the god. Before her eyes was a gold statue of Apollo.

We heard music, slow, melancholy, coming up to us from below. The priests were chanting. And then came the smell of burning barley-grains, bay-leaves, and the smoke was gushing up the steep staircase, through the grating – great clouds of it –

* The sacred navel-stone, regarded as the centre of the earth.

now one understood the necessity for the grating, they'd suffocate down there otherwise, even here the wreaths of it made you dizzy, obscured the dimness of the lamp –

There was a sudden dreadful sound from below, harsh, choking. The music and the men's voices died away. The voice we were hearing was more like that of an animal in anguish, a sudden shriek, a babble of noise, a hissing – if there were words they were nothing like any human speech known to me.

She must be dying. No one could scream and moan and choke like that and live. What were they doing below – holding her down as she writhed and her face blackened, and foam passed her grinding teeth to gather on her distorted lips?

It was horrible. I sat there shuddering, sweating. And suddenly I thought that such sounds of agony could mean only one thing for Athens.

The screams and the other noises ended. Slowly the smoke began to eddy away. I turned to look at Habronichos. I could not see him well in the gloom, but from the glint in his eyes he shared my feelings. Beyond him Timon, in a strangely rigid pose. I could not see the exegete with any clearness.

I wondered how long we should be there.

My head felt as if it would split in two.

Dully I ran through in my mind the procedure that must be followed. The Pythia, possessed by the god, prophesied. The priest-interpreter had taken down her words. Next the prophetes – the speaker for the god – would give the substance of what she had said, either in verse or prose. And then the exegete would explain the pronouncement to us.

Silence below. Was she dead?

The exegete got up. The interpretation might take some little time. We should leave the adyton, perhaps, and –

'No,' said Habronichos in a scarcely recognisable voice. 'We stay.'

So he did, indeed, share my feelings.

I leaned back against the wall as I had pressed myself against the wall of the cell in Sardis, sick with apprehension. I said

nothing. Neither did Timon. The exegete shrugged, and went
down the steep staircase. Habronichos said after a moment, 'I
don't think we are going to receive the kind of advice we can
take back to Athens.'

'What do we do, then?'

'Wait,' said Timon. (I think we had both forgotten him.) 'Do
nothing rash. Talk things over with me first.' His tone had lost
its usual lightness.

The exegete returned. His courtier's face was fixed in lines of
mechanical sympathy. He stood by the wavering, dipping flame,
and read the Pythia's answer.

> 'Why sit you, doomed ones? Fly to the world's end, leaving
> Home and the heights your city circles like a wheel.
> The head shall not remain in its place, nor the body,
> Nor the feet beneath, nor the hands, nor the parts between;
> But all is ruined, for fire and the headlong God of War
> Speeding in a Syrian chariot shall bring you low.
> Many a tower shall he destroy, not yours alone,
> And give to pitiless fire many shrines of gods,
> Which even now stand sweating, with fear quivering,
> While over the rooftops black blood runs streaming
> In prophecy of woe that needs must come. But rise,
> Haste from the sanctuary and bow your hearts to grief.'

After the appalling shrieks and sounds from below it would
have been impossible to be hopeful of a good response, but no
suppliant had ever received so crushing a reply, a sentence of
death passed on an entire people. I stood like a dumb ox marked
down for slaughter. The exegete said, 'My task, as you know, is
to explain any obscurity —'

'My God!' said Habronichos. 'Obscurity!'

Suddenly Timon had gripped us each by the arm, was hurrying us out of that dreadful little room, out of the temple, past the
line of other suppliants. I shall always remember the look of
horror on the face of one portly man, mouth agape, jowls
aquiver. I don't know how we looked, but he got the message

sure enough; the god was not in a comfortable mood that day. 'I think,' he stammered, dropping hastily out of line, 'I will come back later.'

I have wondered since what particular problem he had intended to place before the oracle.

The storm had passed while we had been in the temple; outside the flagstones steamed beneath a hot sun. We did not speak a word until we were in Timon's house. Then the silence seemed infinitely worse than when we had been hurrying down the Sacred Way. I didn't want to be alone with Habronichos, with no excuse for avoiding discussion of what we had heard. I hoped Timon would be – well, obtuse, I suppose, that he'd stay with us.

And Timon was indeed staying with us. Now that I really looked at him, I saw that he was as white-faced as Habronichos – and, presumably, myself. But he was white-faced with anger – I have rarely seen eyes more furious.

'Sit down,' he said, in a voice worlds removed from the tones he usually adopted. 'Now tell me what you propose to do. Obviously you're not going to return to Athens with this – this –' He struggled for words.

'We can't take it back,' said Habronichos, 'but what in the hell *can* we do?'

'Listen to me for a start,' said Timon, 'and have a drink, both of you. I think the time has come for frank speaking.'

'My God!' I said. 'Hasn't there been enough frank speaking?'

'That!' he said. 'But no more talk until you've had some good wine inside you.'

He went out, calling to servants. Habronichos and I sat side by side, staring at our hands. At one point he said, 'Well, if we never have to go through anything together worse than this –'

'Did you ever think – ?'

'That the answer would be like this? Never, in my blackest moments.'

Timon was back. 'Drink this,' he said. 'Don't talk. Listen. And if I don't express myself very well, remember I've never been so angry in all my life.'

Some of the anger was apparently directed at me, for once he'd put the cup in my hand, he said violently, 'That you, of all people, should be looking so hangdog – you, who were chosen for the reason that you're an Alcmaeonid!' and then, when I stared at him he went on exasperatedly, 'Have you forgotten how members of your family bribed the authorities so that every time a Spartan appeared as suppliant all he got was, "Athens must be freed", so that eventually Spartan nerves cracked, and they sent an army to help drive out the tyrants?'

'You mean,' said Habronichos, eyes and voice murderous, 'that *Xerxes* – '

'Has paid our young friend's kinsfolk the compliment of imitating them? Oh, no. I don't think it would enter his head – and although there's a permanent whiff of corruption in the air of Delphi these days, after the sensational exposure of *that* bit of bribery no one here is going to risk being found out in a second such affair.'

Habronichos said suddenly, 'That woman wasn't playing a part. Those cries – my God, I can still hear them! She was seeing something quite appalling.'

'No,' agreed Timon, 'the Pythia wasn't acting a part. They're too artless, these women, for any kind of deceit. But their very artlessness is the root of their power, danger – call it what you like. Only such a person could let herself be truly possessed by the god – as she believes. Certainly I believe that in the utter surrender of her mind, it can be invaded by the thoughts of those close to her – possibly by the thoughts of the suppliants, more probably by the thoughts of the attendant priests. Have I made myself clear so far?'

'Yes,' said Habronichos. 'You are saying that while the Pythia believes she speaks for the god, in reality she voices the thoughts of the priests. And they – '

'Ah!' said Timon. 'Now we approach the root of the matter. For months now two thoughts have been paramount in the minds of the priesthood here. First, the invincible power of Persia.'

Habronichos and I said together, 'Marathon!'

'Which brings me to the second thought which obsesses them. They are convinced that the forthcoming expedition is aimed against Athens alone.'

'Half a million men!' said Habronichos. 'Complimentary to us, I suppose, if true, but —'

'I know, I know. I myself have argued enough with the chief priest, Aceratos, but his mind is fixed. Xerxes is launching a punitive expedition against Athens alone, revenge for Marathon, and Sardis. Athens made her bed when she sent those ships to Ionia; why should all Greece lie in it? Let Attica be laid waste; why should the rest of Hellas be devastated — the rest of Hellas that sends a constant stream of gift-bearing suppliants in this direction?'

After a moment, Habronichos said, 'I take it that Aceratos was with the Pythia today?'

'He was.'

After another moment, I asked, 'And I take it you don't agree with his views?'

And at last we saw the real Timon. All his easy manner had left him now; he was a very formidable man indeed. His eyes glinting, he said, 'The barbarian means to conquer all Greece, and he must be resisted. If he's allowed to get past the northern mountain barrier he'll come this way — if our priesthood knows about his resources, I'm damned sure he knows what he can lay hands on here — it's not two years since he took that eighteen-foot statue of Bel-Marduk from Babylon, eight hundred pounds of solid gold, and melted it down to finance the jaunt he's contemplating to the West. My idea is that he'll look to Delphi to recoup the running expenses of the expedition — and that he won't look in vain. In fact, Aceratos'll have the whole damned selection laid out in the forecourt of the temple ready for Xerxes to take his pick.'

'If, of course, he gets here.'

He got up, and began to stride restlessly up and down the room. 'Be clear about this,' he said. 'I'll fight the damned barbarians, but I'll fight for Delphi, the village, the shepherds

124

and goatherds, their wives and children. And I'll fight for the true Apollo, not the Apollo of a corrupt and cowardly priesthood, but the god bringing reason, order, the far-shining one, the god of the daring mind, of lucidity, clarity, *light*! I'll fight for him to the death. While you've been making your plans in Corinth, we have been making our necessarily more modest plans here in Delphi (I except of course the sixty-strong staff of the temple). Should the enemy approach, we send our women and children across the water to the Peloponnese. Then we climb Parnassos. We carry what valuables we have to the Corycian cave, sacred to Pan. And then Apollo's people, whatever Apollo's priesthood may do, will fight. We know every rock, every ledge above the gorge. More to the point, we know every rock that can be easily loosed. And they will be loosed for good when the barbarian passes below.' And then he laughed suddenly. 'Have you noticed that patriotism is thirsty work? Have some more wine. And don't think that for a moment I've forgotten your present problem.'

'We can't take such a message back to Athens,' said Habronichos. 'I'll speak as frankly as you've spoken to us. *We* — Themistocles and we who think like him — will fight as you will fight. *We* are prepared to defy the oracle, if we think the oracle's advice is disastrous for Greece. If every other state in Hellas submits to him, our fleet will be waiting for him in the Salamis Strait. But there are others in Athens, and —'

'No need to say more. So let us be practical. Obviously you must approach the oracle a second time. Approach as suppliants, of course, but let your supplication be hardened by a little defiance. Say you cannot and will not carry such a message back to Athens. Even threaten. Say that rather than carry such a message, you are prepared to starve to death in the temple forecourt — that should scare them, particularly since one of those threatening to pollute the holy precinct is the kinsman of those who built the temple. Meanwhile, I shall see what I can do.'

Habronichos said bluntly, 'Do you think you can do anything?'

'Well,' said Timon, 'I mentioned my friend, Telecles, the

man afflicted by Spartans as other men are afflicted by boils. He actually has one staying with him now on some official mission or other. I'm going to talk to him.'

'With what in mind?'

'I'm going to tell him what the oracle has replied to you — that the only hope Athenians have of avoiding total destruction is to get clean out of Greece. The Spartans won't admit it, but in their heart of hearts they admit that there's no hope of successful resistance to Persia without the Athenian fleet. So no Spartan's going to like *that* advice. I don't propose to bemuse poor Telecles' thickwitted guest with my theory of the origin of prophecies, but I think I'll be able to convince him that you should be given the chance of receiving further advice — and that necessarily means better advice. And he'll go off to see Aceratos — and the priesthood hates offending Sparta.'

So some hours later we stood again in the forecourt of the temple under a brilliant sky. The storm clouds had cleared completely, bees hummed happily about the sun-baked stones, we could hear birds calling from tree to tree, the plumage of the soaring white eagles seemed to shine.

Aceratos appeared. 'You are fortunate. You have already been privileged —'

Privileged — to hear such screams and receive such a message? I lost what he continued, but Timon touched my arm, and he and Habronichos were re-entering the temple. The Spartan, whoever he was, had played his part.

The darkness and the smoking lamp and the glittering statue. The music and the chanting and the choking smoke. Was it worse knowing what might come, or to be unprepared?

'Lord Apollo, *we'll* take them on single-handed in Salamis Strait if the worst happens, but if Athens were united . . . Lord Apollo, we of the fleet will fight them alone in Salamis Strait, but what of the rest of our people? Lord Apollo, our ships will try to stop him at Salamis if no one else in Hellas withstands them, but if even Athens isn't united . . .

'Holy Maiden, protect your city!'

I was praying so desperately that it was with a shock that I realised that though there was noise below, it wasn't screaming. Muttering, even whimpering – but no screaming.

'Lord Apollo, lord of light, you know we'll fight to the death against the things I saw in Sardis. So if it comes to that – only our ships making a last stand in Salamis Strait – let us take with us as many of them as we can . . .'

'This is stupid,' a part of my mind said. 'The oracle ordered us to leave Attica, leave Greece. You defy Apollo's oracle, yet you pray to Apollo himself to give us the courage for that last fight in Athenian waters – '

But my thoughts went on pounding like blood in my veins, 'We'll fight alone . . . if they come to Attica, we'll be waiting for them . . . narrow waters of Salamis . . . our only hope since we'll be so outnumbered . . .'

'Stand up,' whispered Habronichos. 'Here's the new message – '

The exegete looked at me curiously. 'Are you well? Were you fainting?'

I shook my head.

He read carefully from the tablet:

'Not wholly can Pallas win the heart of Olympian Zeus,
Though she prays him with many prayers and all her subtlety;
Yet will I speak to you this other word, as firm as adamant:
Though all else shall be taken within the bound of Cecrops
And the gold of the holy mountain of Cithaeron,
Yet Zeus the all-seeing grants to Athene's prayer
That the wooden wall only shall not fall, but help you and your children.
But await not the host of horse and foot coming from Asia,
Nor be still, but turn your back and withdraw from the foe.

Truly a day will come when you will meet him face to face.
Divine Salamis, you will bring death to women's sons
When the corn is scattered, or the harvest gathered in.'

After a moment's silence — 'That,' said Habronichos evenly, 'is a message we *can* take back to Athens.'

'Well,' said Themistocles, 'a few shreds of hope. Were you really contemplating fasting to death?'

'I don't know whether I'd have gone in for anything so lengthy,' said Habronichos, 'but I know I'd have cut my throat rather than bring back that first message.'

'Thank God for Timon,' said Themistocles, adding thoughtfully, 'His name's useful, too.* Did you learn the Pythia's name?'

'Aristonice.'**

'Better and better — my dear fellow, face facts, the second message was not so bad as the first, but even so we'll be scraping the barrel to get much out of it to convince the unconverted — and they tend to be a superstitious set, don't they?'

'Do you know what I believe?' asked Habronichos bluntly. 'I think they'll say that either you dictated the whole message or that you added the last two lines — rather, the last line but one.'

'What, the line about Salamis? That's fairly obvious, isn't it? The priests didn't want to offend the Spartans, yet they're convinced the Persians will win. So we get line after line of vagueness not all that different from what had been said before — and then the sop to the Spartans, the line about Salamis. If the priesthood at Delphi is as well-informed as it's supposed to be, that reference isn't surprising. Timon told you they're convinced we're Xerxes' prime objective. *Our* party's made it clear we'll fight. So the Persian army comes down on Attica, we'll have evacuated our people over to Salamis and other places — and Salamis Strait is the best, the only place for us to take on

* Timon, son of Androbulos, meant Honour, son of Manly Counsel.
** Noble Victory.

their fleet if we have to go it alone – as the Delphi priesthood apparently hopes. It's as simple as that.'

'So the priests added the line to whatever the Pythia said?'

'I don't doubt it.'

I sat in silence. Again I was back in that dark constricted room, praying desperately, so desperately that – it was only now that I realised it – there had been, vivid in my mind, a picture of Salamis, but never as I had seen it before, for the silver-blue of the narrow strait was almost completely obscured by squadron after squadron of ships engaged in battle. It had been almost as if I could see it painted on the dimness there before me.

Had the mention of Salamis been no more than deliberate calculation by the priests?

'Wooden walls,' said Habronichos. 'That's another invention on your part, they'll say. Obviously ships.'

'Not so obviously ships. That's going to be something any mother's son can interpret as he chooses. Can't you see what a careful job they've made of it? They don't say we'll *win* at Salamis, do they?'

I hadn't thought of victory at Salamis; I hadn't been that hopeful. I just prayed that we'd take as many of them as we could with us.

'You're nearly falling asleep,' said Themistocles suddenly to me. 'My God, *you're* not going into a trance, are you?'

'He nearly did when we were waiting for the second message,' said Habronichos. 'I tell you, he scared me.'

As I left them they were agreeing that, 'When the corn is scattered or the harvest gathered in,' was another piece of masterly vagueness, signifying any time except midwinter – when, in any case, not even Xerxes would contemplate fighting.

In one way we were handicapped in the debate before a single speaker opened his mouth. The very setting of the Pnyx fought against us. You sit facing downhill towards the City. Immediately behind the speaker's platform is the Acropolis; behind the Acropolis the hills, Lycabettos and Pentelicos, behind them,

Marathon. Who of the opposition would deny himself the telling gesture towards the natural fortress clear in view, the battlefield out of sight but never out of mind where not ten years before an Athenian *army* had conquered?

There was an extraordinary aspect to this Assembly – or perhaps, on reflection, it was not so extraordinary after all. I have attended Assemblies enough, and before any one of them got down to business there were the invariable preliminaries of private grumbling – the countrymen would grumble about having had to get up at the crack of dawn to make it in time, unlike the damned townsfolk who just have to stroll up at the last minute, and then fall to bemoaning the state of their crops, wheat or olives, to which unutterable things were probably happening in their absence. The men from Salamis would grumble terribly about the infrequency of the ferry service; if you wanted to catch the only boat that would get you here in time there was no opportunity for a decent meal, and if the damned windbags held forth as usual, you'd be here until it was too late to have a decent supper at the end of it all – not even time for a drink on the way here. And they would fidget as they grumbled – and yawn until the proceedings began.

But today there was none of it. Stillness, silence, tension, until prayers began the meeting.

And then Habronichos read out the message we had brought back from Delphi.

It was, predictably, greeted by a storm of cheering from the opposition.

The wooden wall. Land defence.

As for the reference to Salamis . . .

For month after month they had fumed, watching the 'sailor rabble' manoeuvring in those narrow waters. 'If the worst comes to the worst,' Themistocles had argued time and time again, 'we evacuate Attica, and fight at Salamis.'

And now the oracle had spoken of Athens' only defence being a wooden wall – and Salamis bringing death to women's sons.

My God, they were exultant! Their enemy was delivered into their hands.

I saw my father sitting among them. He was laughing. I had not seen him laughing for a very long time.

The seers and soothsayers held forth first. Like their professional brethren in Delphi they were defeatist. The god's meaning was clear. Athens and Attica must be abandoned. These oracle-experts were particularly vehement when they interpreted the reference to Salamis – above all, battle must not be risked there. No more explicit warning of disaster could have been given. There was a moment of hysteria when one orator, with waggling white beard, declared that the sacred snake of the Acropolis, which had been off its food for days, had now disappeared.

In their last argument, they had common ground with the other section of Themistocles' opponents, the resistance-on-land diehards, but in that alone. For the Back-to-Marathon movement were patriots. The soothsayers accepted the oracle's prediction wholesale; abandon all Attica, don't fight at Salamis. The Marathonists were delighted to accept the advice about Salamis, but were prepared to defy the earlier part of the prediction; Attica should not be abandoned – above all, the Acropolis must be held, for had not there been on it from time immemorial a wattle wall, a token defence, no more, but clearly the wooden wall that would prove the City's salvation?

As I had foreseen, there were the predictable gestures with the outflung right hand towards the Acropolis, even more gesticulating to the plain hidden by the mountains where less than a decade before the gentlemen in heavy armour had saved Athens.

Themistocles, when he got up, didn't gesticulate. If my heart were pounding, he seemed matter of fact enough. First he took on the soothsayers at their own game, and beat them. The auspicious names of Timon and the Pythia. The disappearance of the sacred snake – well, the sacred snake was showing us the way. The Acropolis was indefensible. But *Athens* – and Athens was not the actual city, stones, bricks, mortar, the inanimate possessions within, but her people – was not lost. The wooden wall was her fleet. As for Salamis, a god of Hellas, speaking to Hellenes, spoke of *divine* Salamis, where men would die. Would Apollo, Hellenic Lord Apollo, speak in this way of a place clogged with the corpses of his own people? Never. He would speak of it with loathing. It would be accursed Salamis. But a Salamis choked with the corpses of the race that in the ruin of Ionia plundered and burned the god's own holy shrine at Didyma – and there too had been an oracle – *that* would be divine! Impossible for the god to have forgotten Didyma. Did they not manage to rescue some of the temple treasures to send to Delphi itself – before the end, and the sack and the burning and the sending of the god's own statue as a trophy to Ecbatana? Would the god forget that? Would the god, remembering that, foreseeing a reckoning for the sacrilegious barbarians, not call the place of that reckoning divine?

(Suddenly I remembered that he had said to me once how his Carian mother had told him how her father had taken gifts to the oracle at Didyma; he and his wife had longed for a child, now she had found herself pregnant, and they had wished to thank the god. 'She said she remembered they told her about it on her last birthday before the Persians came. There was a sacred spring, and a statue of the god, and the shield of Menelaos, that he dedicated on his way home from Troy, although by this time only the ivory facing was left.')

And now he turned to face us, the convinced, the eager-to-be-convinced, the men who had voted the money for the ships, who had sweated and strained in those ships.

'The god says leave Attica. Well and good. We cannot hold Attica against half a million men. But we do not forsake Athens. That part of Athens that cannot fight we send to Troezen or Aegina or Salamis. That part of Athens that *can* fight will man the wooden wall, the ships that are the defence spoken of by the god. I say that we should resolve this, no matter what our allies decide. I say that we must resist even if in all Greece we stand alone. I pray that, whatever the outcome of the matter, we Athenians shall be remembered, so long as one free man remains alive, because, at the worst, we stood firm while others faltered and fled, or, at the best, we, after the gods, saved all Greece.'

And, rank after rank, we rose to him, cheering, shouting his name, weeping with excitement and exultation. In little groups, oases of silence, the opposition, realising the game was lost, drifted away. The passing of the motion was little more than a formality.

'Resolved by the Council and People.

'Themistocles son of Neocles made the motion

'To entrust the city to Athene the Mistress of Athens, and to all the other gods to guard and defend from the Barbarian ... The Athenians themselves and the foreigners who live in Athens are to send their children and women to safety in Troezen (*little Troezen, you could just see it in the extreme distance between the mountains of the Peloponnesian coast, if you stood on the Acropolis and looked southwards*) – the old men and movable possessions to Salamis. The treasurers and the priestesses are to remain on the Acropolis guarding the property of the gods –

'All the other Athenians and foreigners of military age are to embark on the two hundred ships that are ready and defend against the Barbarian for the sake of their own freedom and that of the rest of the Greeks along with the Spartans, the Corinthians, the Aeginetans, and all others who wish to share the danger –

'The generals are to appoint, starting tomorrow, two hundred captains of triremes from those who have land and home in Athens –

'When the ships have been manned, with a hundred of them they are to meet the enemy at Artemision in Euboea, and with the other hundred they are to lie off Salamis and the coast of Attica and keep guard over the land –'

('Which may,' muttered Themistocles later, 'never be more than wishful thinking. We may never get the other states to come so far north. But if I can go back to Corinth with this resolution to brandish under their noses, it may make all the difference.')

And after this vote had been taken, he put forward another proposal.

'In order that all Athenians may be united in their defence against the Barbarian those who have been sent into exile for ten years are to go to Salamis . . . those who have been deprived of citizen rights are to have their rights restored . . .'

Xanthippos and Aristeides returned immediately, Hipparchos remained with Xerxes, and was condemned to death in his absence.

So the evacuation began. We had time in hand, so could make it leisurely, orderly. There was grief, but not panic. It was agreed that the ships' crews might attend to their families' needs before we set sail for the north — if, indeed, we sailed north, for the reference to Artemision was sheer optimism, linked inextricably with that other hopeful phrase, '. . . along with the Spartans, the Corinthians, the Aeginetans, and all others who wish to share the danger . . .' The morning after the decree had been passed, Themistocles was off to Corinth, grimly resolved to transform hope into reality. In the days that followed, which I seemed to spend mostly standing on the quay knee-deep in bawling babies, bleating goats, hens raucous and indignant in coops, nevertheless I felt I was better off than he.

The actual transport of the evacuees was, of course, only part of the over-all picture. There was the problem of the harvest. There was the question of which people were to remain in Athens to keep the City running for the time being, which shopkeepers and tradesmen were to remain, how many farmers should stay on in the countryside. You must not think that the babies and the baskets arrived at the quayside overnight. This was a planned, orderly evacuation. We found out from Troezen and Aegina how many refugees they were prepared to take, all the arrangements were completed before a single woman set foot on a ship – we even had time to work out a system by which, whenever possible, a man's family would be carried on his own ship.

It was a phased evacuation; it was also a partial evacuation. Most of the wealthier families did not participate; in fact, the whole operation might have been very unpleasant indeed, accompanied as it was at the dockside by vituperation from Themistocles' more stupid opponents. As a matter of fact, the opposition verbal attacks helped: I thought, at first, that they might depress the men and their families unutterably, but instead they only made them furiously angry.

At some point during those hectic days I literally bumped into Cleandros. 'You've heard?' he said. 'Hipparchos isn't coming back?'

'Did you ever think he would? It doesn't alter things so far as your family's concerned, does it? You'll have to get the women over to Troezen.'

'I know – I'm expecting them here in the City any moment. They're out at the farm – I sent word the moment the decree was passed. It'll be a hellish job with my stepmother, of course; she could practically sink a ship with her jewellery, so persuading her what to leave behind – '

I imagined he might have trouble in other directions when his stepmother arrived in Athens.

Meanwhile, in Corinth, another obstacle to Spartan co-operation appeared, one which, remembering Marathon, we should never have forgotten. The Carneia, the great Spartan religious festival, would soon be due. They could not campaign then. But after a moment's thought, one of the two Spartan ephors present said heavily, 'To show our good faith, we'll send on ahead a small force to Thermopylae even though it means they'll lose their places at the Carneia.'

'All Greece will thank them for their sacrifice,' Themistocles said blandly.

After another moment's thought, the ephor continued, 'We

want to assure you of our good faith. Therefore, one of our Kings shall command the advance-guard. Leonidas. With other allied troops, of course—and a full Spartan contingent the moment the festival's over.'

'Forty sea miles between Thermopylae and the fleet at Artemision,' Themistocles said to me. 'The usual kind of communications—beacons, smoke-signals—of course. But I'd like something more than that, so I'm detaching the thirty-oar galley under Habronichos for special liaison duty with the Spartans.'

I wrenched my thoughts away from cleaning up the decks of my own galley—the last evacuee had just been safely deposited at Troezen—to look commiseratingly at Habronichos. He was putting a good face on it, I thought. In fact, he was smiling broadly.

'And you,' said Themistocles, 'are to be the errand-boy in the Spartan camp itself.'

Habronichos burst out laughing. 'Mouth already watering for that first connoisseur's sip of black broth?' he asked.

12

There was a marsh to the right of the defending force, which
ensured no enemy attack from the sea. It also ensured no direct
help from us, but there was a little creek to the south where our
fast galley could be stationed. And where it now jettisoned me.
I felt as depressed as any kind of débris must feel.

We had made the crossing at dawn. As I left the ship and took
the road northwards, the rising sun cleared the mist from the
sea, and reddened the waters. Then came the sheer gaunt height
of Callidromos, the eastern ridge of Mount Oeta, crested with
oaks and juniper on my left hand – 'God!' I thought. 'What a
horrible place!' – and finally Thermopylae itself and, wrinkling
my nose, I said to myself again: 'God! What a horrible place!'
For it is not – strange how one wants to say *was*, as if the
Thermopylae to which I came doesn't exist now – it is not a
pass, that is, not a road running between mountains. It's not
even a pass between mountains and sea. You have the great
prolonged ridge of Mount Oeta, the northern slope of which
comes so close to the sea, or rather to the marsh between land
and sea, that the space for a track is so narrow it can take only
single vehicles. This is the first, the east 'gate' of Thermopylae.
After this for a mile or so the road widens, but then the mountains close down again, and here you come to the second 'gate'.
Between 'gates' it's not easy to cover the ground, if ground you
can call it – mostly it's crusted, stinking mud produced by the
hot sulphurous springs that give the place its name. In fact, a
little simple engineering could have made the whole area one
vast impassable marsh, but there's nothing easier than to be
wise after the event. As it was, the only fortification was a wall
built by the Phocians so many years before to keep out Thessa-
lian raiders that now it was half ruined by age. As I came up, the

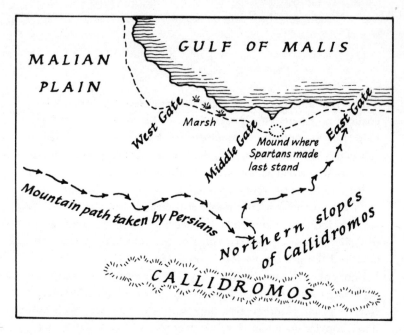

Thermopylae

Spartans were doing what they could to renew and strengthen it.
It was a horrible place.

It would have been horrible even if there wasn't a single
Persian trooper this side of the Hellespont. Though the nights
are cool enough, the days are so hot that at noon it was agony to
handle any metal that had been exposed to the sun. What an
ante-room to the Elysian Fields, I thought – but not seriously.
And the marsh gave, not only fever, but a disease of the eyes, an
inflammation that leaves men blind. Already two Spartans had
succumbed – that, in fact, was my first view of the Spartan
camp – two stumbling figures being led away by slaves. And
then I was past them, and among the red tunics, and, oddly
enough, my first impression was one of sound, of deep, harsh
voices. In the Persian camp, the voices had purred like great
cats; here I might have been among a pack of mastiffs. And they

looked at me as surly mastiffs might eye an unwary dog of another breed that had strayed too close to their kennel. What would they do? Pull me down and savage me? Was this how Actaeon had felt? As two big figures approached me I had an almost uncontrollable desire to call out, 'Down, Thymas! Stay, Stibon!'

'Theron of Athens, sent by Themistocles,' I said loudly instead.

They not only sounded like mastiffs, they looked like them. So Pantites' looks and ways had not been unique; Sparta didn't breed individuals.

'The King had better see him,' said the larger of the pair.

So I should see – what? The Unindividual of all Unindividuals ten feet tall? Well, there he was, taller even than the rest of them, although not ten feet, beside him the sacred insignia of Castor and Polydeuces, his house gods.

But he didn't look like a Spartan.

Not that he wasn't tall enough, or that his face wasn't scarred enough. It wasn't even that his hair wasn't the usual Spartan yellow, but the colour of rust, the colour of a fox. But his eyes weren't the eyes of a fox. They were the least subtle eyes on earth. They were hot, aching eyes, eyes that ached with weariness – not merely physical weariness, but the weariness that follows endless, fruitless mental gropings after the solution of an insoluble problem. There was a double gash between his straight brows so deep that at the time I took it to be another scar. Later I realised it was a perpetual nervous frown. At this first meeting I thought – quite detachedly – that the Spartan King hadn't Themistocles' air of confidence. And then – not at all detachedly – and with a curious ripple of the nerves – 'But if he goes down, I want to go down with him.'

There are two kinds of allegiance. There is the cerebral allegiance I gave to Themistocles, whom I admired more than any other man on earth. Therefore I saw myself as being perpetually on trial before him, proving myself in courage, intelligence. This is an allegiance of the mind, profoundly logical. I wanted – God, how I wanted! – his respect. And there is the other, the instant unthinking allegiance. No logic about it. 'This,' I can remember quite clearly telling myself, 'is reduced to the instinctive feeling a dog has for his master. It doesn't matter how stupid his master may be –' I argued back, 'You don't even know that he *is* stupid,' but then agreed dolefully, 'although the odds are that, being Spartan, he is. It's as degrading as that. One glance from a weary, not particularly intelligent-looking stranger –'

But it wasn't degradation, it was exaltation. My mind wrung its hands; my heart soared. I was glad I had been sent to the stinking mud of Thermopylae.

'Well,' said Habronichos some hours later. 'You don't look as worn coming as you did going. How are you getting on?'

'I felt,' I said, 'like a deer about to be savaged by hounds. But instead I got a – a rough friendliness.'

'What else did you expect? Pantites didn't say much, but he thought you didn't do too badly at Sardis.'

'Oh!' I said, startled. 'Is *that* why I was chosen?'

'Just woken up to it? Did you think it was all because of your beautiful eyes? Someone who'd got on fairly well with a rather difficult Spartan in somewhat trying circumstances was the obvious choice for liaison with a few thousand Spartans in circumstances we hope won't be so trying.'

'Three hundred,' I said. 'With helots.'

'Well, yes, the advance-guard at present, but the rest won't be long in coming up. What did you think of Leonidas, by the way?'

'He didn't say much.'

Habronichos burst out laughing. 'What do you expect a Spartan King to be except laconic? Well, what did his staff officers say?'

I gave figures. The King had brought with him from the Peloponnese three hundred Spartans, five hundred men from Tegea, five hundred from Mantinea, one hundred and twenty from Arcadian Orchomenos, one thousand from the rest of

Arcadia, four hundred from Corinth, eighty men from little Mycenae. On his way north he had gathered up seven hundred men from Thespiai, struggling for independence from Thebes.

Habronichos said, 'That's the entire Thespian striking force. Well, what about Thebes itself?'

'Four hundred men. He – the King – became almost loquacious at this point. He said he knew that with most Thebans pro-Persian, to ask for troops was a challenge. At the same time he thought he'd get more than four hundred.'

'Were they volunteers?'

'Yes.'

'Every pro-Hellene in the damned place, no doubt. Go on.'

'A thousand men from Phocis – they're holding the path over the mountains. Every able-bodied man from Locris – a few hundred.'

'Locris? I thought they were ready to submit.'

'They were, but the King sent round messages that he's brought only the advance-guard with him, the main army's expected any day, our people control the sea, and Xerxes isn't a god, just a man who's more or less accident-prone. It brought the waverers in.'

'For someone who doesn't talk much, what he says seems to the point. What about Thessaly, though?'

'He had Pantites with him. He sent him into Thessaly with the same message.'

'Well, I'm sorry you're bereft of the company of an old friend. Anything else?'

'Last night he sent his men forward on a night raid. He told them to spread out all over the countryside and, when he gave a signal, they set fire to farm buildings, cut down trees with as much noise as possible.'

'To give an exaggerated idea of numbers, eh? More imagination than I'd expect from a Spartan. Was it his own idea? Which officers has he with him?'

I ran through names. 'There's a Dienekes,' I added doubtfully, 'who's supposed to be something of a humorist.'

'Well,' said Habronichos, 'keep your tablets ready to note down his witticisms. You might be able to dine out on them for the rest of your life. Well, I'm for Artemision, and you're for your mud patch. I'll be back at dawn tomorrow.'

I went back to my mud patch. To my astonishment I was told I was to regard myself as a member of the royal mess. And that really was an extraordinary business – extraordinary and illuminating. Say Spartan, and what do most people think it denotes? Bravery. Physical toughness. Indifference to discomfort. And military necessity excluding everything else – war first, war last, war every time. War is the Spartan's profession. Yet – and this was the revelation – no Spartan is businesslike about war. We, the Athenians, the amateurs, the dabblers, are far more realistic, practical in our approach. They are so many sentimental schoolboys.

That first evening was – I'm sorry, I can't escape the word – extraordinary.

They might be further out of Sparta than any Spartan army had ever been, but any territory where they encamped was forever Laconia, as they saw it, and the approach of most of Asia in arms wasn't going to make them alter their ways. They had their evening exercises. Then they had supper. So I was introduced to the famous black broth for which Pantites had yearned when chicken cooked in saffron had been placed before him. I had seven companions; they shared Pantites' passion, eating with avidity. I managed to choke down the portion ladled out to me only by trying to recite mentally all the choruses by Aeschylus I could remember, and thereby divorcing my stomach from spirit.

> 'The driven oar, the flaxen gear,
>   A tower full-orbed against the brine,
> Have borne me un-stormconquered here:
>   I blame not nor repine;'

I said to myself between gulps. At my side a gruff voice described to me the subtleties of the Spartan cuisine. 'Pork,' he said, 'cooked in blood, seasoned with salt and vinegar.'

'Thou ancient law of pity, that bindest Heaven,
This crimeless exile see!'

I thought desperately.

'. . . so good,' said my neighbour – hopefully? – 'that the older men never eat anything else. All the younger fellows get is the meat.'

I turned and took a good look at him. He was definitely approaching middle age. I said, 'Well, being a younger fellow, may I offer you –'

I had no need to end my sentence. He upturned my bowl of Stygian liquid into his own – emptied already – then offered me his lump of pork. I chewed on this resolutely.

Well, I might have been afflicted by this ludicrous attachment to their King, sitting silent at the head of the table (I sat nervously at the foot) but I was paying dearly for my pleasures.

My companion, whose name was Maron, was being rallied, if one can use the word, by his comrades on his adroitness in effecting his swap with me. Half a dozen harsh voices said their owners would sit next to me in future. Struck by a sudden thought, I looked hastily around. I hadn't noticed it before, being so much oppressed by the thought of being encompassed by three hundred Spartans in the mass that I hadn't noticed individual faces. But now I realised that there wasn't a single young man among my present companions – and, as far as I could remember, members of the other messes weren't any more youthful. My only reaction at the time, however, was to feel more like a fish out of water than ever, surrounded not only by Spartans, but Spartan veterans.

We had wine. No passing round of the wine-bowl here; we were strictly rationed. A slave measured into each cup about one-twelfth of a pint. I couldn't altogether conceal my surprise; 'Deliberately done,' grunted Maron. 'It keeps us sober.' I took one sip and blessed the custom. The stuff might have been the vinegar with which they seasoned their black broth. The cup was unusual in colour and design, too. I turned it about in my hands, seemingly so absorbed in the receptacle I overlooked its contents. 'The design's deliberate,' said Maron. 'With that colour, you can't see if water's impure, and the shape makes the mud cling to the sides.' 'What a good idea,' I said, false as hell. 'Oh, there's more to it than that,' he said. 'Our potters don't have to waste time on anything needless, useless.'

Suddenly I remembered Xerxes' drinking habits. 'My God!' I thought. 'If we captured him, the worst punishment we could give him would be to make him a member of a Spartan mess for life.'

A huge barley cake on an earthen plate was set before me. At least it helped to settle my queasy stomach.

Dinner being finished, they rose and sang the thanksgiving hymn. Ignorance of it prevented me from black hypocrisy. 'Now what?' I asked myself. 'Night exercises?' But instead they had a competition – again, apparently, a regular procedure. Each man had to sing a song by Tyrtaeus. 'You've heard of *him*, of course,' said Maron. I had, but what I had heard was extremely odd. When the poor devils of Messenians had risen in revolt against Sparta over a century and a half before, reducing them to the state of oppressed servitude right and proper in Spartan eyes had been a lengthy business. The story went that the Spartans, sending to Delphi for the oracle's advice, had been advised to import a poet (they having nothing of the native sort) to inspire the sons of Laconia for the struggle. And they'd imported Tyrtaeus. According to one account, he'd been a lame schoolmaster in Athens with no great reputation in Attica who, the moment he set foot on Laconian soil, was inspired by the Heavenly Muse. I had never believed a word of it and after that evening, and my first hearing of Tyrtaeus' effusions, believed it less than ever. No Athenian could write such stuff. If he *were* a schoolmaster, his mentality was no more advanced than that of the most retarded of his pupils. But the Spartans adored his outpourings, and sang them on the march – that I knew. I hadn't known, however, that they gave solo renderings after supper.

Up sprang a grizzled commander and bellowed:

'Up, in free-born hardihood,
Soldiers born of Spartan blood!
Guard your left with shields a-swinging;
High the gallant spear-shafts flinging.
Hoard not life nor stint to pay:
Such was never Sparta's way.'

Fine, stirring stuff, and they loved it, joining in the refrain, and stamping their feet.

'Hoard not life nor stint to pay:
Such was never Sparta's way.'

I thanked the gods that Aeschylus had not been sent in my place.

Maron contributed a number of lines, only one of which I remember clearly. 'In nakedness his blood-wet members clutching.' I think anyone will agree it is indeed a memorable line. They liked that too.

But the lines they really adored were the most appalling morbidly sentimental rubbish I'd ever heard. A youth's fair form was fairest when he died in battle. A corpse on a battlefield was more beautiful than the living boy. This boy, dying in youth's bloom – I stared about me – scarred, weatherbeaten faces, most of them men around the forty mark, wallowing in this unhealthy nonsense. It was only now that I really comprehended how many centuries they were behind the rest of Greece. It wasn't merely a case of still keeping a monarchy (and not one king, but two). It wasn't merely having iron bars for currency. It was an attitude of mind. They'd never grown up. This was how schoolboys felt about fighting – and very young schoolboys, schoolboys who hadn't got down to Homer yet. Homer knew what war was like. It was a bad business, an evil. It was an interruption of the good life. But Spartans thought it the noblest form of activity in which men could indulge. They thought dying in battle *attractive*, God help us –

My meditations were interrupted by sudden realisation that the singing had died away. Silence. And – good God, they were all looking at me. Had I spoken my thoughts aloud? But, no – the looks cast in my direction were friendly. And beside me Maron said gruffly, 'Go on. They don't often ask outsiders.'

Had it been the words of the last song that had caused them to invite the only youth in the assembly to participate?

'I don't know any of Tyrtaeus' songs,' I said.

'Sing another, then,' said Maron. As coaxingly as a Spartan could, he said, 'The man who sings best is given an extra piece of meat.'

A few hours before I had been insanely happy because I'd come to Thermopylae.

But it seemed that in the cause of good inter-allied relations, sing I must. The question was – what? Drinking songs in Athens were about passing brimming bowls, and coronets of violets, and dancing girls. Had Spartans ever heard of dancing girls? And then, in my panic all I could remember was a song by Sappho, of all people. Spartans would never have heard of Sappho, but they'd gather the lines had been written by a woman if I suddenly piped up with:

'Sweet mother, let the weaving be,
    My hand is faint to move.
Frail Aphrodite masters me;
    I long for my young love.'

In an appropriate falsetto, of course. What would they do? Drown me in black broth?

Maiden of Athens, for your City's reputation, help me to *think*! (To make a fool of myself before him –)

And through remembrance of my first sight of him, she sent inspiration to her hard-pressed votary. Another poet from Lesbos:

146

'Come, sons of Zeus, from Pelops' isle,
    Leda's children valorous –
Castor and Polydeuces, smile
    With gentle hearts on us.

O'er earth's broad lands and every sea
    Your racing horses' reins you hold,
And men you rescue easily
    From death in freezing cold.

When on trim ships astern you spring
    And climb the thwarts, a far-seen light,*
A lantern to black ships you bring
    In the despairing night.'

I found myself the social success of the evening. 'Who wrote it?' 'Alcaeus of Mytilene.' I was awarded the extra meat, protested my unworthiness, gave it to my neighbour, was summoned before the King.

So he *could* smile.

'Come outside a moment.'

Outside to the glow of watchfires and two big figures rigidly at attention, guarding the two upright bars fastened together with horizontal bars, the sacred insignia, Castor and Polydeuces, beside which I had first seen him.

'Did you think of this?'

'Yes, sir.'

He gave his faint smile again. 'We're supposedly descended from the Heavenly Twins. People believe they lead us, possess us almost, in our functions. When a Spartan King goes to battle, Castor is supposed to accompany him in spirit; Polydeuces, the inactive brother, stays at home.'

That struck me as odd; Polydeuces, the divine twin, would surely be the better protector in battle. But I had enough sense

---

* Towards the end of a storm, the Dioscuri, Castor and Polydeuces, were thought to appear in the form of lights (the form of electricity known nowadays as 'St Elmo's fire') denoting that the danger was passing.

not to indulge in Athenian quibblings. If it came to that, I wasn't indulging in much conversation at all; I realised I hadn't said anything except 'Yes, sir.' I'd been more loquacious before Xerxes.

Uncannily he seemed to know what I was thinking. 'Did you have more to say to Xerxes?'

'I'm sorry,' I said. 'I didn't think Spartans wanted people to talk. And – well, I haven't been told the procedure with a Spartan King.'

'Nor, I should imagine, the procedure followed with regard to a Persian King.'

He was smiling again, and suddenly I burst out laughing. Heads swivelled in our direction, but I went on laughing. 'I should say not! He's terrified of disease, you know – before he arrived they – they had a kind of general fumigation, smoking spices held under the chins of everyone as a safeguard, and anyone speaking to him has to hold his hand before his mouth so that his breath can't reach Xerxes' face. And – oh, yes, before being fumigated you have your hands and beard washed in rosewater!'

And he was laughing, too. 'I must remember that – spices and rosewater. Pantites didn't tell me that.'

'Were you scared?' he asked after a moment.

The temptation to lie was immense, but I resisted it. 'Very much, but I tried not to show it.'

There was another brief silence, but this time it did not worry me. Then he asked, 'What is he like, this Persian King? As a person, I mean. Pantites never really got beyond describing his painted eyelids.'

I thought for a moment, then said, 'His vanity is the chief thing I remember.'

'Vanity?'

'Personal vanity. He always has to have someone admiring him – even a prisoner like me.'

He looked at me thoughtfully. 'That's worth remembering . . . *Did* you pretend to admire him?'

'No,' I said. 'Not even for strategic reasons.'

'Are you Athenians good at concealing your feelings?'

'Not as good as Spartans, but we try.'

They gave me a corner among the rocks in which I rolled myself in my cloak and lay staring up at the sky. First I hurriedly ran through my repertoire of songs lest I was called upon to perform next evening. There was a Cretan song, *A Soldier's Riches* – '*I have great riches, spear and sword*' – which should appeal to this most uncompromisingly masculine and militaristic of all audiences.

Were the red tunics the only patches of brightness and colour to be seen in Sparta?

How could they bear such a life? Yet they all seemed contented enough. Except Leonidas. I went over our conversation. It would be the last, I thought. Tomorrow or the day after the rest of the Spartan army would come up to join the advance-guard, and I should be merely one face among thousands.

I didn't sleep at once. The new moon went down, and the stars came out. There was the bright constellation of the Twins, Castor and Polydeuces, one divine, one human, but when the human died, the divine brother could not live without him, and begged that their fates might be joined: Heavenly Twins, swift riders cleaving through the air to the aid of men in ships in winter gales or on the battlefield. (Odd how the deities of a state not renowned for skill in horsemanship or navigation should appear as riders and at sea.)

The inseparable union of brothers . . .

13

I awoke to the sound of harsh Spartan voices, decided they spoke as they did because they talked from the backs of their throats, realised that in such a milieu no time should be wasted on idle speculation, sprang up, and looked about me. It was dawn. All around me they were combing their long hair; no one took any notice of me. They went through various exercises, sat down, were inspected by a senior officer. I felt unbearably scruffy and dishevelled, would have given much to freshen myself up in the cold sea, so much more pleasingly aromatic than the mud surrounding us. This being impossible, I made myself as presentable as I could. As I combed my short hair, I realised I was now being watched by amused Spartan eyes. Presently one of them came across and asked me to have breakfast with him. To my relief I was not to subsist on a diet of bull's blood, but was given bread to dip in that deplorable wine. My host announced that he was Pantites' brother-in-law. It appeared he was intrigued by my behaviour: Pantites had said I wasn't a bad fellow, but I insisted on asking questions. Yet I hadn't asked any questions since my arrival. Not wanting to let my old comrade down, I said, 'Well, I suppose the questions will come when the main army turns up,' a pointless remark in fact, but it gave Pantites' brother-in-law the opportunity to instruct me a little.

'Yes,' he said, 'you're not seeing us in normal conditions.' He sketched for me the way things should be done. A proper camp, not in this hellishly confined space, should be circular – *circular*, he repeated firmly. Obviously it was my cue to ask, 'Why circular?' in order to receive the crushing retort, 'What – have a square one, with four useless corners?' The Spartan army consisted of five regiments, corresponding to the territorial divisions of the state. On campaign one of the kings was always commander-in-chief, and the regimental commanders were part of the royal mess. 'It's different here, of course, with just three hundred in the advance-guard. It's nothing like the staff he usually has with him – regimental commanders, surgeons, quartermasters, commissariat officers – ' He gave further details. My wholly selfish reaction was, 'When that lot comes up, there'll be no more royal mess for me.'

And then he said gruffly, 'Not like the way the Persian King carries on, eh?' At the time I could not understand the expression in his eyes; it is only now that I realise what it was. It was that of a child asking to be told a story.

(*This all reads as unforgivable superciliousness. You must remember that I was young, and prided myself on my sophistication of mind. I did not then truly appreciate the value of simplicity. I did not realise the goodness, the fundamental virtue of which a straightforward man of action is capable. I had not then seen Spartans fight. And I had not then seen how Spartans could die. May they forgive me from the further shore.*)

On the previous night I had thought them schoolchildren, but I had been wrong. At least, they were not like Athenian children, brought up on Homer. Education for a Spartan boy meant two things – physical fitness, and obedience to authority. The finished product was the toughest thing, mentally and physically, the world has ever seen. It obeyed orders, and said little. Ideally, it should think little. Ideally, it should not do what an Athenian product like myself had done – which had so markedly impressed Pantites. I had asked questions. But even in Sparta perhaps the system broke down sometimes. A man might wonder. Wonder about the world outside Sparta – which he, except when campaigning, could not leave on pain of death. As my present companion wondered. Pantites, from what the King had said the previous night, had not said much about our experiences in Sardis, but he had whetted the appetite of his brother-in-law, and here I was, the talkative Athenian who had been part of Pantites' personal odyssey into the unbelievable world of

Asiatic monarchy. And from me Pantites' brother-in-law might learn more. I had entirely misunderstood his motives when he first approached me.

So I described to him Xerxes' court, and was heard with close attention. 'He wouldn't last long as a King of Sparta, would he?' he asked, his eyes fixed on a tall figure in a distinctive helmet with ram's-head cheek-pieces.

'No,' I said. 'He wouldn't.'

My companion went off with others to relieve advance pickets. He had told me he did not mind being at Thermopylae; in fact, he said, most Spartans enjoyed being on campaign – 'When we're on campaign, the physical exercises are cut down, so war means a rest for us.' As he left me, a comrade addressed him as Dienekes. So he was the wit of whom I had been told. Doubly a rarity. A Spartan with a sense of humour, and a Spartan with curiosity as to what lay outside the frontiers of his state.

A second interpolation. I find that in describing these days I make no mention of the contingents from the other states, brigaded there with the Spartans. This gives an unfair and unbalanced picture, perhaps. The injustice is particularly unforgivable in the case of the Thespian contingent. No men were more gallant than they. I talked with them, moved about their positions – but the point was that, even if they came from the most remote hillside state north of the Peloponnese, we had so much in common. I suppose it really amounted to this – even if a man never set foot outside the borders of Phocis or Locris, he knew he could if he chose. The outside world was not forbidden to him. The ideas of the outside world were not forbidden to him. They could come to him, if he would not go to them. But to be with the Spartans was like going on a journey of mental exploration, a unique opportunity. Strangers were rarely permitted to enter the forbidden territory of Laconia, but a segment of Laconia – and it was the people of Laconia, not the land, that surprisingly fertile, gentle countryside that makes Sparta – had been moved north of the physical frontiers. Any time I chose, I

could visit Phocis, or Locris or the other states that sent contingents.
But this was probably my only chance of getting to know Sparta.
What I didn't realise at first was that these particular men did
not give a balanced picture of Sparta. They were Sparta at its
best: Sparta at its worst remained south of the Corinthian Isthmus.

It was in search of the Phocian contingent that I climbed up
the shoulder of Oeta – a miserable business. Thick bushes,
strong and thorny, hid, but did not soften, the razor-sharp rocks
below. If you left the thickets of thyme and juniper, there were
boulders and stones of a kind to break an ankle on, and it was
hot, swelteringly hot.

I should point out in honesty that I had made things needlessly difficult for myself. I could have got up to the Phocian
bivouac by a track leading up from the east gate over the northern
slope of Callidromos, the track, in fact, to secure which the
Phocians had been posted high up over the Spartan west flank.
But I must show my toughness, and start marching up a slope
that at times seemed like a sheer wall. More than once I missed
my footing, and started a slither that threatened to send me slid-
ing nonstop into space; I may say that even more poignant than
the thought of hurtling down to the base of the cliff, was the
thought that, hurtling, I should hear laughter from below. As I
grabbed at a juniper bush and wondered whether it would take
my weight, I hoped that if it didn't and I went smack into the
mud, I'd smack all the life out of me.

I found the Phocians camped in a meadow above an oak
forest. It was a pleasant position – a little breeze made it cool,
brought the pleasing scent of hay. The Phocians were roasting
meat – mutton – and offered me some; I thought they were
excellent fellows. So relaxed as they lounged on the warm grass,
laughed and talked. They offered me good wine. I picked the
thorns from my flesh, bathed my cuts and bruises in a little
stream running down one side of the meadow, and went back
down the track which the Phocians were guarding. My feet
rustled comfortably among the oak leaves which were just

beginning to fall. It was still blessedly cool in the shade of the forest. Very different from the blistering rocks and steaming mud of Thermopylae.

The crew of our galley greeted me with some hilarity as I came to the cove. 'He's changed already! Real snap in the way he marches! Look at those shoulders! Eyes front all the time, too!'

But Habronichos was not smiling. He took me to the far end of the cove, drew out the tablets on which yesterday he had noted down all the information I had given him, and said: 'Read through this again. You're sure you've left nothing out?'

Somewhat surprised, I said, no, although I could amplify a little. For example, I'd just come from the Phocian camp, and —

'To hell with the Phocians — concentrate on the Spartans. What people does Leonidas have with him?'

I was pleased by the question, after Dienekes had unwittingly briefed me so perfectly to answer. 'Well, in an advance-guard, he hasn't his full usual staff, but he has a soothsayer, a surgeon, a quartermaster, the bearer of the sacred fire, a commissariat officer, his personal squire —'

'No one else?'

'Well, there's one regimental commander —'

Habronichos said again, 'Listen. This is important. He has with him three hundred Spartans and the staff you've mentioned. No one else?'

'No, but they're expecting —'

He wasn't listening. 'Be back here at dusk,' he said. He turned on his heel, made for the galley in haste.

'But what's happening?' I asked, hurrying after him. 'I'll have to report to Leonidas, won't I, what's going on in the fleet.'

'Oh, here,' he said, turning briefly to thrust another writing tablet into my hands. 'From Themistocles to the Spartan King. Just as well you reminded me — I almost forgot.'

He was on board before I had collected my wits. How cheated I felt! I had looked forward to a leisurely chat with the galley-crew, myself giving a detailed account of the singing contest I had won the night before, a witty description of the horrors of Spartan food. I had thought up an extended metaphor of myself as the man who, beset by savage mastiffs, held out the back of his hand without a tremor of unease, was sniffed at, circled, generally inspected – accepted.

And now the galley was shooting off across the slightly muddy waters of the little bay, and I hadn't even had time to ask if they could spare me a skin of wine, a few figs.

Well, after a brief swim, I had better tramp back in the malodorous heat – it was now so oppressively hot that the weather must break soon – and give Themistocles' message to the King.

I was told he was with the advance pickets. I found him talking to Dienekes. Talking was accurate enough. I realised that all the time – all the time? One whole day – I'd been at Thermopylae he'd always talked quietly whereas everyone else bawled at you as if you were a deaf recruit at the far end of the parade ground. I don't suppose I'd ever really been unaware of it. Voices are important. You can ignore a face, so long as the voice isn't unpleasing, but a rasping voice kills everything.

So I reflected, standing in neck-stiffening rigidity, and he read Themistocles' message, the frown marks between his eyes deepening. He made no reference to the contents of the letter, but turned to question me about the Phocians. Where were they bivouacking? In a *meadow*? What about their outposts? Their sentries? He said to Dienekes, 'Someone must be sent to see to this. These people play at war.'

'They volunteered,' said Dienekes, 'and they're the local experts. They're used to mountain fighting, we're not. In any case, we haven't men to spare to stiffen 'em.'

'You're right, of course. This is the route by which his main army must come. I can't spare a single man.'

Suddenly memory of the lounging figures in that hay-scented meadow lost its savour. I said, 'If you could second only one officer –'

They gravely turned to look at me. 'From an Athenian that's flattering,' said the deep, quiet voice. '*One* Spartan to make all the difference?'

It was I myself who felt the silly schoolboy now. I was reduced to muttering, 'Then, when your main army comes up –'

Their eyes met. I could not read their expression – were they laughing at me? I said, 'The Festival –'

'The Festival,' said Dienekes, 'will be over soon enough –'

From the King a jerk of the head, evidently indicating dismissal. Dienekes saluted and tramped off. The King looked at me with a gleam in his eyes. Humour?

But he remained silent. I was becoming used to Spartan silences. They were not necessarily sullen or stubborn. They simply arose from the fact that Spartans never talked for the sake of talking. If they had nothing worth saying they did not mind admitting it.

And then it happened. Dienekes, a dozen paces or so ahead of us, called out, pointed. Before us the plain stretching towards Lamia shimmered in the heat. And, in the distance, there was a kind of dewdrop of brightness in a cloud of dust that came steadily nearer.

'Well, here they are,' said Dienekes.

'Here *it* is, rather. One man, I should say.'

'Orders, sir?'

'We take no notice of him. Here he can get no idea as to our strength – or lack of it. So when he is able – for he can't see us yet with all the dust about him – let him take a look at our advance post, find us as relaxed as Phocians – and with any luck he'll go back with a report that because we're taking things easy, we must have plenty of confidence, and to Xerxes you have plenty of confidence only if you have plenty of troops.'

Dienekes grinned, moved about, giving orders. The sentries stacked their spears, sat down, some yawning, some combing their hair, others indulging in a desultory exercise or two. None of them looked towards the plain at all. In the shadow of the rocks stood the King and Dienekes. They watched the oncoming rider with no change in their usual expressions. There was, after all, no need. Always they had that air of watchfulness. A Spartan until he reached the age of sixty was eternally on active service.

Long before he came within arrow range the rider had slackened his pace to a cautious canter. He came quite close, near enough for us to see him clearly, a dark, bearded face, a soft felt cap, a saffron tunic with embroidered sleeves, a light wicker shield, a bow and quiver.

'Median cavalry,' I said.

He was puzzled. No one tried to interfere with him, no one, in fact, took the slightest notice of him. The few men he could see were absorbed in hair-combing, leisurely exercises. Behind them rocks and the hastily rebuilt wall, concealing how many troops? All that he could be sure of was that the pass was held, and I think he must have suspected a trap, for suddenly he bent low in the saddle, wheeled his horse round, and galloped off fast. I remember how the white dust rose under the beast's flying hooves almost like a cloud of snow. We heard the hoofbeats die away, watched horse and rider dwindling into a distant speck, into nothingness, and no one spoke. Heat and silence, except for the small noise of grasshoppers, brooding heat, brooding silence over the entire plain, it seemed. Then the King asked, 'How long before the main army arrives?'

I had to lick my lips before I could answer. They were salty with dried sweat. 'Three to four days, at least,' I said. 'It took seven days to get the lot of them over the Hellespont. It's a very large army, sir.' I wanted an excuse to grin at him. 'And your royal colleague doesn't exactly travel light. He always takes with him boiled water from the river at Susa, for example.'

'No!' from a startled Dienekes.

'Oh, yes, for his use alone, in silver vessels on special carts drawn by mules. And somewhere they're carrying his gold and ivory throne.'

The King of Sparta sat on a rock, and laughed at me. 'And I couldn't even sit on this if it hadn't been in the shade,' he said.

Before us the Spartans took up their weapons, strong, square-wristed hands seeming to grip them more tightly than they had before — if that were possible.

I must say I was glad to see a messenger being sent off, urging a speedier march to those coming up to join us, the enemy now being close. I hoped my face did not show my relief; the Spartans, as ever, were quite inscrutable, although I gathered there was something of an altercation as to who was to go. Dienekes, I knew, had been the King's first choice, but in the end a trusted royal slave was despatched. I had enough nerve to ask Dienekes why he hadn't gone. He said he had pointed out he was a poor horseman.

As the news spread, the allied contingents talked excitedly, the Spartans showed no emotion whatsoever. I reported that I was going to keep my rendezvous with Habronichos, and got in reply a nod, but no spoken acknowledgment. I set off for the cove, leaving early, for in the shadow of such cliffs it grows dark quickly. I can remember that the first sight of the enemy had left me scared, but excited. I was in a hurry to give the news to Habronichos because it *was* news. I wished afterwards I had taken my time, so that I could have preserved that mood a little longer.

It was almost dusk when I reached the cove. At first I thought the figure pacing impatiently up and down must be Habronichos, but as he turned and came towards me the tilt of the head, the quick stride made me recognise him — and gasp. Themistocles. Themistocles had left the fleet to come across the forty miles of water —

'Themistocles!' said I, showing I had not yet acquired a Spartan distaste for the unessential.

'I haven't much time,' he said in a low, rapid voice. 'The clouds are coming up fast, and we're expecting to sight the enemy soon, but what Habronichos said you'd reported to him was so incredible I had to come to check for myself — '

I didn't understand what he was talking about; to be honest, I was hardly listening. Bursting with infantile one-upmanship, I said, 'We've seen the enemy. A cavalryman on reconnaissance. He —'

'That's scarcely news,' Themistocles interrupted me impatiently. 'It was bound to happen. What concerns me is not the enemy who was bound to come, but a man — or men — who *should* have come, and haven't. Now, for God's sake, Theron, did you make a mistake when you reported to Habronichos? Did you leave out someone when you told him who'd come north with Leonidas?'

Nettled, I began to go through the Spartan staff again. 'Soothsayer, surgeon, bearer of the sacred fire, quartermaster —'

'Are you telling me there's not a single ephor?'

'Why, no,' I said. 'Should there be?'

'*Should* there —' he began in a kind of despairing anger, then broke off. 'No, I can't blame you because you didn't see the significance. I set you to learn all you could where the enemy was concerned, not the customs of an ally. But no ephor!'

After a moment I said awkwardly, 'You'll have to tell me — why it's so important, why I shouldn't have missed it.'

'What do you know about the ephors of Sparta?'

'There are five of them — they're magistrates elected every year. They take office at the beginning of winter and —' I began to laugh; it was the last time I laughed for a long time — 'the first thing they do is to order all Spartans to shave their moustaches and obey the laws.'

'My God, they're not a laughing matter,' came the low, furious voice beside me in the darkness. 'There's nothing funny about the ephors — and there's nothing funny in the fact that not one of them has come north with Leonidas. They've done for him — and don't give a damn that in doing so they may have done for all Hellas too!'

'Why — would they want to do for him?' I asked haltingly.

'I haven't the time to give you a lesson on the power and policy of the ephors; you'll just have to take my word for it that the one is absolute, the other is aimed primarily at the destruction of what power remains to the Kings. They destroyed Cleomenes, this man's brother, only a few years ago.'

'But what has Leonidas done?' I cried, aghast.

'To be ruined by them? Nothing. The implacable hostility's always there. The other royal line must be more easy-going, acquiescent generally – they don't seem to produce men as able as this one. But, my God, Theron, the ephors never lose a chance to stir up rivalries, jealousies – or to make it clear to both houses that it's a horse-rider relationship, with the ephors holding the reins. Every month – *every month* – the Kings have to take an oath to uphold the constitution, and the ephors take an oath guaranteeing their remaining in office so long as they act constitutionally – which means continue amenable to what the ephors decree.'

'What does a man get out of being King, then?'

'Honour. He is genuinely revered by the ordinary Spartan because of his divine descent. And he is commander-in-chief in war. But that's only nominal. Theron, listen – this is the whole point of what I've been saying. If the power of the ephors is great enough in time of peace, it's far greater in time of war. It's they who mobilise the army, give the generals their orders. And in the past they've always kept their feet on the King's neck during a campaign. Always two of them with him to make sure he obeys orders. That was why, when I asked Habronichos what ephors were with Leonidas and he said, according to your account, none, I decided I must come to find out for myself.'

'They've – deliberately abandoned him?'

'It's the only explanation. Of course, they're killing two birds with one stone. They never wanted to send any troops north of Corinth, damn them.'

'Do you think he knows?'

'He must. He's had ephors breathing down his neck since he succeeded his brother; why has he suddenly been left to go it alone? He's not a fool.'

No, he was not a fool; my idea was that he thought too much

for a Spartan. Yet – 'Why, then, when we saw that first Persian did he send off a request that the main force should speed up its march?'

'Well, he had to, hadn't he, to keep up the spirits of his unfortunate allies? And, human nature being what it is, no doubt the poor devil hoped a miracle might happen yet, the ephors might forget their feud against his family.'

We were both silent for a moment, so silent that I could hear the regular rhythm of the waves hissing on the beach, and then retreating. I don't think Themistocles heard it, being too deep in thought. 'I'll have to see him,' he said hurriedly. 'I –

'Look!' I said. '*Look*! There's no time –'

Darkness had fallen while we were speaking. He stood with his back to the sea, and so it was I who saw, over his shoulder, and miles away, something one might almost take as a god kindling a fire in the sky – a sudden blaze of distant yellow fire. And then another.

He swung round. 'The beacons! Their fleet's moving! I must go. *You* must speak to the King.'

'I?'

'Well, mustn't you?' he demanded, and had gone, running down the beach, calling to Habronichos.

I raced after him. 'What – tell him I know that his coming here is all a farce?'

He paused momentarily at the water's edge. 'A farce? The Spartan temperament doesn't run to farces. You're going to be involved in another kind of drama.'

He was on board, voices – Athenian voices that sounded almost strange to me – were shouting orders, another beacon flared up into the night, the enemy squadrons were coming, but Themistocles had an entire fleet behind him when he faced it, and the enemy land hordes were coming, and Leonidas had three hundred Spartans.

I felt myself weak at the knees, sat down abruptly on a rock. I was appalled at what confronted me. As I may be judged one day, I swear that I was scared, not so much by the thought of

Xerxes' half a million, as by the task laid on me by Themistocles. I must look into the grave face with the unSpartan eyes – and now I could understand their expression – and say, 'We know that you have been betrayed.' I sat there trying out the right phrases in which to say it, trying it out aloud, but with no success. All that I heard in the end as I sat head in hands was the sound of swear words run together. Easier to curse the ephors than to face the King.

It was quite dark now. As Themistocles had said, the clouds had come up fast. There were no stars, and only the faintest of glows showed where the young moon was beginning to rise. Now that the galley with its lantern had gone, there was just enough light in the blackness for me to see the shifting silver line where the waves broke on the shore. I sat on there, scared, sick and shivering.

I heard the man before I saw him, the firm, slow step, the betraying little clanging noises of armour. But he said nothing. And I was furious. I wasn't thinking clearly, of course; the only idea in my head was that this was a Spartan sent to spy on me. In that damnable state it seemed no one trusted anyone. One couldn't blame a betrayed King for seeing treachery everywhere, but the thought that he believed me to be faithless hurt like hell.

I said, 'It's all right. Tell him I've been talking to Themistocles; I'm not a spy for the ephors.'

There was silence. A little wind had risen, and for a moment – only a moment – the clouds parted – and in that moment I could see a horse-hair plume and then, with a quiver of the nerves I still remember, that brief shaft of moonlight showed the helmet itself, in the shape of a ram's head. Only one man wore a helmet like that.

Beside me Leonidas the King said, 'When you foreigners think of Sparta, you think of drilling on the barrack square at midday – under the sun. It's not typical, you know. If you want to know what Sparta's really like, think of a night like this, and people queasy in the stomach – as you were – because they don't know who's moving about in the dark. We have our crypteia, our secret police. They lie low by day, but at night they come out and they murder helots. There is some discussion among the ephors as to which is the better method of encouraging the helots to adopt a permanently submissive frame of mind – the liquidation of potential leaders or the quite indiscriminate extermination of any helot the crypteia may come across.'

It was dark again now, dark as the night when the crypteia would choose to go hunting. I said, 'There are other methods of secret assassination – and not only of helots.'

His voice was quite expressionless. 'You guessed, then?'

'*I* didn't. Themistocles did – the moment he heard there was no ephor with you.'

'Yes, they slipped up there; other people beside Themistocles may put two and two together. Later they may regret that the last election didn't produce an ephor ready to dedicate himself to the task to the bitter end. Then no questions would be asked, would they? Even Themistocles might be fooled.'

'How long have you known?'

'From the moment I left Sparta, and no ephor came with me. That was so much out of the pattern that even I suspected.'

'You take it coolly.'

'Coolly? How little you understand Spartans. Even if I could be cool, as you put it, about what's being done to me, do you think I can forgive what's being done to the three hundred men who've come with me?'

I said with sudden realisation, 'They know, don't they? That's why Dienekes refused to go this afternoon.'

'Apart from other reasons, Dienekes dislikes waste of time, energy. Yes, they all knew. If an Athenian can see the significance of no ephor, what Spartan could miss it? I said I would bring with me only men who have sons; that told everyone I knew there would be no returning home. Every man who came with me volunteered.'

'You have at least the consolation of their devotion.'

'Consolation?' He came and sat on the rock beside me. 'I thought you Athenians were expert in choosing words. In any case, it's not all devotion to me; I've inherited some of the devotion they gave to my half-brother. You know something of Cleomenes, I suppose?'

'A little,' I said. Cleomenes had died at the same time as Miltiades; to us in Athens the news from Sparta had seemed of minor importance. With sudden enlightenment, I said, 'I know what people outside Sparta were allowed to know — he was over-ambitious, went insane, killed himself. Do you mean it's not the truth?'

'I thought it was the truth once. Then I began to doubt it. That's one of the reasons I'm expendable.'

Briefly he told me of his brilliant elder half-brother, with gifts unusual in a Spartan, vision, imagination, the qualities to make a deep impression on a serious, conscientious younger brother absolutely lacking in self-conceit.

And then the ephors had told him these qualities were dangerous, that Cleomenes was a traitor and a revolutionary. They spoke of a suspicious visit he had recently paid to Thessaly; seven years later, Cleomenes' brother believed he knew what was behind that visit; 'If the barbarians were going to invade by land, there was every reason for a Spartan King to come north, take a look at the territory he might soon be defending, get some kind of unified resistance. Dienekes said to me when we first came here that if Cleomenes had lived and been allowed to carry out his policy, then the frontier of Hellas we're defending would be far to the north of Thermopylae. But they — the ephors — twisted everything. I didn't know him well, we were half-brothers, I didn't have much confidence in my own wits. If the ephors said he was a danger to the state because of what he was doing in Thessaly, I was half prepared to accept it. But what clinched everything was what the ephors told me he was doing in Arcadia and among our helots. They said he was plotting revolution. I suppose that, as they saw it, this was precisely what he was doing. They wouldn't accept *why* he was doing it.'

Cleomenes had become obsessed with the inevitable attack from Persia. No doubt ambition to be the leader of a united

164

Greece played its part; there was also a restlessness, an energy about him that made the ephors see him as the greatest of threats to their dominance. 'But, as I realise now, his first thought then was the threat from the barbarians.' He'd been recalled from Thessaly, he couldn't organise resistance there, so he thought nothing could stop the Persians north of Corinth. And if they got to the Peloponnese, what was to stop them there? A minority of Spartans; a majority of helots held subject by terror; the Arcadian highlanders, always resenting the Spartan newcomers who treated them as second-class allies.' So Cleomenes had gone into the Arcadian mountains, and told the clans there that for such first-class fighting material as they were, only the best was good enough. He offered them the chance to enlist in his personal bodyguard. And to the helots he had spoken man to man, offering them an improvement in their conditions. The Peloponnese, dominated by a small minority master-race had no chance of standing up to the Persians, he said. And the ephors had come to his younger brother and denounced the King as a traitor to Sparta and to the whole of Greece.

'I said I did not believe that.

'He was going to meet the chief men of Arcadia, who were prepared to take oaths of loyalty to him. The ephors had to move fast. They tricked him into coming back — sent him a message of reassurance, support. He thought he'd won. So he didn't go to the meeting. He came back. And they had him now.'

For a time there was silence. I thought, 'A Spartan giving his confidence is the equivalent of an Athenian appealing for help. But what can I do to help? What could I do, in any case, and now with the Persian armies a few days' march away —'

'It was now that they said he went mad. He lashed out at people with his sceptre. I don't think he was mad; I think he was frantic. He realised he'd been trapped, and he'd come back thinking he'd won. He was quite alone and absolutely helpless. He reacted like a snared animal, thinking every man was his enemy.'

'Did you see him?'

'Yes, I insisted on seeing him—this was after the ephors told me he must be locked up, being insane. And of course he distrusted me. He tried to strike me. I tried to talk to him, but all he would say—and he kept saying it—was, "I was going to pull down the temple next to the ephors' mess." That is the temple to Fear—did you know there was such a building? "Fear's our chief god," he shouted. "That's the way to run the state, by fear!" I came away believing the ephors—he was mad, he must be shut up. I did ask them why they thought his mind had gone; they said he'd always shown signs of being unbalanced, and since his return to Sparta it had been noticed he'd drunk only wine unmixed with water. I had noticed that when I was with him—a bowl of wine, but no water. A year ago an old slave who was dying told me that even then he was to all intents and purposes under arrest, although it wasn't obvious. And by the ephors' orders, he might be given wine—but no water. That would have its effect.

'So he was shut up as insane. Not long afterwards he was dead. His body was covered with gashes. They said he'd made his jailer give him a knife, and he'd slashed at himself. I think he was murdered, but put up a fight first, and they had to explain away the wounds.'

'When did you begin to suspect?'

'Not until the slave told me about the wine. I think he could have said more, but he was afraid. I tried after that to find out the truth; it was then, I suppose, they decided to get rid of me too, I hadn't given them much cause for alarm before. So they're playing a double game. They can't afford to lose the allies north of Corinth, particularly Athens, so they had to make a feint of protecting the territory north of the Isthmus. They send the smallest force possible, but with it a King. The fact that I'm here should convince the allies of the purity of Spartan intentions. Who's to know the King is the awkward one, the expendable one, sent north for the Persians to do the ephors' work?'

I said in real horror, 'But you are not going to accept this! To stay here, knowing—'

He laughed. 'Do you mean I should retreat? I've been sent here with – understatement – insufficient men for the job I'm supposed to do, but if I left Thermopylae, who'd be the scapegoat?'

'You can show clearly enough that you were given impossible orders.'

'Spoken like an Athenian. I was never any good at arguing, and since I've been here I've been working things out. Do you think I want to go back to defend myself to those who sent me here? No, let the fool die as bravely as he can. I'm a good fighter, and an appalling speaker: let me at least concentrate on the one thing I'm any good at. And laugh for the two of us when the lies they'll spread about me grow into legend. They'll have to make a hero of me dead, you know, to cover up the fact that, living, they've made a hell of a fool of me. Royal self-immolation – that would be a good line to take, wouldn't it?'

(It was. Within months we were all being told that he had heard of a prophecy that Sparta would be saved by the death of her King – that he had even ordered his own funeral games before leaving Sparta.)

'I could never – accept such a situation,' I said.

'Acceptance hasn't come all that easily to me. Do you think otherwise I should have issued that proclamation when I first came here – this was only the advance-guard, at any moment the Spartan army would be joining me at full strength? I suppose I had some stupid idea that this might shame the ephors into doing precisely that. It probably caused them a great deal of quiet amusement.'

He stood up. 'I shall, of course, send all non-Spartans away in good time.'

'I will not go.'

'There is no need for you to concern yourself in what is, after all, basically a matter of Spartan internal politics.'

'For me,' I said, 'Spartan internal politics don't enter into it.'

'Then you yourself are displaying that very puerility you so obviously have thought ludicrous in us.' After a moment he said,

'Possibly because we Spartans don't have so many thoughts as you quick-witted Athenians, we find it easier to conceal the few we do have.'

'We Athenians may also find it easier to change our minds than you Spartans do.'

'I take it that you're better as a trireme commander than a spearsman or swordsman – keep yourself for the job for which you're best suited. And even if you were all that good as a spearsman, when a quarter of a million Persians attack three hundred, the increase in that force to three hundred and one will not make the slightest difference. Nothing would be gained by your dying with us. You can't save us by staying. We shall die just the same.'

'You let your three hundred volunteer.'

'Ah!' he said, 'but remember they are all older men, with growing sons. I don't suppose you even have a wife. Well, if you survive the war, no doubt in due course you'll marry and have a son, and perhaps when he's old enough you'll tell him of a few days spent in an obscure muddy spot called Thermopylae with three hundred Spartans.'

'Three hundred Spartans and their King,' I said.

'Three hundred Spartans and their defeated King – yes.'

After a moment I said carefully, 'Three hundred Spartans and their King won't be defeated at once. Shall I be allowed to take part in some of the fighting before I'm given my marching orders?'

He replied with something to take my breath away. 'That can be managed: after all, I'll want you close to me to identify the troops they send against us.'

So I should be allowed to fight on the left of the Spartan line.*

'But of course,' he added briskly, 'if I decide on a movement needing real steadiness and skill, you're out.'

As he went away up the sloping beach, there was a low growl

---

* A commander traditionally fought on the left of the line because he was protected by his shield on his left arm; if he were on the right, his unprotected right side would be open to attack.

of thunder, almost like some gigantic animal in the sky. Before I followed him the rain was drumming down, and by the time I regained the main body, the thunder was ear-splitting. The rest of the night was spent working on the further strengthening of the wall. I don't think I spoke much to anyone, if at all. I can remember torches hissing in the rain, and tall men in cloaks and the clink of trowels, and myself glad that Spartans were a silent race, and almost hoping that the main Persian attack would come next day, so that I should have less chance to know them well.

14

But the Persians took their time. The weather may have slowed them down. It continued foul, a north-easterly gale with — unusual for the time of year — violent flurries of rain. I saw Habronichos only twice during the period of waiting, and such information as he gave was patchy. The enemy had stolen a march on us — if one can use the phrase about a fleet. A detachment of fast Phoenician vessels had made a night attack on one of our patrols at Skiathos, taking them by surprise because they had steered direct across open water.* Luckily the men manning the beacon on the heights were able to send off warning. But then, as the main Persian forces started moving, the storm had risen. Themistocles, in his delight at this, had been less careful than usual not to shock his uncongenial colleagues. 'Good for Boreas!' he said. 'What's the use of having a god in the family unless he pulls his weight occasionally?' Then surrounded by scandalised faces, he had had to explain laboriously that the Athenians believed that the north-east wind, Boreas, had married an Athenian woman, the daughter of King Erectheus, and they therefore usually referred to Boreas as 'the son-in-law'. This scarcely helped matters. Heads were shaken at the incurable frivolity and lack of piety of the Athenians, but Boreas, it seemed, had taken no offence. He had played his part well enough. Our fleet retired to the lee of Euboea to ride out the storm, but watchers on the height kept sending heartening news of heavy damage being done to the enemy, and then wreckage began floating past to confirm it, spars, and drowned men,

* The Phoenicians probably steered by the stars. The Greeks were surprised; their navigation and tactics amounted to island-hopping by daylight, and so they would never expect to be attacked before dawn in open water.

swarthy, hooknosed, and messages came that, where the main enemy fleet had been drawn up, dozens of ships that had foundered looked like so many buoys.

There seemed to me more fury in the weather of those three days than I have ever known. There was thunder and rain on the first night, but the full force came next day. It was odd, that storm. It seemed to die away on the first morning; not for long, just long enough for those ignorant of that iron coast to be unwary enough to continue sailing again. For a brief spell there was a break in the clouds, a few patches of watery sunlight, and then the light became yellow, eerie, the black thunderclouds were back, blotting out the sea, spindrift was flying, and there was lightning, and a bellowing everywhere, thunder above us, the sea itself seeming to hurl defiance back up into the sky. So much I knew, standing on land. Habronichos, who had made a run for it, and just managed to gain the shelter of the bay in time, said that in the last hour of his trip the spurts of spray and rain made him feel that Poseidon was throwing giant handfuls of wet sand in his face. As we talked, the hiss of the great angry rollers added to that feeling of fury.

But at the back of our minds we knew that whatever destruction the storm brought to the enemy fleet, to the enemy army it could bring no more than delay, that such storms in any case had always blown themselves out on the third day, and even if the gods fought for us at sea, they seemed, at the best, neutral on land. And on the third morning there were tattered clouds in the sky, sunlight falling sullenly on the sea. All the enemy ships couldn't be sunk, and once they'd re-formed, the land army would feel safe to resume its march along the coast road.

And so came the day when we saw an immense dust cloud stretching across the entire breadth of the plain before us and the parched earth shuddered and trembled beneath the enemy advance, and, later, at dusk, I stood on a height overlooking the plain and saw a great swarming of men that almost seemed to make that dusk appear a living, moving thing. There was a clamour of

171

noise, menacing and dreadful, almost like the recent roar of the stormy sea on the shore, with now and then discordant individual yells. There were hundreds of camp fires reddening the night. It would have been an appalling enough sight if we had had a thousand times our numbers. And all the effective opposition would be offered by three hundred Spartans. And their King.

They did not attack for four days. We never knew why. The bad weather may have disorganised them badly. Xerxes may have been hoping that if his fleet could destroy ours, we should have to retreat. There is another possible reason, which I have heard dismissed derisively by those who have never met an absolute monarch. Simply that Xerxes believed that at the mere appearance of his hordes, we should run away. Absurd, say the logical thinkers, knowing that a Spartan King stood within the gates of Thermopylae. But they have no knowledge of that very different creature, a Persian Great King. I had seen myself how this barbarian believed that his most fantastic whim had only to be expressed, and it was accomplished. I had known that atmosphere in which the sour stench of fear fought a winning battle over the odours of musk and scented oils. The men of the West knew he was coming to eat them up. Very well, when his armies appeared, they would run away. Absurdity to a logical man is logic to an absurd monarch.

Remember too that the man was cruel as a great cat. Even supposing that what I believe to be impossible actually happened, that someone among his courtiers (there were, after all, Greek exiles accompanying him), persuaded him that, against all imperial reasoning, the enemy would stand and fight, knowing his overwhelming strength, and confident of victory, he would move very deliberately in to the kill. That is what he had ordered when we had been captured in Sardis, 'Let them have time to think, ample time to think.'

I myself think he would have given us time to think even if no storm had brought destruction to his fleet and disorganisation to his armies.

172

'And then,' said the Spartan King, 'when our time for thinking is up, what will he do?'

'Attack us head-on.'

'Inefficient. He's cancelling out his great advantage, numerical superiority. Once they get into so narrow a space – '

'With his disregard for human life, he can do quite a lot. He'd sacrifice thousand on thousand to get through. He'd lash them on to your spears until his dead were piled high as Callidromos.'

Over the plain during those days of waiting an incessant hum came to us, as from a swarm of furious bees. But when you climbed the heights and looked down at all the deliberate, mindless bustle of those myriad distant figures, you thought of another insect. You thought of ants. And that thought was particularly horrible.

After three days, we saw a party of a dozen men galloping across the plain. It almost blinded you to look at one of them; even in the distance we could see he was carrying on his person the average Greek state's annual revenue. There was gold everywhere – bracelets, ear-rings, necklace, embroidered crimson robe, stiff cap.

The gorgeous personage had with him an escort of brilliantly dressed soldiers, one man dressed in the Greek fashion, and another carrying a herald's staff. They stopped well before they were within any kind of range, and waited.

'Pantites said you look well on a horse,' the King said to me, 'and you know the language. Go out, and bring him in, but slowly. Whatever he gives as his reason, he's probably been sent to take a good look at us.'

So I mounted and rode out. As I drew closer, I realised I knew both the personage and his Greek companion. The Ionian recognised me, even if he didn't show it; the Persian, who had similarly seen me at Sardis, had not bothered to give a second glance to a wretch condemned to death sooner or later.

'Leonidas, King of Sparta, asks your business,' I said, laconically enough, I trusted.

The Ionian's eyes flickered. They had known that long-haired Spartans held the pass, had not been sure that a Spartan King was here too. The Persian reacted not at all; to him one western tribe was the same as another.

'I am sent by Xerxes the Great King, King of Kings, King of lands containing many men, King in this great earth far and wide,' he said.

'A highly responsible position, no doubt,' I replied. 'Do you bring a message from your King?'

'A proclamation,' he replied, frowning.

'I will find out if the King of Sparta is prepared to hear it,' I said, and cantered off.

They had brought up every available hoplite to the front part of the gorge. As far as the eye could see, that narrow front bristled with spear-tips. Three hundred red-tunicked Spartans in the front ranks; with luck it would not be noticeable that in the distance there was no long hair to be seen beneath the helmets.

'A proclamation from Xerxes,' I said.

'Do you know the men bringing it?'

'There's an Ionian I saw at Sardis. The Persian —' gratefully I suddenly remembered the name — 'is Xerxes' own half-brother, Habrocomes, no less.'

'Bring him along.'

As I returned with Habrocomes, I tried to see the pass through his eyes. I think that, accustomed as he was to gaudy luxury and profusion, the sight of rank upon rank of grim, silent, heavily armed men, must have had some effect. Even a stupid man might have realised that these troops were here for business.

A little ahead of the rest, tall beside his standard, stood the King.

'What is your message?' he asked briefly.

I translated, and got in return, 'Xerxes, the Great King, King of Kings, King of lands containing many men, King in this great earth far and wide, orders you all to give up your arms and to

174

submit to him. After this you may go away unharmed.' I might remark here that Habrocomes possessed an extremely high-pitched voice.

There was a moment's silence, then the King's deep voice replied tersely, 'If you want our arms, come and get them.'

The naturally bulging eyes almost started from Habrocomes' head. He panted, 'You – you, the ruler of a contemptible state that will cease to exist within weeks, to – '

'What is he saying?' asked the King.

I translated. Beside me Habrocomes spat out curses and predictions.

'Tell him,' said the King, 'that Sparta will never be smaller than the length of our spears.' And he turned away and began to talk to Dienekes. The audience was over.

Habrocomes tugged at his bridle; inwardly I winced for his horse's mouth. I saw him off. As I left him, he said, his face distorted with rage, 'Tell him there will be no further chance for him. He'll be brought before the King and – '

'There will have to be certain preliminaries,' I said. 'I presume our King will not have the pleasure of a personal meeting with your master in – er – those encounters?'

My meaning took a moment to penetrate. Then he snarled – he really did snarl – 'Impious dog!' and his hand fell on his dagger hilt.

I laughed.

He gave me a brief prophecy as to my own future, and galloped away.

Beside me the Ionian said below his breath, 'His master has brought his throne with him. Seated on this, he will watch your destruction.'

'I'm glad he's brought a few simple creature comforts,' I said. 'A travelling detachment of the harem too, I hope – anything to help him to bear the future pangs of chagrin with some equanimity.'

He gave me a curious look, half wistful, before he galloped off after Habrocomes.

175

There had been altercation in our camp. Some of the allies felt the Persian offer should have been accepted, but the Locrians supported the King. Impassively, he sent back another urgent appeal for reinforcements. I managed to dent the impassivity a little by telling him Xerxes had indeed brought his throne along with him so that he might view the conflict in appropriate style.

Next day they attacked early in the morning. It was the noise that gave us first warning; from their camp the heavy murmur, always menacing, grew into an appalling clamour, yells, howls, shouts of a vast mob lusting for slaughter. Then came the dust, whirling towards us, and the earth shook.

That first Persian attack was, in its way, oddly deliberate. Assured in their overwhelming strength, and therefore of victory, they did not hurry overmuch. This was to be not so much a battle as an entertainment for their King. Later we learned they had waited until the light was good enough to give him a clear view. Then they moved in – almost ceremoniously – for the kill.

'Stand by me,' said the King, 'and identify what he's sending against us the moment you can see them.'

Could he hear my heart hammering? I shaded my eyes.

Brightly coloured trousers and jackets, felt caps, wicker shields, short spears – 'Medes.'

'What's their rating?'

'Only his Immortals are supposed to be better.'

But after this I was aware only of first the shouting, and then the faces. They were laughing as they came at us, white teeth against dark faces and curled beards. And – my God, they were excited! Excited at the prospect of easy victory, easy killing. ('Clear the pass,' Xerxes had shouted to them, we learned later. 'Capture those men and bring them to me!') I felt little drops of sweat running down my upper lip. And then, suddenly, for me, it all became personal. I had only one wish now, to get close to them, to drive the spear home.

The yells grew louder, the dust cloud was vomiting thousands,

176

about me the Spartans stood in absolute silence, locked their shield line, settled their spears.

That day's fighting may be easily described. Only three short sentences are needed. They advanced along a front only fifty feet wide. They advanced against spears nine feet long; theirs were shorter. And they advanced against Spartans – towards the end they were driven on; we saw the whips being used against them.

They would have found it simpler, and infinitely safer, to charge a wall of iron.

This is what happened all that day, as the dust rose up like clouds of smoke from the parched ground, and they broke and reformed and came on again, and broke and reformed and charged, screaming all the while. We fought in silence. Apart from any other reason, you need to save all the breath you have for driving home the long spear. We coughed in the dust, panted with the effort of heaving forward, our whole bodies straining behind the thrusting right arm and the spear. In all my life I have never been so tired. When the opening of the gorge vomited another yelling crowd of attackers, the business of keeping spear straight, shield locked, absorbed me to the exclusion of everything else, but when that onslaught broke, I was conscious of exhaustion and pain, aching calves, thighs, back, shoulders, a right arm that throbbed with agony of effort, lips dry and cracked from thirst, but there was no time to relax grip on shield or spear, even to wipe the sweat that trickled into your eyes and threatened to blind you before the yelling recommenced, and they were back again.

And then for a moment there was comparative silence.

I had no idea how much time had passed. I squinted up and there, through the branches of the trees projecting from the sides of the gorge, was the sun, directly overhead. We had fought all morning.

We had sustained casualties. A few attackers had been able to get in between our spears, to hack with their shorter swords, but not many. One hadn't noticed it in the fighting; they hadn't

177

dented the line, for when a man fell another took his place, and as long as the line held, that was all that had mattered. But now one became conscious of the casualties. No dead, but some men with shattered arms, one or two limping, or putting hands to faces livid with blows. We dragged the wounded to what shade we could find for them. They would have to lie in their blood and sweat until they could be carried back to the rear position. Someone brought round bread soaked in wine and water for us and for them.

'They're coming again!' someone called.

'The same?' asked the King.

'No – others.'

'What regiment?' He turned to me.

'Cissians. Their clothes are like the Medes, but their caps are different.'

'How good?'

'Rated as good as the Medes.'

As they ran at us, they screamed even more shrilly than the Medes had done, but otherwise the pattern was the same. When they finally broke, my right hand was blistered raw, my right shoulder was torment, the back of my neck all pain, and I felt that if I thrust my body forward once more it would crack in two.

Dienekes said to me, 'Still on your feet, then!'

'I feel as if my back's broken.'

'Don't worry; I don't feel all that much better. It's not the usual kind of fighting, this. Generally it's a short, sharp business, over soon enough. We've never had to take on most of Asia before.'

There was one consolation in my existing condition: with every muscle in my body screaming with agony, if in the next attack I had an arm or leg sliced off, I'd scarcely notice.

But against the next attack I played no part. Through a haze of exhaustion I heard the King talking. Sooner or later even Xerxes might realise that sending in men with shorter spears and smaller shields would not work. On the other hand, it was up to us to see he kept sending them in to fight at close quarters –

Dienekes shook my arm. 'Out of the line fast, lad. This is work for Spartans. Get to the rear. A long way to the rear.'

'What are you going to do?'

'Next time they attack, we fake a retreat. Out of the line!'

I got out of the line fast. A feigned retreat is the most risky of all manoeuvres. The only troops in all Greece who could do it were those to whom war was life itself, and not an interruption to it.

'Tell us who they're putting in next, and then get to the rear.'

I stared out over the plain, saw the telltale dust cloud, line after line of men becoming clearer through that cloud. A wild flurry of colour that even the dust could not hide, yellows, blues, purples, stars, squares, circles, and gold – bracelets, ear-rings – and silver- and gold-ornamented spears.

I gave a yell. 'He's sending in the Immortals!'

'Dressy, aren't they?' said Dienekes. 'Off to the rear!'

I went to the rear; I should only be in the way. And at the rear I leaned on my spear, and learned that warfare can have a perfection, almost a beauty, of its own.

If you see it waged, not merely by Spartans, but by Spartan veterans picked by their King.

I wondered how much Xerxes could see, from his throne. I wondered if he stayed seated on his throne. When he saw that feigned retreat, I should think he'd jumped up in such excitement he almost sent the royal umbrella-holder flying. Perhaps he yelled, as the Immortals yelled as they rushed forward in pursuit. They yelled – from exultation – almost like men in physical agony. And then the Spartans turned, and the Immortals found they were rushing on to a thrusting, unswerving hedge of spear points, already reddened.

That Spartan line was glorious. I found myself babbling Homer – 'As a man joins the compacted wall-stones of a high house and shuts out the raging winds, so was joined the wall of helmets and shields.' They threw down the first disordered rank of the Immortals, the second, and on, and on, steadily, relentlessly, inevitably. And the Immortals broke and shrieked and ran for it.

He sent in others; there were, or had been, ten thousand Immortals, all told. By the time that dusk fell every attack had been thrown back, the enemy coming fresh to the attack against men who had fought throughout the day were mauled as badly as those who had made the first assault in the morning. Xerxes pulled back those he could. The pass was littered shoulder-high with Persian corpses.

'Tell me about the Immortals,' said Dienekes. 'Those spears had *silver* on them, and they were dressed like — like —'

Words failed him. I could have supplied a term, but felt it might be meaningless, such a profession not being followed in Sparta.

'They are very special,' I said. 'On the march, they're allowed to take their concubines and servants in wagons, and baggage animals carry special food for them.'

'So there'll be some bleeding hearts over yonder tonight?'

'I think,' I said, 'the heart that's bleeding most belongs to the King in this great earth far and wide.'

It rained that night, and there was a high wind, this time from the south-east. There were violent peals of thunder and in the distance we could see the lightning flashing about Mount Pelion. I suppose I should have been wondering what was happening to the fleet, and the Athenian vessels in it, but all that I could think of was the situation here. Being overtired did not make for sensible thinking; after the awesomely brilliant performance of the Spartans that day, I was beginning to hope a little. I lay there in the driving rain and thought that with only double our numbers we could hold the pass indefinitely, that the ephors, for shame's sake, must have sent at least another token force to reinforce us, but a Spartan token force was really a battle-winning force.

If Leonidas had twice the amount of men, he could hold the pass, and Xerxes would have to give up. He couldn't stay in front of us indefinitely; Leonidas had swept the plain bare of supplies before ever the Persians came in sight. Xerxes' large army would starve, so he'd have to retreat, and if he left a small force behind we would come out of the pass and beat it. It was as simple as that. And then our fleet could go over to the attack.

All that was needed was the despatch of another small force from Sparta.

If anyone had bothered to take a look at me as I lay sleeping that night, I have no doubt he would have seen an idiotic grin on my face.

The rain eased off before dawn, and the sun rose in a clear sky. We could have wished it otherwise. Under a harsh sun, the thousands of corpses would soon stink and rot, and God knew what pestilence might break out.

The other allies claimed their right to defend the pass that day. Some of the Spartans, although they must still have felt their bones cracking with weariness, objected, but the King gave permission. I think I know his reason; he must have been aware of how the Greek spectators had felt after his repulse of the Immortals the previous day. To equal the feat of the Spartans was something approaching the superhuman, but pride will often help men to do the impossible. And this the allies in turn did throughout the morning, driving back attack after attack.

In the afternoon the Spartans, being rested, took over. Perhaps it was as well they did; the attack now came from a composite force; Xerxes must have included in it picked men from every regiment. God knows what threats and promises they were treated to before they advanced; I should think the threats outweighed the promises, for when we threw them back we found that he'd stationed a special reserve force in their rear to block their way, and force them back into the attack. They screeched and howled, turning this way and that. Some tried to make a dash for the marsh. They were cut down either by us or by their own people. Others were trampled to death. The mud edging the sea turned red, soon the shallows were rust-coloured, and the foam was blotchy pink. Every stone in the front portion of the pass was covered with blood, and there had scarcely been any need to build up the old wall. The enemy had built their own wall of dead. Before they could get at us again, they would have first to move the great mounds of their own corpses.

It did not rain that night, and there was some moonlight. It made all the bloodstains look black. I found it hard to sleep; I was excited, I told myself Xerxes assuredly wasn't sleeping either, he was wondering desperately what to do, our reinforcements hadn't come up today, but surely they would come tomorrow, the King's last messenger would meet them on the march, his news that Leonidas was under attack would speed them up. I should be glad to see them; every day we held the pass we had counted a victory, but it would be good to know that real and final success was at the end of it. I was not like the Spartans; they were disciplined to shut their minds to fear, I had managed to screw myself up to a fairly successful imitation of their cool, steady courage for two days, I hoped I could carry on, but didn't know. It would be hard to go on being brave when one was becoming increasingly tired. Or was tiredness really an advantage? Automatically one went on doing the same thing, and —

I fell asleep.

I was roused before dawn to go on duty, having volunteered to take the place of one of the three hundred who was wounded. Thermopylae was a grim place to awaken to — so many enemy corpses, and even our own ranks of sleepers looked like the dead under the moon. It was very cold, and I was still drowsy.

The voice came from the darkness about half an hour later. It said, 'For God's sake let me speak to your King. The Persians are coming along the mountain pass.'

It was an Ionian voice.

We sent for torches and told him to come forward, and he did so, his right hand high above his head, the palm towards us. It was the Ionian I had met in Sardis, the Ionian who had accompanied Habrocomes. He had with him another man, who looked terrified.

'I am Tyrrhastiadas of Cyme,' said the Ionian. 'I must see the King.'

'The King is here,' came the quiet voice I now knew so well. 'What is your news?'

'He's sent the Immortals — what remains of them, but still enough to do the job if they get through — along a mountain path to take you in the rear.'

'There'll have to be reinforcements for the Phocians. Rouse the sleepers,' the King flung over his shoulder to Maron. To the Ionian, he said, 'Go on.'

'They knew there was such a pass, but they couldn't find a guide and without a guide they could do nothing; it's a narrow winding track with frequent forks. They sent messengers all over the countryside, promising vast rewards to any man who'd act as guide, but nobody answered. Then yesterday a farmer turned up, a Malian. He said he'd act as guide.' After a moment he added, 'They asked him what he wanted as reward. He said he didn't want a reward; he just wanted to get them — and you — out of the neighbourhood, because armies meant ruin for farmers.'

'When did they start?'

'At about the time when the lamps were lit in the camp.' An hour after sunset.

'When will they reach the Phocian camp?'

The man who had accompanied Tyrrhastiadas said, 'I come from Trachis, and I know the path. Where is the Phocian camp?'

Eyes turned to me. I described the meadow — the only open place among the forests.

'I know it. They should be there just about dawn.'

'It's a narrow track. He's sent some thousands of Immortals — how many men abreast?'

'Two at the most, but often they'll have to march in single

183

file. But they should be able to make good time; once you're on the ridge it's not bad going.'

The King said, 'I'll thank you both later.' He turned back to Dienekes. 'I'll keep the Thespians and the Thebans with me here; we'll have to rush the rest to support the Phocians.' Dienekes hurried off.

Tyrrhastiadas said, 'Xerxes is taking such a gamble because he's desperate. He's had to risk the Immortals because all the rest of his army is completely demoralised. Even with the Immortals, he knows that if they meet any real opposition, with that long straggling line –'

I said, 'I took a short cut up the mountain when I first came here. I think I could find my way again. I might just get to the Phocians in time –'

'Or you can bring back news. Yes.'

I left a camp feverishly alive, men hurriedly forming line, grumbling, heavy-eyed with lack of sleep. 'What's up, in God's name?' one shouted at Dienekes. He said grimly, 'While we've been guarding the door, they're trying to get in through the roof.'

I began my climb, while they made ready to file off along the easier ascent.

Scree, tangles of thorny bushes, gnarled roots. In my desperate haste I was taking paths a goat would never risk. Much of the time I crawled, sobbing with the effort. So much exertion should have made me sweat like a pig, but my broken-nailed, bleeding hands remained cold. My head swam, but I would not, dare not let myself rest, gasping, for even a moment. Already in the east the sky was a dim grey.

There was another crawling, clutching animal, sobbing with fear and exertion on that mountain side. He was making better haste than I, for he came crashing downhill. It could only be a Phocian.

'Friend!' I croaked. 'Theron of Athens – I came to your camp the other day. The Persians –'

'They came on us – caught us unawares – scattered us –'

'*Scattered* you!'

'They came on us without warning – we were asleep. Then one of us heard this rustling – we thought at first it was the wind in the trees, the beginning of another storm, but it was them kicking up the fallen leaves in the oak forest –'

As I had done, carelessly, only days before.

'What about your outposts, your sentries? A Spartan came up a few days ago –'

'He blared orders at us. Some of us thought he was comic; he got other people's backs up.'

So they had done nothing. 'Be quick in telling me. You were still bivouacked in that meadow, and you heard the Persians coming because the leaves rustled –'

My God, *I* was sounding like a Spartan.

'We put on armour – we didn't have our weapons by us –'

'But you rushed to get them, and then, bearing in mind the fact that you'd all the benefit of a good night's rest, while they'd been marching for nine hours –' I was savage.

I never knew how old he was, it being still too dark to see his face under the trees, but from the whimper he gave then, he was young.

'When they saw us – it was just light enough for that – they drew up in line –'

'Which would take some time, since they were coming in single file –'

'We had to run to get our weapons,' he said. 'They shot arrows at us –'

'You were a nice open target in that meadow. And so you ran. Where?'

'To the hilltop above the meadow.'

I said in cold incredulity, 'Leaving the track open to them? Why in the hell, if you had to run, didn't you run into the forest to the east, and hold that? They'd never get through then.'

He said, his teeth chattering, 'We thought they were out to finish us, so we made for the hilltop.'

'You thought *you* were their target, when there was a Spartan

King below!' He gave a yelp as my broken-nailed fingers dug into his arm. 'Get up to that damned hilltop and bring your late comrades down! An Ionian came across and warned us; nearly three thousand of our men are on their way up to meet them. If another thousand attacked them from the rear, *they'd* be trapped as they thought to trap us. Get going.'

I gave him a shove in the right direction.

I never saw him again. I don't know whether he even tried to take the message to the Phocians.

If I had climbed in desperate haste, I clawed my way down in a frenzy, slithering, falling, taking crazy leaps, filthy, bleeding, bruised. How long had it taken me to come down from the meadow where the Phocians had set up camp? According to my frantic calculations, if the enemy came down unopposed they should be at our backs by mid-morning. They would have worked the time out very carefully. When they were at our rear, Xerxes would launch his last frontal attack.

But of course they would be opposed, and it wouldn't happen. Feverishly I began to take a mental roll-call of the allied contingents. Who'd been kept back? The Thespians and the Thebans. Two thousand, eight hundred men hurrying up the mountain, then. Ample to keep back an enemy struggling along the narrowest of fronts. And then the Phocians would come down on them from above. As they were bound to do, to wipe out their folly and cowardice.

Except for my gropings and crashings, I came down at first in the stillness, that uncanny stillness, of early dawn. But then, in the greyness, the first birds began to sing, and in a moment there was gold in the sky, the sun was up over Pelion, his first beams fell on Callidromos' eastern ridge, and every bird in those wooded heights was singing, as the light and colour of day came flooding across the mountainside.

There was not a breath of wind in the bright air. It was going to be a fine day.

The brightness even managed to strike through into corners

of the pass. That was a pity. It showed only too clearly faces
wearied with pain and fatigue, stained bandages, some with the
blood still welling through.

I made my report to the royal headquarters behind the stone
rampart. The Phocians, surprised, had run, but I'd sent one of
them back to tell them to follow the Persians down. My reports
were terser than they used to be.

'Get some food.'

I didn't want food; I felt sick, but I went off obediently, and
found Tyrrhastiadas and the man from Trachis were with me.
I didn't really want company, but Tyrrhastiadas had been kind
to me in Sardis.

'When did you decide to come over?' I asked.

'We talked months ago at Sardis, didn't we?'

'Yes, but –' I hesitated.

'You didn't think I'd ever have the guts to leave the comfort
of Cyme? Well, I raised my foot to take the decisive step after
the embassy the other day; I sent off my slave then – you
remember him perhaps – to get my family into safety. And I
took the step when the Immortals started off last night.'

The man from Trachis was some distance from us, on the
other side of the fire, eating wolfishly. I said in a low voice, 'He?'

'I don't know. I fell in with him when making my way here.
I'm better armed than he is; that may have decided him in the
rôle he's decided to play.'

'Humble well-wisher in place of spy?'

'Humble discourager, rather. His line is pessimism.'

'I told you to get some food.'

The King had come up. I sprang to my feet. 'I'm not hungry.
I'll get a meal when –'

He jerked his head in the way I now knew well. I followed
him off. He said, 'Eat now; your next meal may be in Hades,
where the diet may not suit you.'

I said I didn't understand; one shouldn't expect too much
from the Phocians, perhaps, but we had sent nearly three
thousand men to deal with the Immortals, and they had plenty

of time to seize the lower track before the Persians could come out in any strength.

'They have gone home,' said the King.

'Gone *home*?'

'They have a fair start. From here a mile and a half before they're out of the pass at the east gate, after that easy country for travelling. In the first hours they'll run the risk of being cut to pieces by Persian cavalry, but the fight we'll put up here should delay things enough to give them a good chance. You're looking astounded. I told you I didn't intend the non-Spartans to suffer, didn't I?'

'You take it coolly,' I said, as I had said – how long ago?

'Coolly?' he replied, as he had also replied – how long ago? 'How little you still know Spartans. The Spartan in me recognises the importance of not wasting the lives of good spearsmen. But otherwise –' He looked swiftly up at the gaunt rocks clear in the sun, the thick forests higher still. 'Up in those woods – somewhere – the enemy is being led down towards us by someone who'll be branded as a traitor – a farmer who wanted to get all the invading armies off his soil. Is he a traitor? Why should a man from Malis feel love for Sparta?'

'I was not thinking of him.'

'No, you were thinking of Tegeans, Mantineans, other Arcadians. And why should they feel love for Sparta?'

'They fought well enough, yesterday.'

'They wanted to show they could fight as well as Spartans. And there was still hope yesterday.' Suddenly, in a gesture extraordinary for him, he beat his hand against the rocky wall of the gorge against which we were standing. 'We kept this pass for two days, the Ionian says Xerxes was in despair yesterday. God, if we've come so close to a successful defence, what couldn't we have done reinforced?'

I said nothing. I was becoming Spartan in my speaking habits; if there were nothing to say I held my tongue.

In his old calm manner he resumed after a moment, 'Why are you so surprised?'

'When I started off at dawn, they were filing off eastwards; I thought they were obeying orders.'

'I believe that was their original idea. In any case, they'd been roused roughly, they were moving like sleep-walkers at first. But then they really woke up to what was happening, that they were being surrounded by the enemy – because they'd been deserted by Sparta.'

He sat on a boulder, as he had sat when we first really talked together. 'You're looking amazed still – do you think I shouldn't waste time in talking? But there's all the time for talking now – when nothing can be done.' And then, as I still stood shaking my head in rage and disbelief, he said again, 'Why are you so surprised? Have you been deaf and blind all the time you've been in the camp, and kept your mind closed to everything but those strange animals, the Spartans, and their curious customs?'

'You said something like that days ago, and I told you the truth. That may have been my attitude in the beginning, but it altered soon enough. Yet what you say now is partially true, I suppose; I haven't talked much with the non-Spartans.'

'And didn't take the hint when I told you about my brother's ideas – no more second-class treatment for the Arcadians and our other Peloponnesian allies? Didn't it occur to you to reflect, surrounded by those allies, that when Cleomenes was done for, his plans were done for too, that the allies still get bad treatment – and resent it? And didn't it occur to you that, if Themistocles grasped the point about no ephor coming here, that men with first-hand knowledge of the power of the ephors might get the point too?'

'I have been unforgivably stupid,' I said.

'It might have been a good thing for you yourself if you had shaken your mind free from your preoccupation with one state alone.'

'Will you tell me what happened?'

'It seemed as if they were going off up the track. Then the front ranks halted, and began to shout. They had been deserted by Sparta. They had done enough, they were going home. I sent

Maron. He asked if they were going to desert their comrades. It wasn't a good choice of words.' (*Had it been Maron who had gone up earlier to the Phocians?*) 'They shouted that they had been deserted first. And who were they deserting? Spartans – the very race that had sacrificed them.

'In a way they were right, of course. The spirit of Cleomenes is being avenged.

'Maron sent for me. When I got there, I asked for volunteers to stay. No one moved towards me. On the other hand, for the moment no one moved on towards the east gate. I mishandled things then. If I had waited a little, I might have had some volunteers, some of them, I think, were uneasy in mind. The two days' fighting together had made them think differently, if not of Sparta the state, at least of the Spartans who are here. But I couldn't wait, the sky was grey already, and so I lost my temper. "Very well, then," I said. "*Go!*" And I knew then I'd made a mistake, there'd been doubt in many minds, fear of dishonour, but I'd solved their problem for them. "*Go!*" I'd said, and in future they'll be able to salve their consciences by saying I gave them a military order, and you don't disobey a Spartan King giving a military order.'

He got up.

'Remember!' he said. 'It's not the blackest desertion. That's the desertion of my Spartans by other Spartans. Give this message to Themistocles –'

I stared at him blankly. I had completely forgotten Themistocles, Habronichos, the fast galley.

'Yes,' he said. 'You'd completely forgotten the reason you were sent here. Tyrrhastiadas took the warning to Habronichos while you were going up the mountain.'

I said, words stumbling in my haste, 'Now that Tyrrhastiadas is here, knowing more about the enemy than I ever can, I can stay!'

'You Athenians are the greatest self-betrayers in the world,' he said slowly. 'Your face lit up when you said that. But you are not staying. I had no idea when you would come back, so

Habronichos is bringing the galley round, and, when I give the order, you and Tyrrhastiadas will swim for it.'

'*He* is the valuable person —' I began, but he cut me short.

'I am not acting as a Spartan should; I am allowing myself a luxury in the last hours of my life. You are going!'

I had one last thought. There was still the galley. He could get away in it. I opened my mouth to say as much, but caught his gaze. He knew what I planned to say, and his look vetoed the unspoken thought.

It should never have been thought of.

After this there remained nothing to do, and little to say. The King asked first Dienekes, and then Maron to come with us to the galley, to take his last report back to Sparta. Each refused, in typical fashion. 'I came with you to fight, not to act as messenger-boy!' said Dienekes. 'And what's the use of it? They know we're dying here, as ordered!' Maron said, 'I'll do my duty better by staying here; the news may be better if I stay.'

The galley came in sight. I said, 'When do I go?'

'I shall tell you.'

I nodded mutely. I was all Athenian at that moment, almost gave full rein to my feelings, but managed to control myself. I don't know if my eyes said anything.

Tyrrhastiadas said suddenly, 'I think they've learned their lesson. The very thought of your spears is a bitter nightmare to them. They'll be using their archers today.'

The man from Trachis said loudly, 'They have so many archers that when they shoot their arrows darken the sun.'

'Good news, that,' said Dienekes. 'It means we'll fight in the shade.'

Soon after this the man from Trachis went away to the rear. No one hindered him. Probably he went to meet his Persian masters.

The sun was climbing higher now. The corpses were beginning to stink, and there was the smell of the sulphur and the mud and the brine that had been in our nostrils ever since we had come to Thermopylae.

There was a sudden stir in the rear, and we saw a stumbling figure being guided forward by a slave. It was one of the Spartans who had been sent away when blinded by eye inflammation. The retreating allies had passed through the tiny village where he had been sent; when he had heard that his comrades would soon be surrounded, he had come, stumbling and falling up the narrow, dusty road between mountains and sea, to rejoin them.

They did not question his coming. They gave him a spear and a shield, and his old place in the line. If you disregarded his dreadfully inflamed eyes, he looked in better shape than his fellows. It was only when you saw him, in his polished armour, that you realised how battered and dented everyone else's equipment was.

Torn, muddied, bloodstained tunics. Wounded steady in line with the unscathed.

The awful stink of Thermopylae. What a horrible place to die in.

On the heights there was the smell of myrtle and juniper and thyme. Higher still, in the oak forest —

I had glanced over my shoulder, unthinking, to look up at those wooded slopes, and I saw on that slope the sun flashing on a spear point.

I said, 'They are there. On the lower slope.'

The King poured out a libation to the Ferryman, to whom he and his comrades were bound that day. And then he addressed us.

'It is not the fashion for a Spartan leader to address his troops before a battle. There is no need of this, in our case —'

This was true. Non-Spartans needed the eve-of-battle speech, to encourage them, give them confidence. We didn't have the constant drill that shuts the mind to fear. We could stand watching an enemy, wondering, 'What in the hell am I doing here? How did it happen?' Such thoughts did not trouble Spartans. Ponderings as to why and wherefore never troubled them. Duty and obedience to orders were enough.

'—but this is a strange battle for us. It is a battle we have no chance of winning. It is not that death threatens us. Certain death awaits us. We must see to it that it is death in battle rather than the shameful and slow death that will come to us if we are taken alive. When your spears are broken, use your swords. When your swords are broken, use your daggers. When your daggers are broken, use teeth and nails. The gods were more considerate in the creation of fighting animals than in the creation of fighting men, but even if human teeth and nails are a poor second best to fangs and claws, we must use them if nothing else is left to us, and use them so that even Spartan nails and teeth will be something to trouble their dreams at night.

'We shall, of course, take with us as many of them as we can. That means attacking on as wide a front as possible. File out now, and take up your position before the wall. For the killing we need as much room as we can get.'

The men guarding the entry to the pass came running back. 'They're coming!'

The Spartans began to file out into the wider space before the wall. I made as if to follow them. The King detained me for a moment. 'I didn't finish my message to Themistocles, did I? Tell him always to be wary of the ephors' acts and promises. If they can betray a Spartan King and his men to their death, what will they do to a foreigner?'

'I'll tell him.'

'He must not judge the Spartan soldier by the actions of the Spartan government.'

I nodded.

'He must try to prevent the fighting men—all the fighting men—from being used and duped again.'

I could say nothing.

'May you Athenians, sea animals that you've become, meet better luck than we land animals have had. You must go soon.'

We could see the first Persians coming into sight. It was not a speedy charge; they were being lashed on from the rear, but even with whips they held back from the Spartan spears.

And Tyrrhastiadas had been right. Over the screaming heads poured a storm of arrows. To escape them the Spartans would have to close with their enemies. I tightened my grip on my spear. But briefly his hand touched mine.

'*Time to go,*' he said.

One of the arrows struck him in the face, and it was I who cried out. He instantly pulled it out, but it left a terrible wound. I could see the white of his cheekbone.

'*Time to go, Theron. Good-bye, comrade.*'

He turned his head, shouted an order, and the Spartan line went forward.

I began to thread my way through the mud and the blood and the mess of the stinking Persian corpses, down to the water's edge.

'*Ah, my friend, if after living through this war, we could be sure of ageless immortality —*'

'What did you say?'

I had not known that Tyrrhastiadas was with me.

'Nothing.'

Behind us a sudden clash of shields. I threw down my own shield, my spear, helmet, took off my breastplate.

'*— in we go whether we yield the glory to some other man —*'

In I went, into the water, away from it all, pushing my way through the dead, sprawling Persians, the drowned, bobbing Persians, through the foam stained and sticky with blood, into the water muddied with blood, and then clear water and the side of the galley, and hands hauling me aboard. Tyrrhastiadas was already on the deck.

I asked Habronichos, 'Do we stay to see the end of it?'

'Until it's certain,' he said.

'What else can it be?'

So we sat and watched for a time.

Fortunate Achilles, who could be out of the battle, yet terrify the enemy by his war cry.

I do not expect anyone to believe this, but I knew when he died. A few minutes later Tyrrhastiadas said, 'There is a tremendous struggle going on — there — do you see?'

'I think the King is dead. The Spartans are fighting to drag his body away.'

' *—think it infamy that the dogs of Ilium should have Patroclos for a toy—*'

They drove the Persians back four times.

And then we saw them retiring, decimated, but in good order, and carrying something, back to the narrowest part of the pass, behind the wall. No need to ask what that meant. The attack was beginning from the rear.

Some men did not go back with them, and surrendered. These were the Thebans.

Just behind the wall there is a little mound. Here the defenders made their last stand. Finally they were overwhelmed with missiles; even Spartan nails and teeth were enough to keep their enemies at a distance. It had lasted until the mid-afternoon.

'They are branding the Theban prisoners,' said Habronichos. 'Let us go.'

15

We had covered half the distance to Artemision when we met a speeding thirty-oar galley. 'News for Leonidas from Themistocles!' called the captain. 'The enemy attacked this morning – it's been a murderous business, but on the whole we had the best of it and –'

Habronichos shouted back in an almost unrecognisable voice, 'The enemy attacked at Thermopylae too this morning. The Spartans –' He stopped, groping for words. Then he resumed, 'The Spartans – didn't have the best of it –'

But I think it was the air of dreadful depression and misery about us that told our story better than any words could do.

'Defeated?' said the other captain in sudden horrified realisation.

'Dead,' said Habronichos. 'All dead. Leonidas and every Spartan with him.'

And the oar-beat seemed to echo the words. Dead. Dead. Dead. The other galley turned and accompanied us back to Artemision. Its crew must have noticed we weren't doing Athenian oarsmanship much credit. Some of our men were weeping as they bent to their oars.

Evening had fallen like a pall when we reached Artemision. The beach was a gloomy sight in the dusk; the long strip of shore seemed alight with funeral pyres. They were still picking our dead out of the water, from the wreckage of ships as well as humanity, balks of timber, broken oars.

Half our Athenian vessels had been disabled, five had been captured. At first sight the ships still afloat looked like the vessels of a beaten fleet – all the scars of defeat seemed there, hulls stove in, being hastily and desperately plugged with sail-cloth, broken rams, great gaps in the banks of oars – great gaps too on the rowing benches, decks blotched by blood, wounded lying where they could – and, along the beach, the corpse fires. And every unwounded survivor was exhausted.

Yet we held the battle station; *we*, and not the Persians, could retrieve our dead from the sea. It had taken some time for the ordinary sailor to appreciate the significance of this, but just before our galley appeared the mood at Artemision was swinging from desperation to hope – we had not done too badly, after all, in fact, we had done better than we had really dared expect. The Phoenicians had tried the diecplus trick, and the countermeasure thought up by Themistocles had worked. When battle was resumed next day we should meet with even greater success. Spirits rose most swiftly in the Athenian contingent. Our raw, mass-produced squadrons that had been derided by ally and enemy alike had held their own. It was the enemy who had retreated. It wasn't quite Marathon all over again, but it was a beginning. The great Persian fleet was no more invincible than the great Persian army had been. Themistocles, conferring with his staff officers, heard a man laugh suddenly. The laughter spread from group to group. There was even some singing.

And then our galley had come in, manned by a crack crew that was rowing badly, quitted by three men in stumbling haste, who hurried up the beach so blindly that, like sleepwalkers, they almost blundered into the watchfires. All that we said, apparently, was, 'Where is Themistocles? We must see Themistocles,' and the little groups before us parted, fell silent, stared after us, still in silence, and hope swung back to desperation.

Our faces told them of catastrophe, our rowers, lying almost unmoving at their benches, supplied some of the details. Behind us as we went up that beach, silence, but then the whispers began to spread, following us. 'Thermopylae taken. All the Spartans dead. With their King.'

There was Themistocles staring at me. The fire at which he had been sitting gave light, but I felt no warmth from it. Before I could speak, he said flatly, 'I was a fool. I clung to a hope I should have known was illusory.'

'They are all dead,' I said. 'The King and all his Spartans. The enemy found a path over the mountains and took them in the rear.'

Still staring at me, he put his writing tablet in my hands. 'Don't tell me the details,' he said. 'Write them down.'

He may have said it because he did not have time to hear more at that moment; he may have said it because of pity.

'This is Tyrrhastiadas of Cyme. He brought us the warning. I told you about him, I met him in Sardis.'

They clasped hands. 'We'll talk later,' said Themistocles. 'Now's the time for action. If they're through the pass, our position here can't be held. We'll have to move out. Tonight.'

There had been physical exhaustion. Then there had been mental elation. And now it was shattered. Now there was depression and bitter anger. We had been robbed of our reward. We had fought and endured for nothing, it seemed.

I sat scribbling. Someone came up to me. 'Where's your equipment?'

'The Persians have it now. I had to swim for it.'

'... *your beautiful burnished armour is in Trojan hands* ...' It was too much to expect Thetis of the Silver Feet to surface in the bloodstained waters of Artemision, pushing aside the wreckage and Persian corpses to offer me fresh armour from Hephaestos himself.

Suddenly the beach was invaded by terrified islanders and herds of bellowing cattle. The news had spread; they were hoping to be evacuated. Themistocles said, 'Our poor devils deserve one good meal before they pull out. Take the cattle. Better for us to have them than the enemy. Build the fires up high with wreckage, and leave them burning after the meat's been roasted. If *they* think we're still holding the station, we've a better chance of getting away.'

Someone gave me food. 'Come on. When did you eat last?'

When the Spartan King had said to eat a good breakfast, the next meal might be in Hades.

'You'll sail with Themistocles.'

'Why not with Habronichos? And where's Tyrrhastiadas?'
Suddenly, above all, I didn't want to be separated from Tyrrhastiadas, who had shared that morning across the straits.

'Habronichos has gone, and if you're talking of the Ionian he's gone with him.'

Within the hour, the ships began to stream away, the Corinthians leading, the Athenians bringing up the rear. It was hard going for men already exhausted.

After I had finished writing, I sat on for a little while on the deck of the speeding vessel, staring across the forty miles of water. Above me the stars were bright. There swung the Heavenly Twins, Castor and Polydeuces, who bring help to ships in danger, flashing through the air on speedy wings. On land they had scarcely proved efficacious as helpers and deliverers.

I wondered if the Persians had stopped slashing and defiling the dead they had not dared approach when living.

I wondered why, when the crew of the galley had wept as they bent to their oars, I had been unable to weep.

I wished I had been able to weep.

I went down to take a turn at the oars.

'Hard luck about Cleandros,' someone said next morning.

'Cleandros?' It was still difficult to remember much that had happened before I went to Thermopylae.

'You saw the beacons flaring, didn't you? That was because the three-ship patrol in the harbour at Skiathos was taken by surprise. The first ship taken came from Troezen; the Persians dragged the man who'd fought best to the prow and cut his throat. Then they captured the next ship, from Aegina. The third ship was one of ours; Cleandros was second in command. It tried to get away, but ran aground. We don't know what happened to the crew, but there doesn't seem much hope.'

Themistocles encouraged the oarsmen onward with words. 'The news will reach Athens before us. There are beacons, and Habronichos has gone ahead. But we mustn't be long behind him.

God knows what's happening there—remember that all who think as we do are here in the fleet, the people left in Athens who can carry the Assembly now we're away, are the opposition—'

The sea was quite smooth as we fled south, unshadowed, the colour of milk as the dawn haze rolled away. And behind us it remained empty, empty for mile after mile of burnished water after the sun had risen, glittering, flat, still.

'How long?' said Themistocles, looking back.

'They were badly mauled?'

'Yes.'

'Then they won't be in any hurry to chase us, will they?'

'The army?'

'He'll have to bring the army on ahead, won't he, to seize harbours and watering-points?'

'Yes. How many days would you say we have left to us before he's in Attica?'

I said painfully, 'It depends how long he takes to—celebrate taking Thermopylae. Then a day and a half from Thermopylae to Thebes, a day and a half from Thebes to Athens. He'll send his cavalry first, of course.'

'Then,' said Themistocles evenly, 'we must hope that he'll celebrate his triumph at Thermopylae in no uncertain manner, mustn't we?'

'Yes,' I said.

Those who had died there would agree. They'd delayed him living; they'd delay him dead.

But we never dreamed how much of a festival he'd hold in that bloody, muddy hole of a place. Later we learned what he had done during those days so precious to us.

His men did not dare approach the dead until evening. Then he had the Spartan bodies mutilated; the head of their King was struck off and impaled on a pole.

The following day was occupied in shovelling into holes all but a few score of his own Persian dead. The holes were covered over with leaves and loose earth. He meant to advertise his victory—but not the price he had had to pay for it.

Once Thermopylae was tidied up, an invitation was sent to the fleet, which had now gingerly advanced to Artemision. 'Friends and fellow soldiers, the King grants leave for anyone who wants it to go and see with his own eyes how he fights against the madmen who thought they could beat him.' So, all next day, his sailors were being ferried in small craft that forty miles from Artemision to Thermopylae, the forty miles back. They were encouraged to mock and desecrate what remained of the Spartan dead, but at intervals were called to attention by Xerxes' staff officers, who delivered to them Xerxes' own version of what had occurred. No one appears to have queried a word of it – no one being bent on suicide. But no one could have believed it. Sailors are necessarily practical people. They rarely have a high opinion of military men, but, much as they may have despised the land forces, they must have wondered why, if the soldiers had suffered so few casualties, it had taken them three days to clear the pass.

It was only next day, when the boatloads of visitors had been ferried back across the strait, that the army resumed its advance.

So the dead Spartan fighters gave us time to save Athenian civilians. I have often remembered that.

'We must get down to Athens like bats out of hell for two reasons,' said Themistocles. 'It's not one crisis but two. What are they doing in Athens – and what are they doing in Corinth?'

'Building their wall over the Isthmus.'

'I don't know if you're saying that seriously, but I think it's the most likely thing in the world. More. They'll want the fleet to fall back on Corinth. So it's up to me to persuade the Spartan admiral to call in at Salamis first, while we evacuate what are left of our people in the city. Eurybiades can't refuse that.'

'And afterwards?'

'With any luck the Persians will have caught up with us by then, and we can't slip away.'

The waves were dancing now on a dazzling morning.

And at last the light shone on olive groves and hills and sandy coves we had known all our lives, and we were approaching Athens – an Athens on the verge of panic.

The men with the fleet before going north had carried their families over to Troezen, but the men who had opposed Themistocles throughout had been unwilling to leave their homes and possessions. They had always been convinced that this Persian invasion, like the last, could only be shattered on land. Since Athens had gone insane, and put her trust in the fleet, salvation could only come through the Spartan army.

When the news of Thermopylae arrived, therefore, the first reaction of the opposition-dominated Assembly was to send off a vain appeal to Corinth asking the Peloponnesian army to come north to defend Attica. 'They're too damned gentlemanly in their attitude towards Sparta,' was Themistocles' comment when he heard this. 'Just as they're too damned ungentlemanly in their attitude to me.'

'And too damned stupid both times,' I said. 'I should have thought that any fool could see that if the Spartans weren't willing to risk their main armies north of the Isthmus *before*, they're hardly likely to do it now.'

It was the news that the Spartans had (as the opposition saw the matter) betrayed them that did more to create panic, a breakdown of nerve, than any grim news of the battering our fleet had taken. They were as hysterical as a doting woman whose husband has proved faithless.

At least they admitted now that the army of Athens alone could not defeat Xerxes, but even so some of them could not stomach the fact that their safety depended entirely on the abhorred fleet. Their obsessive hatred for Themistocles and his policy was so great – and all the greater because that policy was now proved the right one – that they were no longer quite sane. They did not want victory, if victory were won by Themistocles. Almost they did not want safety, if safety were achieved through Themistocles.

But there was a second group, that reacted differently. After our ships had come slowly into Phaleron Bay (leaving the rest of the fleet to make for Salamis) and, very stiffly, weary men left deck and rowing benches, there were wild-eyed hysterics plucking at our arms, clutching at hands blue with oar-weals, and crying, 'The Spartans aren't coming! They're fortifying the Isthmus and letting everything else go! They've turned down our appeal! They've cut us off altogether – the Spartans are destroying the Bad Stairs!' And then would come the inevitable appeal, 'Get us to Troezen!' But there was no time now to take them to Troezen. Some might get as far as Aegina, if Aegina would take them. Most of them would get no further than Salamis, and Salamis, barren, rocky Salamis only ten miles long, was more like a serrated mountain ridge rising out of the sea than an island. If we didn't limit the number of refugees going to Salamis, there would be a time limit to the number of days they could be supplied there.

They had brought their families with them down to the waterfront. This would be nothing like the orderly evacuation we had planned and supervised before going north. These groups of people, huddled individually on the ground, or clinging together in distraught groups, were as incapable of rational thought as men and women rudely awakened from sleep. In that burning heat, the chill of fear was almost tangible.

And feverishly the hands came out to us.

Themistocles looked at the women and children with pity; his contempt when he turned to their menfolk who had brought them to this I recognised in the narrowing of his eyes, the hardening of his jaw muscles. I was not so reticent. 'The sailor rabble has its uses after all,' I said.

'I hope we *can* be of use,' he said. 'Maybe they've cut it too fine. And with confusion and panic already here, discipline already gone for good – my God, it's what I was always afraid of, a last minute evacuation just as order collapses and madness sets in. Still, we'll have to try, won't we? Anyhow, I've another job for you to do. Quite a few well-known faces aren't here. Get up into the City and find out what the hell's going on.'

As I picked my way through that crowd, always hands plucked at me, strong, urgent hands, which I could brush violently away, and timid hands, aged hands, feeble hands, which I must detach gently.

The others had decided to barricade themselves on the Acropolis. The oracle-mongers and priests had been right; the wooden wall was the old wattle palisade, they would take themselves there with all their portable treasures. They would, they told me, be doubly safe — the temples themselves would be sanctuary for them as for the priests and priestesses who naturally would stay. I admit I was not a particularly impressive ambassador — impressive to them, I mean; others might have viewed my appearance differently. My tunic was wet from the sea, my cloak faded and stained. My hair was thick with salt, my eyes smarting and heavy from sleeplessness. They sat freshly barbered in purple or scarlet himations clasped with golden brooches. Their sense of affront that I should thrust myself upon them in my dishevelled state showed in their eyes and voices.

I could not induce them to change their minds. They were the Deucalions of Athens. Zeus, in justifiable anger, might destroy their impious countrymen, but they, the righteous, would survive, and when the flood of barbarian savagery had swept us all away, it would recede, and they, and they alone, would descend from the Acropolis to resume the inheritance that ungodly men had taken from them. From the Acropolis they would have witnessed our destruction with complete equanimity, and to the Acropolis they were going that evening.

And there was the last interview — to which I went sick at heart, and with lagging feet.

I knew it was futile. More than one of those I had visited, after lashing me with his tongue as a traitor to my class, had gone on to speak of my father. He too was going up to the Acropolis.

It had been late afternoon when we had docked, so it was

nearly dark when I went to what had once been my home. I was almost too late; my father was already sitting by the entrance, waiting for friends to come with a litter. The hall was dark; earlier in the day there had been a sacrifice to the gods, but the fire on the altar had died long before. A single lamp burned, and I could only see his face dimly by its light – dimly, yet only too clearly. It was as cold and hard as a stone in winter.

'Father,' I said, 'will you let me carry you down to the harbour?'

He said nothing.

'Father, I have seen the Persian army – I was with the Spartans at Thermopylae. We can't withstand them on land. Any chance of victory lies with the fleet.'

He had not even looked in my direction, but when I took a step towards him, his head swung round sharply and he gazed at me in hatred. 'So you'd try to take me by force? I swear to you that if you dragged me aboard your ship, I'd find some way of throwing myself into the sea rather than owe my life to you and your half-breed friend.'

I knew he would do it.

'Father,' I said for the last time, 'it's unbearable that we should part in this way. Will you grant me one request? I lost my equipment at Thermopylae. Would you let me have yours? Your son will do his best not to disgrace the armour you wore at Marathon.'

'I have no son,' replied my father, having turned away from me.

It could not be a tidy evacuation of the others. Panic made a messy job inevitable. And it wasn't that we had simply the task of transporting human beings, we had to transport the means of keeping them alive – and the crews of the three hundred ships we must somehow detain at Salamis. We had managed to get the corn reaped by the end of May, but threshing is a lengthy business, going on through July and much of August, and mobilisation had put paid to most of that. And who was left to bring it on mules and ox-carts into the City? Yet we must find food for the crews of three hundred triremes, double that number, it seemed, of refugees.

The very old, and the very sick, could not be taken. They were carried up to the sanctuary of the temples on the Acropolis. And household pets must be left behind. Soon the despairing howls of deserted dogs running up and down the waterfront drowned even the shrieks of women and the wails of children.

But I did not see the end of the evacuation. I stood with Themistocles watching that scene of terror and confusion — swearing, sweating sailors, many of whom still bore the scars of battle, argumentative refugees, despairing refugees, possessions dragged from the handcarts that had brought them down — and he said, 'We're cutting it fine, but we'll just do it, I think.'

I said, 'Let me ride out towards Cithaeron; they'll come that way. I'll see them at a safe distance enough — burning farms or just their own cloud of dust. We'd have some idea then if we've days or merely hours in hand.'

He raised one eyebrow and looked at me quizzically. 'Care to be honest?' he asked.

I said, 'Well, I've had my bellyful of running away from the Persian army.'

'Don't chance your luck,' said Themistocles. 'I don't want to lose a damned good trireme captain. You're not fit to go off tonight; start at dawn tomorrow.'

I spent part of what remained of the night trying to get hold of fresh equipment. On a sudden thought I hurried through the dark streets to Cleandros' home, but the street door was locked, and the house was quite silent. The family must have gone to Troezen in the first evacuation, after all.

I ended up by looting. It was strange to plunge into the armourers' alley, and find that, too, dark and silent, no fires glowing, no hammers clanging. Every little workshop was quite deserted. They had, of course, taken with them almost all their stuff, but luckily what little they had left behind was cavalry equipment. So I picked up a light breastplate, not too ornately worked, a helmet of the Boeotian type, which gives not only the best protection, but the least obstructed vision, a light shield, a machaera,* for on horseback a weapon that slashed and not the cut-and-thrust type of sword was necessary, and two light throwing spears. I went back to my own house to pick up a pair of riding boots. It was, perhaps, better that it was dark when I saw it for what was undoubtedly the last time.

* A heavy, curved sword.

16

I started off in the morning coolly enough – in every sense of the
word, fairly alert in mind still, and comparatively physically
comfortable in body if not in thought. I can remember looking
about me at familiar territory and thinking, *Attica's a naked
land, with all her bones showing.* I'd never thought of it in
this way before; I realised with a sudden pang that I was
looking at it all with a new clarity in the knowledge that possibly I was looking at it for the last time – but this caused less
pain than the thought that succeeded it – *These may be the last
days anyone can see it a as free land.* After this my mind was in
torment.

Strangely enough, mental relief came from sheer physical dis-
tress. The sun, which tortured the body, was like an infusion of
poppy to the brain as the heat of the day increased. A shadow,
when you saw one, was black as cuttlefish ink.

And yet, not knowing why, I galloped.

I rode into a countryside less and less familiar now that the
crops had gone, so featureless in its bareness that one's memory
clawed desperately after past excursions.

A torrent bed, boulder and pebble filled, with occasionally a
tenaciously surviving oleander. A clump of laurel, equally tena-
cious. And then it was blazing noon, and I was crossing a shelterless plain, and suddenly I was dreadfully aware of how much
this abandoned countryside was bereft of life – no goat bells, no
ass braying, only the endless buzz of myriads of crickets –
almost a roar that noise seemed in the prevailing quiet. Silence
and stillness, not a breath of wind. And burning hot. In that
countryside drained of life and sound, movement and colour –
bleached stones, silvery white thistle-heads, pale corn stubble
like the first attempt at a beard on the chin of a tow-haired boy,

white dust everywhere – in all this ghostly landscape only the heat seemed living and real.

The heat beat down and one's eyes were darkened, the blood drummed, and the brain was stupid. This was the moment to imagine one saw Pan.

Wincing as I touched the burning metal, I took off my helmet to ease my aching head. I realised I wasn't thinking clearly. If there were Persians ahead, I felt too stupid and too dazed to cope.

Lunatic to have travelled in such furious haste in the midday heat of Attica.

Would a few hours make such a difference?

Just because something within me now kept saying, 'Make haste! Make haste!'

But if an action, a conviction, were, humanly speaking, unreasonable, did this not mean they came from some divine prompting?

I slid down, fondled my poor beast's sweat-darkened neck, told him I'd walk him a little to rest him.

Of course, one shouldn't forget Pan. 'God of the countryside, my apologies for disturbing your noonday rest, but the damned Persians are here again. Help us with your favour now as you did ten years ago. Be beside *us* – and let *them* see you!'

We plodded on. Limestone, stubble, dust, dried up twigs, stalks; with a shock I realised I was stumbling on, staring at the ground, never looking up –

Was that a sound? Someone laughing?

I raised my head. The sun darkened my eyes, so I had to shade them with my hand before I could see – see rocks ahead, and, above them a sudden flurry of movement, a goat, bounding effortlessly from boulder to boulder. In that unnatural silence you could even hear the clatter of its hooves.

My horse, too, had raised his head, and begun to trudge towards the rocks. And then, on the other side of them, there was colour, the green of plane trees and sound. There is no other sound like it on earth, Holy Maiden, I can't be mistaken –

pebbles, and green moss, and there, in the shade of the plane trees, a trickle, just a trickle, but cold, cold – and it was cool in the shade . . .

My horse drank. From above came the bleat that I had mistaken for laughter. I'd forgotten him, but he didn't intend to be forgotten. There he stood on the topmost rock, beard cocked at a jaunty angle so that he looked ludicrously like some of the swaggering sailors you met down in the docks. His slanting amber eyes, blazing bright, stared down at me, almost with humour one would say, the kind of derisive humour that springs from affection and long familiarity. Then with another of the bleats that sounded like laughter, he leaped down from his perch like an Olympic athlete, landed close to the horse – who took not the slightest notice – stared down at me, lying prone, with the same air of jocular knowledge, and was off again into the sunlight in a series of tremendous bounds. I could hear his neat little hooves clicking away into the distance, but I did not think there would be any prints in the little patch of mud and soft ground where he had paused momentarily by the spring.

An hour later, I realised with a shock that I must be in the neighbourhood of Cleandros' farm, the farm I had visited only once, that single meeting with his stepmother having been more than enough for me.

I wondered how she liked being a refugee in Troezen. Her domineering ways would scarcely endear her to her hosts.

There was a sudden flurry of dust ahead of me, the sound of flying hooves. A single rider. I tightened my grip on my javelins, although reason told me no Persian scout could be riding so furiously. A man rode in this wild haste only in flight.

An elderly man, a groom, whose face I remembered vaguely from meetings with Cleandros. He remembered me, gave a great cry of relief. 'They're here!' he stammered. 'The Persians. I saw them a mile from the farm –'

'What in the devil were you doing at the farm? You should have gone to Troezen weeks ago!'

He said, gasping for breath, 'The master told us to – but when he'd gone *she* took over. We weren't to go. She'd had a message they'd be coming this way –'

Yes, her father would have seen to that.

'We – the master's slaves – couldn't do what he'd told us because *her* slaves outnumbered us. The young mistress –'

I had forgotten there was a sister.

' – wanted to get away, but her stepmother kept her with her all the time. But she managed to get a message to me to keep a horse ready, so that the moment they were sighted, I could take the warning to Athens –'

'They were a mile away, you said, when you left?'

'A dozen riders, coming from Eleutherae. They'll be at the farm soon.'

'Your horse is fresher than mine – get ahead with the warning, tell Themistocles I'm following behind. You've done well.'

'We wanted to do what the master said, but they were too many for us. When he hears –'

I said as gently as I could, 'His ship's missing. He may be dead.'

His face crumpled in sudden grief. Then he said, 'Just as well, perhaps. If he knew that his sister –'

'Get back with the news. Then wait for me. There'll be room for you in whatever household's left to me.'

He nodded, raised his hand in salute, jerked his reins, and his horse, a good one, broke into a gallop again. I turned my own beast's head to follow him, and then halted.

I have never been able to decide why I changed my mind. I had found out what I had come for; I'd been right, they were coming by way of Cithaeron and Eleutherae. It was now up to me to retire as speedily and discreetly as possible.

But I went on riding forward until I came in sight of the farm.

The sun was still high enough for me to have to shade my eyes against the glare. No need to strain my ears to catch the sounds, though. Women screaming. Men shouting, laughing. The barbarians were already here. And, I imagined, might stay for a time. The patrol might have been sent out for reconnaissance purposes only, but the defencelessness of the farm, women and servants only — well, for the time being they'd forgotten their original purpose.

Or had the patrol been sent in this direction partly in reply to a request from Hipparchos? The women's screams had little real anguish — they knew there wasn't much to fear. Their mistress only had to say *I am the daughter of Hipparchos*, and she, with her household, would be restored to her father intact.

I took cover in a clump of trees, tried to think.

This reads more calmly than I thought at the time. This, remember, was my first encounter with the invaders in Attica. All my blood cried out against a hurried, stealthy retreat — if I could only give a shout of anger and defiance — let them see one armed man — know it wasn't all going to be women tranquilly waiting to be taken.

Hardly knowing what I was doing, I rode out into the open again.

It wasn't heroic — I had a good start.

So I rode out, and shouted a war cry.

And then, instead of retreating hurriedly, began to gallop forward.

Because suddenly I heard a scream that was anguished enough.

Because a struggle was going on there in the roadway before the farm, and when I shouted again, a figure broke away and came running towards me in agonised flight. Two Persians came galloping in pursuit.

It was a girl. The sister who had argued about *The Suppliant Women*, the desperate women in flight from loathed barbarian pursuers . . .

Odd how, as I galloped forward, above the rhythm of hoof-beats on the sunbaked earth, I could hear, quite clearly, line after line from that play.

She kept her head, that girl. As they bore down on her, she swerved suddenly in her run like a swallow in its flight. They could not pull up in time, were past her, tugging at their reins, I could see their faces quite clearly now – open, shouting mouths, like men enduring ineffable pain, one might think, but it wasn't pain, it was delight, delight in killing, they'd kill her if they caught her – she who'd dared to run from them. They were screaming, screaming like wild beasts, you almost expected the swarthy faces to be the faces of beasts – but beasts' faces can't show with such clarity the lust for blood.

And then my left side went forward, my right arm went back, I was rising from the thighs, and the first cornel wood javelin cut through the air. It got the leading man in the chest, carried him out of the saddle. If it didn't kill him outright, his neck broke in the fall.

I had been watching the men and not the girl after she swerved aside. I'd hoped she would go on being sensible, would try to take cover, to hide, instead of carrying on with this crazy run in the open, but here she was again now, coming on towards me, diagonally. The second Persian could have run her through, but for the moment he was ignoring her, he was galloping towards me, yelling, waving his sword above his head. I could almost imagine I heard the whistle of it through the air.

I swung my horse over a little to get closer to the girl, and drove the second javelin through his neck near the collarbone. He went over with a shriek and a crash of bracelets they ought to have heard in Susa.

And then, for the moment, the only sound was the rasping of my breath.

Two dead Persians, the girl speeding across to me, two horses running wild. No one else, living or dead, close to us. Persians enough at the house, but they'd thought two pursuers could easily deal with her. Now there were furious yells from the distance.

I dragged her up before me. 'Can you ride?' 'Yes.' 'Then we'll get one of those horses.' Time enough to seize a bridle, dump her on to the horse. 'For God's sake, hold on.'

No time to get my javelins back.

I hoped she could stay on the horse – Persians drape their horses with something more like bed coverlets than anything else. It makes for comfort and softness, but not the securest of seats.

'I'll stay on,' she said, as if she read my thoughts.

'You'll have to – my horse is too tired to carry us both. Now, *ride!*'

If she had to wrap her arms around her mount's neck to stay on, luckily Persian horses have massive heads, heavy necks.

This was the most furious gallop of all. The blood beat behind my eyes, I had to keep watching her all the time for fear she fell, but she was sticking on well enough. God knows what my expression was like, wild, I'd say, but her face looked oddly serene, just as her voice had been steady in our brief exchange of words. But there was a tell-tale little pulse beating in her neck, and I remembered the momentary tight grip of her hand as I'd caught her up – the nerves were quivering under that surface tranquillity. I said, 'My name is Theron. We met once.' She said she remembered, but did not turn her head.

We managed to outdistance them and no one saw us when we came wearily to the little spring among the rocks, and dismounted and drank. She asked if I had met the groom. I said I had – and then I told her about Cleandros.

She said, after a moment's silence, 'You must go on without me. I can hide here and follow as soon as I can. It was – selfish of me to run to you.'

I asked, 'Why did you? They'll treat your stepmother with honour, and she'd protect you, no doubt – '

'I know,' she said. 'She said as much, as we waited for them to come. We'd been doing that for days – just waiting. Even when we heard their horses, she told me to sit with the other women – waiting. But I couldn't. I thought, "If I were an old woman, then perhaps I'd do it, sit with my hands folded, waiting for – whatever they decided to do to us." And then I thought,

"But I'm not old — *and I'm an Athenian*! I can't wait — and submit!" '

'You were struggling with them before you saw me.'

'Yes. I tried to get one of their daggers. And then, when I saw you in the sun, I ran . . .' She stopped suddenly, then said, 'I must wash the dust from my face.'

It didn't have the blurring roundness you see in the faces of so many young girls — the good bones showed through her flesh as the lines of the land are clear in our Athenian landscape. She thought I was watching her impatiently, and flushed. 'You must get away,' she said again. 'Their main cavalry isn't far behind — I heard them telling my stepmother that.'

'Why shouldn't you come with me?'

'That horse can't keep going for long — he's going lame, I think.'

I swore under my breath, and went to inspect him. Yes, there was a swelling.

'Your horse can't carry two of us,' she said.

'And what will you do?' I asked angrily. 'Go on running?'

'No, I'd hide.'

'Like a hunted hare? Have you ever seen one? I saw one once — she'd heard the dogs, and she crouched there in the grass exhausted, her eyes — '

'Please — ' she said, flinching.

'She was so still she might have been dead already.'

'And — you picked her up?'

'Yes, I picked her up. If hares think of gods it must have been as if a god had reached down from heaven to snatch her to safety. But don't think a god will reach down from heaven for you!'

'No, but sometimes the hounds lose the scent.'

'Sometimes,' I said. 'Not often. And of course, for Cleandros' sake, I'm taking you with me.'

But she was not listening to me — and then I heard it too.

A noise like distant thunder. I actually thought, 'An earthquake?' for the ground seemed to tremble. And then a great cloud of tawny dust, the lion-coloured dust of Attica, and a great

murmur like a gigantic hive of bees, and flashes of almost unbearably bright light in the dust. The main Persian cavalry had
come.

I had no javelins left. My horse, bearing two of us, could not
move very fast. There were so many of them they could outride,
outflank, surround us.

Two hares would be trying their luck.

Our only hope was that they would not come too close. If
they kept the course they were on, they would see only bare
rocks, the green of the plane trees was secret on our side. They
were too far away, their horses' hooves making too thunderous a
sound for them to hear the trickling of the spring.

If it hadn't been for the goat, I remembered, I shouldn't have
come near myself.

Of course, I whispered later, as they came as close as they
ever would — with luck — what we needed was a camel. Horses
stampeded at the smell of a camel — did she know that? That's
how the Lydian cavalry had once been routed. She managed a
smile as she nodded.

And then, drawing a deep breath long minutes later, 'Well,
no need for a camel after all!'

A whisper came back, 'They must have been moving quickly
— yet it seemed so slow.'

'It's like that before a battle. Time goes crazy. We'll move on
when it's dark — you'd better get some sleep now.'

'I don't want to sleep. If I did I should only see things —
things over and done with, beyond all help now.'

I saw her point.

'Well, rest at any rate.'

The sun, as it sank over the horizon, had the look of a distant,
dying fire. Next day, I thought, the Persians would be in the
deserted streets of Athens itself . . .

But the master of driven slaves need not wait so long. After
a time I drowsed off, to be awakened by someone whispering —
'Wake up,' and at the same time pressing a hand tightly across
my mouth.

'Please be quiet!'

The hand over my mouth was withdrawn. It was the girl whose name I'd forgotten. I had suddenly thought of that in the tense moments when the Persian cavalry had been passing – if we'd been detected, it would have been odd to die in the company of someone whose name I didn't know, I'd thought, and I'd resolved to ask her her name if horsemen turned aside and galloped towards our refuge. But they hadn't, and I still couldn't remember it.

'Quiet!' she whispered. 'Listen! And – Oh, look!'

Beyond our barrier of rocks, a reddish light. And noises. The creak and groan of wood, the crack of whips. Oxen bellowing. Men shouting. Others – many more – groaning, sobbing, cursing –

I crawled forward.

Livid, flaring torches, showing many naked slaves and a few oxen, men and oxen alike roped, chained to carts, dragging them forward, men and oxen alike streaked with sweat and blood from the lash, men and oxen alike showing the whites of their eyes in terror and pain and exhaustion, groaning, stumbling forward – terror, pain, exhaustion, terror, pain, exhaustion – the slavery of the East that reduces man to a beast had come to Attica.

It had been horrible enough in the late afternoon to see the Persian cavalry grinding our poor parched Attic soil into powder beneath it, making the very earth seem to shake beneath the tens of thousands of hooves. But the sight of slaves and oxen chained together, lashed onward together, was something the Eumenides might desire for the torment of the worst of sinners.

'I was in Sardis before they crossed from Asia,' I said at last. 'I saw there things worse than this. But to see this in Attica . . .'

If never before, now one truly began to hate.

The next day was one of roundabout, furtive journeying along little tracks, of hiding behind rough walls marking boundaries between farm and farm, beneath overhanging bushes in dried-up river beds, in little, remote olive groves. And all about us Attica was ablaze.

I could remember wondering at our first meeting how a girl with so soft a voice could have so hard a mind. Now I discovered another paradox – how little bones and fragile flesh could be driven on by courage like adamant.

Her feet bled as we came cautiously down a dusty path towards the coast. The horse we had left in a little deserted settlement with a spring, and green growths about it.

It was the late afternoon. The earth was burning beneath our feet, eyes winced against the bright sun. Not a breath of air stirred. We had seen nothing of the invaders since noon; we must now look for a place to hide until the evening, when we could make the crossing to Salamis.

There was a little grove of trees just ahead of us; as quickly as we might we made our way towards it. I was so tired again now that once more I could scarcely lift my eyes from the ground, and the contemplation of the two moving shadows, a slight one, faltering now, a taller, slightly steadier one behind.

I was tired but I had slept a little the previous night; I think she had never closed her eyes. As we rested again I tried to persuade her to sleep, and again she refused, with a kind of despairing wildness.

'What did they do at the farm?' I asked suddenly. 'Your stepmother was in no danger –'

No, she agreed, but some of the older men slaves had shown fight. 'Those who'd been there before she came – they never really accepted her as mistress, so though she said we were to do nothing . . .' She shook her head blindly, then tore a strip from her tattered dress to bandage her foot. I couldn't get her to talk again, and eventually I sat silent too.

The sun began to sink. Birds started to call to each other from the branches above our heads. The noise of the crickets was deafening.

And then, uncannily and instantaneously, there was absolute silence. The birds made no sound, even the crickets seemed struck dumb. There was a tremor — not so much in the earth as in the air.

'Is it — an earthquake?' she whispered.

'Look!' I whispered, licking my lips, pointing.

It seemed as if the entire horizon was moving where the road ran along the line of the coast. It was a day of burning heat, the air was windless, yet suddenly there was a great shimmering cloud of dust, more than man-high, a saffron cloud, for not only is our dust of Attica tawny, lion-coloured, but the rays of the setting sun fell directly on it.

From the cloud came the sound of a myriad feet and voices.

'Persians?' she whispered. 'Their entire army? I can hear men marching.'

'The light would shine on armour, spear points. And the voices are — Greek. Can't you hear them?'

She said, 'They're singing.'

I wiped the sweat out of my eyes. 'The direction the cloud's moving — '

'It's going towards Eleusis.'

'They're singing the hymn of the Initiates. It — my God, it's the day!'*

I was standing now; she was kneeling, bending forward, straining eyes and ears to see, to hear, to begin to hope, for we both knew that we were the only human beings in that deserted part of Attica.

And then it had gone, vanished in the direction of Eleusis. The setting sun sent a clear amber light swimming over the entire landscape. And a little breeze played about my face, infinitely cooling, bringing with it the scent of a thousand fresh herbs that had soaked in the sun all day, although the only herbs about us were poor dried twigs. I have never smelled anything

---

* The day of the Great Procession to Eleusis. No Athenian would ever describe the Mysteries of the goddess Demeter celebrated at Eleusis, but to Initiates they brought happiness, and the belief that the end of life might also be its beginning.

so glorious. It was not a sweet scent, it was wild, tingling, aromatic, at the same time as refreshing as the little spring had been on the previous noonday of blistering heat, and as enlivening as a cup of hot spiced wine after a long weary ride on a bitter winter's night.

'Do you feel it?' came a startled whisper. 'I —' And then, quite without warning, she had fallen asleep with the sentence unfinished.

And the thought of Eleusis had made me remember her name at last. Cleisidice. From the Homeric Hymn to Demeter — '. . . Cleisidice, the loveliest of that virgin company.'

17

At night we went over to Salamis to confirm the evidence of eyes straining homewards from the island. The whole of Attica was ablaze. And astonishing news met us. Others had made the crossing by night, not long before us. The crew of Cleandros' ship had not been lost after all; the moment she had gone aground, they had leapt ashore, evaded the Persians, stolen horses (having providentially landed in Thessaly) and made their way home. By good fortune they had chosen to make the last part of the journey by Tanagra and over Parnes by way of Decelea, whereas the enemy had chosen the Eleutherae route. Whether they would have escaped if they had come over Cithaeron is doubtful, for they had a wounded man with them — Cleandros. Their escape from the ship had been a near thing; the enemy archers had been shooting before they leaped ashore, and Cleandros had been hit. His condition had grown steadily worse as they came south, but they would not leave him.

All this I learned from Hormos, his captain; Cleandros' sister had gone at once to the tent they had rigged up for her brother. As he stopped speaking, I said, 'When you were in Thessaly, did you hear anything of a Spartan, Pantites, who was sent by the King for liaison duties with the loyalists?'

'We heard that there was a Spartan who had been sent by the King. He too was trying to make his way home.'

(Ultimately he managed to get home. He was met with such hostility — because, through no fault of his own, he had not died with the King — that he killed himself. I have often wondered what stories the ephors spread about him so that on his return he was treated as an outcast. Certainly they would want his mouth shut. He knew the real reason for the loss of Thermopylae.)

The enemy fleet, burning coastal villages as it came, rounded Sunion Cape and came into Phaleron Bay at the same time as the Persian cavalry entered the streets of Athens – nine days after the fall of Thermopylae.

Our fleet was now larger than it had been at Artemision. When the news reached the reserve ships at Troezen that the main squadrons had put in at Salamis – against orders – there had been furious argument. The reserve fleet itself had been instructed to use the harbour of Troezen as its base, with a view to establishing a defence line south of the Isthmus; the argument now was, since Themistocles was obviously taking his own line without consulting what remained of the Congress at Corinth, what was the reserve fleet to do? If heated, the debate did not last long. The commanders of the Athenian vessels said from the start that whatever the others decided, they were going to join Themistocles at Salamis. Since Athenian ships made up the greater part of the reserve, the others eventually decided to follow suit, and nearly a hundred vessels came sailing into Salamis Strait, to join the survivors of Artemision in the three eastern inlets of the island.

So here we were entering on the last act of the drama, taking our stand in the last ditch – whatever metaphor you prefer. Perhaps that of the last ditch is the more apposite. To Xerxes, the narrow streak of water of the Salamis channel must indeed have seemed the last ditch to be leaped before the final triumph. There on one small island was concentrated the manhood of Athens – sailors, troops, magistrates, old and young. To him Salamis must have seemed like nothing more than a rugged sort of paradise – the name they gave to their hunting parks, the great enclosures where wild beasts were penned awaiting destruction at their master's pleasure.

Yet, again, when talking of Xerxes' designs on Salamis, it gives an inaccurate impression to speak of the Great King leaping a ditch. Great Kings do not proceed in this manner; theirs is essentially a stately progress. In fact, his first action after reaching Athens – and presumably having his gold and ivory throne installed – was to order the construction of an immense causeway to bridge the straits so that his army could simply march over to the kill. We could see his soldiers throwing rocks into the sea in the narrowest part of the channel; a look-out brought news that at Phaleron they had started to lash ships together before towing them into place. Themistocles burst out laughing. 'He thinks it'll be an easy job after bridging the Hellespont! Well, at some point one of his generals is going to pluck up the nerve to tell him it's not a practicable proposition here – particularly once they got into deep water and within arrow-range. But it'll never get so far. Someone'll have to tell him they haven't the time. After Artemision they haven't enough ships to divide their fleet and send off half to attack the Peloponnese, and they must be worried about supplies. Within weeks the autumn gales will be setting in – no more provisioning, then. So they must be aiming for a quick decision.' He looked about him at the ring of gloomy faces. 'That's what we have to remember – that they have their difficulties too. They must get a victory before the autumn – and they're not at all sure it can be done.'

He was speaking at the first full council of war after the reserve ships joined us, and met with little response. No one yet was prepared to say, 'Any battle we fight will be a lost one,' but the defeatism there was so thick you felt you could cut it with a knife. Themistocles was the only admiral who made plans on the assumption of a Greek victory; the ideas of the others ranked no higher than panicky if at present silent calculations as to how in the hell they could get away in double quick time, having been trapped by this Athenian swine into danger of being bottled up here by the enemy.

The Commander-in-Chief's Spartan rigidity of mind was something of a help, however. Demoralisation might be settling in hard and fast, but Eurybiades had called a council of war and, by God, it would follow protocol and custom. But first there was a wrangle where the council should be held. There is nothing like demoralisation, defeatism, to breed hysterical suspicions. The Peloponnesians were particularly vociferous here. So many allied contingents – strangers – you didn't know a tenth of the men you met – enemy agents – every word reported to Xerxes – well, you can imagine it. Meetings must be held within a heavily guarded perimeter. Themistocles opposed this, was shouted down. So they withdrew to secure isolation, each commander of a contingent being allowed two or three aides personally known to the other admirals. From Adeimantos of Corinth's angry glare when I was introduced it was plain he knew me only too well.

So at last we settled down, and Eurybiades asked for suggestions as to the most suitable place to engage the enemy fleet – immediately setting the tone for the meeting by declaring flatly that this would have to be in some part of Greece still under our control. 'We can't consider Attica, it's already Persian territory.'

Then at last the pessimism became vocal and came thick and strong. 'Sail to the Isthmus while there's time, fight to defend the Peloponnese.' 'If we're beaten *here*, we'll be bottled up on an island where no help can get to us.' 'If we're beaten at the Isthmus, we can at least find refuge among our own people – '

Themistocles interrupted, 'But can't you see you're all arguing on the assumption that we're bound to be defeated?'

They turned on him then. He'd tricked them into coming to Salamis, but he needn't think he could keep them there. He wouldn't get away with his defiance of orders, he wasn't running the war, he –

Here the commanders of the contingents from our neighbours, Aegina and Megara, intervened vigorously. They too were determined to keep the fleet at Salamis.

The result was practical, if not technical deadlock. The commander of each contingent had a vote – but Athens, Aegina and Megara, although completely outvoted, controlled three-quarters of the fleet. Frustration made Adeimantos more offensive than ever. He launched into a speech expressing such short-sighted self-interest that I muttered rebelliously to

Themistocles. This, at least, made Adeimantos come to an abrupt stop. 'What's he saying to you?' he blared. 'Out with it! If you've something to say, let's all have the benefit of it!'

'I was saying,' I replied, 'that one of your people in the reserve fleet told me your temple prostitutes are praying that their men should be in love with battle. If that's so, I can only say — '

The commanders from Megara and Aegina burst out laughing; Adeimantos looked black as thunder; the meeting broke up in confusion. Habronichos said to Themistocles, 'How in the hell are you going to get the selfish bastards to see that in the long run it's in their own interests to — '

'By patience and tact,' said Themistocles.

'Patience? How long a time do you think Xerxes will give us?'

And the wrangling went on the following day — and the next, outside the council as well as in it. I suppose it was even worse to be excluded from that closely guarded tent; each dawn when you saw the light growing behind the hills you'd wonder as you ate what breakfast you could scrape up, if it would be your last meal. And you'd reflect that, win or lose, some of us would die. Then came the morning when the Persians stopped building the causeway. We cheered at first, but soon enough the shouting died away. For Xerxes had given priority to another target. Before he finished us off, he was going to capture the Acropolis.

There was no military reason for storming the Acropolis. A large garrison of fighting men might have offered some threat in the way of raids and sallies, but Xerxes knew what kind of people had sought refuge there, the old and infirm who had taken temple sanctuary with the priests and priestesses remaining to guard the treasures of the shrines, the religious and political diehards who would not accept that safety lay in the fleet (and they were nearly all middle-aged or elderly), a token garrison of volunteers.

The Acropolis was no strategic threat whatsoever. Militarily, Xerxes could disregard it. But symbolically — Ah, that was another matter. His mode of thought had an atrocious simplicity about it. The choice was submission or extermination. I, who had been at Sardis should have known that, but when I had left my father in his anger and hatred, I believed that there lay only two possibilities before us. If the fleet were destroyed, the Acropolis must eventually surrender. But if the fleet won – and that issue must be decided within days – the people on the Acropolis could last out that length of time. We should all be destroyed, or we should all survive – that was my thought when I had left my father that last evening. My bitterness was because he and I should not endure that common fate together. But I had been thinking like an Athenian. I had forgotten that a Great King does not think logically. I should have known that he was determined to destroy the Acropolis even before he finished us off. There was no escaping that defiant crag. And *we* could see it from over the water. Until he had deprived us of that spiritual rallying point, until, and this was the thought to which he probably gave priority, the Maiden ceased to defy him, he would not rest.

The 'wooden walls' of the Acropolis were in reality a single palisade. There was only one point at the western end from which the defenders believed an attack could come, and this they had barricaded with planks and timbers. The Persians posted archers on the Areopagus rock opposite, they fired flaming arrows into the 'wooden wall', and set it alight. Then there was a pause. The collaborators, those Persian camp-followers, seemed to have come to their senses as belatedly as I had; only now they realised that Xerxes was out for complete destruction, temples as well as people. This – the destruction of the temples, I mean – shocked them. They nerved themselves and interceded for the buildings on the Acropolis. Destruction of a temple might instil a little superstitious uneasiness in Xerxes yet; he said he might spare the shrines if the defenders surrendered. But the surrender call was rejected, and the lese-majesté of the rejection killed any qualms Xerxes may have known. He ordered a direct assault on the western gate, but the defenders sent crashing down among his troops pillar drums from an unfinished building project.

I tell this dryly, but you must not think that I, any more than any other Athenian there on Salamis, straining eyes and ears for sight and sound of what happened across the strait, did not share the agony of those trapped on the rock, did not wonder, sick at heart, when the despair first began. Was it as early as the first sight of that immense cloud of dust drawing nearer across the plain, the dust (the voiceless herald, Aeschylus was to call it) of an army greater than any the world had seen, and then that thunderous trampling of a myriad feet? And everywhere Attica first ablaze, then blackened in the late summer sun. And then the enemy swarming through the familiar streets below.

Thirteen years later Aeschylus produced *The Seven Against Thebes*. The audience wept. They thought, not of the strife between the sons of Oedipus in the dawn of our history, but of something they themselves, like the play's author, had witnessed, and many of us had had relatives and friends to whom that dreadful army of invasion had been more than the distant gleam of spear-tips through the rolling dust. Perhaps it is better to recall it all as in the play thirteen years later, no real Acropolis to stare at, but a painted citadel at the back of a stage, the noises we heard no more than stage effects. The terrified chorus cling to the altars as they hear the shouts of the attackers, the thunder of horse-hooves – 'Do you hear – or do you not – the clash of shields?' cries one woman. 'The noise terrifies me!' cries another. They scream out at the clang of the horses' metal bits, at the noise of the chariots, and the shriek of the wooden axles*, and then the crash of heavy stones flung against the gate, and again the clang of shields, and it's not real, it's only a stage carpenter making a good job of it, it's only play-acting. And it's good literature when they cry of women dragged like unmastered horses by the hair, weep for the ravished, the torn flower – thirteen years have passed since that happened to the priestesses before their throats were cut, and the Acropolis blackened with the smoke of death. Better to think that the cruelty and insanity

* The axles of ancient chariots were made of wood, and wetted with water instead of oil.

227

and blasphemy of war is a clever concoction of words, and the trained voices of actors, and stagecraft, and not something that happened here, to people you knew.

The Persians found a way up the Acropolis. There is a recess in the cliff in the front part, to the rear of the gates, by the sanctuary of Aglauros the daughter of Cecrops. The rock is so sheer here that nothing had been done to guard it. But the Persians — did Xerxes lash them on against the poor defenders here as he had lashed them on against the locked shields of the Spartans at Thermopylae? — climbed the unclimbable as darkness fell.

Some of the garrison, seeing further resistance was hopeless, threw themselves off the rock, to be dashed to death below, with one exception. He only broke an ankle, kept his wits, held his tongue, lay for dead, and then dragged himself off somehow, into the shadows, disregarded, for now the storming party was opening the gates, the whole Persian army, it seemed, was rushing through the entrance, raging, yelling, boasting, laughing. And it was he who told me later of his last view of my father, crawling into the inner shrine of the temple, with death in his heart.

The Persians left him there, with the old and sick and crippled and wounded. They dragged out the priestesses. Later they tossed their bodies back into the temple, piled about it what remained of the wooden walls that had promised salvation, and set flames to the human and building débris they had wrecked and desecrated.

And we watched it all on Salamis. Did we curse and shriek and groan? No, we all sat silent, unmoving, as still as if we had been captured by the Persians, and crucified, pinned down by their spears to lie helpless watching our kinsfolk burn.

Almost I could swear I felt the heat, smelled the smoke.

Almost I thought I heard my trapped father scream.

One could, of course, see little very clearly. All that was visible at first was a dreadful confusion of smoke brightened from time to time by showers of burning ash, but then came flames galloping like beasts in great roaring gusts – I think that perhaps we did after all hear the crackle and roar of the blaze at its height, and told ourselves it was the beating of waves on the shore.

At one point I must have moved my head a little, for I can remember, quite clearly, the sight of row after row of faces – almost like faces in a theatre – but these were no more than stony masks transformed by that distant horror as once men had been petrified by the glance of a Medusa.

At last it ended. All that was left on the Acropolis was the reek of smoke and the reek of death. And as the glow of the flames began to die, the moon rose, calm radiance in the skies above, violent light matching violent death below. I pulled my cloak about me, for I was cold – on a late summer night in Attica.

Habronichos touched my shoulder. Cleandros had been conscious for a little while, and had asked for me. So I went to another death-bed.

He was unconscious again when I got to him. His sister looked up at me. She said, 'I think he's dying.'

Even if there had been no dim lamplight to show me his face, this would have been obvious from his breathing. I knelt at his side, opposite her.

'What has happened?' she asked. 'I heard shouting, but then no sound for hours.'

'They've taken the Acropolis and burned it.' After a moment I added, 'I don't think they left anyone alive.'

Cleandros muttered something. I could not catch what he said, but she did. 'Yes, my darling, I'm here,' she said.

He opened his eyes. 'Poor girl,' he said. 'Where's Theron?'
'I'm here.'

I bent so that my face was in the little circle of lamplight. He looked up at me. 'I shall die soon.'

I nodded. 'On the further bank, salute the King of Sparta for me.'

His eyes rested on his sister's face, then wistfully sought mine again.

'There's no one else I would ask,' he whispered.

'Don't worry,' I said.

He drifted off once more. There was a footstep outside, Themistocles put his head in, looked at me with a question in his eyes.

I got up to follow him. 'I have to go,' I said, 'but I'll come again when I can.'

She nodded.

I said, 'I'd forgotten your name. I didn't remember it until we reached Eleusis. I shan't forget it again.'

18

Themistocles was waiting outside. 'Adeimantos, in view of what he tactfully calls the changed situation, has asked Eurybiades to call a fresh council of war,' he said, expressionlessly. 'By the way, there's a ship for you. Euctemon got an arrow in his shoulder up north, and the wound's not healing, so you must take over.'

It was not a well-attended meeting – in fact, some allied commanders had been so demoralised by the capture of the Acropolis that they had hurried straight on board their ships, had hoisted sail, and were preparing for immediate flight. Of those who remained on land, a majority within minutes of the council opening passed a resolution 'to fight in defence of the Isthmus' – 'Which,' exclaimed Themistocles, 'amounts to the same thing. The only difference between you and those already on board ship is a matter of timing.' He took Eurybiades aside. 'With your permission, I'm going to speak my mind,' he said. Eurybiades shrugged; at least he realised he had as little chance of stopping Themistocles in that mood as he had of checking a volcano in full eruption. 'Once this fleet leaves Salamis, it will disintegrate,' said Themistocles. 'Your command will simply fall apart. There'll be no more talk of fighting for Greece – every ship will bolt for home, and there'll be nothing you or anyone else can do to stop it. And once they get home, the crews will scuttle off their ships to hide behind the city walls!'

Eurybiades stood chewing his thumb. No Spartan could relish the idea of a disintegrating command. 'I'll call a full conference,' he said. 'Get the commanders from their ships. No point in rushing into hasty decisions.'

As we waited, I muttered to Themistocles, 'My God, no need for secrecy or security now – the whole thing's blown wide open.

No use trying to pretend we're not as divided as hell. By the morning Xerxes will know, if he doesn't already –'

'Well,' said Themistocles surprisingly, 'if you find any Persian well-wisher creeping down to the shore, for God's sake don't think it's your sacred duty to break his neck, will you?'

The violent hostility at the reconvened meeting almost hit you in the face as you went in. Themistocles decided the only strategy was to go into the attack at once – he began to speak immediately he entered which brought fury from Eurybiades, that stickler for protocol. 'I haven't opened the proceedings yet!' he bawled, looking as if he were about to knock Themistocles down. 'Hit me, but let me have my say!' said Themistocles. Adeimantos, delighted to see Eurybiades turning on Themistocles, poured oil on the flames. 'Don't you know that a man who starts too soon in a race is flogged?' he jeered. 'Yes,' returned Themistocles, 'but if you're left at the post you've no chance of winning.'

Remember that a little while before he had seen the end on the Acropolis. Remember that most of us had been so stunned by shock and grief we could scarcely think, far less speak cogently. Remember that no man loved Athens more than did Themistocles, who now must be persuasive, convincing, level-headed in the face of constant interruptions, gibes and sneers. Remember those gibes and sneers when you read his argument – and marvel at the cool cogency of it.

'Very well, let's discuss the decision to sail south of the Isthmus. If you fight there, it will have to be on the open sea, and Xerxes won't send his fleet on ahead without land support. If the ships come, so will the soldiers. So when you talk about abandoning Salamis you're really saying you're prepared to take on the responsibility of drawing both the Persian navy and the Persian army down on the Peloponnese.

'I thought we had all accepted long ago that the open sea helps the enemy, a confined space helps us. With our inferior numbers, we *must* fight in narrow waters, and we shall win . . . Yes, I admit that my chief reason for saying we should stay and fight in Salamis is because of our women and children here on the island – should I be human otherwise? But *you* are defending your own people in the Peloponnese better by fighting here than if you withdrew south of the Isthmus. Wherever you go – without a fight – not only the Persian navy but the Persian army will follow you. But if Xerxes' navy's defeated here, it's only a question of time before his army's beaten. If his ships are destroyed, he'll start retreating –'

And so on.

It was, in its way, a continuation of the struggle he had been waging for years, both in content and in quality. Trying to induce rigid, military-obsessed minds to accept the paramount importance of command of the sea. God knows when he had last slept, he had seen the heart of Athens destroyed, weariness or weeping left his eyes red-rimmed, his broad shoulders sagged – but he went on arguing for hour after hour, logically, levelly. But reason was too fine a weapon to use. It was only a threat that began to crack the hostility. Eurybiades said suddenly. 'You've stopped saying "we"; it's always "you".'

Themistocles nodded. 'I'm glad you've noticed that. If you won't defend Athenians, why should we defend your people?'

'So you split from us!' Adeimantos. 'Are you going to fight Xerxes here single-handed?'

'No, but we'll look after our people single-handed. Priority given to getting them out of Xerxes' reach – leaving the rest of you to go to the devil in your own way.'

I don't know how far the majority of them believed him at this point – but, all-important, Eurybiades did. He was beginning to know Themistocles. He had also, I am convinced, been instructed by the Spartan authorities long before that at all costs Athenian naval co-operation must not be lost. He knew he was letting himself in for venomous private tirades from Adeimantos – the old ally being abandoned for the new, and so on – but he dared not risk the loss of the new ally's fleet. Yet he still hesitated. Themistocles took a step towards him and said in a low voice, 'If you move out, at least it will provide a new

233

spectacle for the two Athenians I've brought with me. The last time they saw Spartans in action, they weren't running.' Eurybiades stared across at Habronichos and me. His face went a dull red. Then the dead who died at Thermopylae made victory at Salamis possible. Slowly, grudgingly, but decisively, Eurybiades said loudly, 'We must stay where we are – for the time being, at least.' Even more loudly he continued, 'The meeting is adjourned.' Then, in typical Spartan fashion, as the crowd of furiously dissenting men began to stream away, he turned to Themistocles, and said that since if, after all, we might fight here we must first, while there was still time, send a ship to Aegina to bring to Salamis the sacred images of Aeacos himself and the other tutelary heroes of the island.

In his gratitude for Eurybiades' decision, Themistocles was more than willing to fall in with any excess of Spartan piety. 'You can have a thirty-oar galley,' he said, and then – the old humorous glint back in his eyes – he added, 'And why don't you ask Aristeides if he'll captain it?'

Eurybiades thought it a brilliant idea. So did Aristeides.

As we came away from the meeting, beneath us the earth gave a prolonged shudder. Almost you could believe that you stood on the pitching deck of a ship in a gale. Before us a great column of water spouted up from the sea. The galleys not drawn up on the beach danced crazily. Everywhere there were shouts of alarm. But there was only that one tremor, and within moments the panic was over. And for the Athenians, exultation took its place. Poseidon, Earth-shaker, ruler of the sea, had told us not to forget him.

But the mood of the other contingents was different. Many of them had been aboard their ships, ready to make for home, when Eurybiades had called the fresh conference. Now their commanders told them they must stay after all – but without concealing their own opinion that the decision was suicidal. At first crews stood about in silent groups, then whispers began, spread, finally the three inlets where the ships were based were

alive with furious voices. Eurybiades was out of his mind. He
was condemning us all to destruction. We should get out while
there was still time. Why fight for a land already lost when at any
moment the Persians would be moving on against the Peloponnese? Here we were helpless, caught in a trap . . . and then
someone uttered one word – 'Starvation' and that word was
caught up, passed on, voiced ever more loudly. Xerxes didn't
even have to fight us if we stayed here. He simply had to wait
until we were starved into surrendering.

So it went on all through the morning; the whole Peloponnesian contingent of the fleet seethed with rage, suspicion,
unrest. Our own contingent, with those of Megara and Aegina,
remained aloof, little islands of resolution in a boiling sea of fury.
'We'll be starved out!' the Peloponnesians shouted. 'Starved
into surrendering!' Their commanders laid siege to Eurybiades
with the same arguments. He could find nothing to refute this,
so sent for Themistocles. Themistocles said, tersely, 'Xerxes
hasn't the time to starve us out. What about his own supply
position? And how long before the autumn gales begin?'

'Then he'll by-pass us and make for the Peloponnese.'

'He's based his whole campaign on combined operations. He
won't send his army off without the fleet. He won't send the
fleet as long as we're here. That alone justifies our being here –
we're effectively checking the advance on the Isthmus.'

'He could detach part of the fleet.'

'Never. That's the other factor on which he's based his
entire campaign. Complete numerical superiority.'

If this is repetitious, imagine the effect on a physically
exhausted man of having, hour after hour, to go over the same
points, contest the same arguments. The heat was atrocious. In
the mid-morning we managed to get him to go off and snatch
some sleep. I went down to my new ship, and talked to the crew.

In the late morning the rage and panic reached its height. The
road to Eleusis and Megara and Corinth, that road so often
taken by Themistocles in the past months, runs close to the
coast. Suddenly, from Salamis, men saw a cloud of dust moving

along it, moving fast. Cavalry. At that all hell broke loose. Adeimantos and others came storming to Eurybiades. 'They're making for Corinth! They're cutting us off! Now are you satisfied? We're rats in a trap!' The noise itself was enough to rouse Themistocles. He plunged his face into a bowl of cold water, towelled himself dry, hurried to stiffen Eurybiades' nerve. I remember how his dark-red hair stuck up in wet spikes all over his head. 'It's a feint,' he said. 'Just a feint to make you think we're cut off. Are you going to fall for such a trick?'

'It wasn't a big dust cloud,' agreed Eurybiades. In as low a voice as a Spartan could manage, he said to Themistocles, 'We can't let things go on like this. If the enemy get any idea of the —' he swallowed hard — 'dissension here —'

'A damned good thing if they do. Nothing like it for giving a false sense of confidence.'

Eurybiades was not listening. 'And we can't hold these much longer. If I don't give the order to evacuate, they'll be taking themselves off —'

'You mean that rather than have them disobeying a Spartan you'll fall in with their ideas?'

Themistocles stalked off. We followed him.

'He's weakening again,' said Habronichos. 'I give him another forty-eight hours.'

'Are you surprised? I've always told you the average Spartan's the timidest fellow on earth north of the Isthmus.'

'And he's a *very* average Spartan. My God, and it all depends on him!'

'Well,' said Themistocles, 'as I've said before, don't let's forget the enemy has his difficulties too. Over there everything depends on Xerxes — think of that. At least Eurybiades isn't vanity gone mad. I'm off to resume my slumber. Come to me in an hour.'

'He won't sleep, you know,' said Habronichos. 'That mind of his will go on trying to find solutions.'

I doubted whether any solution would be found.

I went back to my new ship. The crew were expressing loud

doubts as to the ancestry of Adeimantos and the Corinthians – particularly their paternity.

The Ionian Tyrrhastiadas came in search of me, and asked if he might serve in my ship if there were an engagement. I was glad to see him, someone non-Athenian who nevertheless was absolutely committed. We sat in the shadow of the ship, and talked of his plans for the future. He said he might make a home in Athens, once his family had joined him. 'If there remains any Athens,' I said. 'You know that if we're lucky, I'll help all I can; if we're not lucky, then it'll be Sicily and starting from scratch for both of us.'

'There could be worse prospects,' he said. He spoke of his wife and twin children, a boy and a girl, both small. He seemed to love the girl particularly; she reminded him of his sister, taken by the Persians when the Ionian revolt had collapsed. 'I don't know what became of her; I hope she's dead; we were very close.'

After that we sat staring at the channel – a mile wide, just over three miles long, the area of decision, decision whether all free Greece would follow his Ionia.

And other girls follow his sister.

'There are some men,' said Themistocles, 'who suffer from a peculiar affliction of the eyes. They can't distinguish things very well in the dark.'

I said I believed this was so.

'Believe? You know it. From personal experience. *You're* partially blind at night. At least, you're going to be victim to a temporary attack this evening.'

I thought at first that fatigue had affected his wits. But his voice was crisp and, whether he had slept or not, his eyes had lost their weariness. Perhaps I was the one to be befuddled with tiredness.

Then I thought my eyes as well as my hearing had been affected – though not in the way Themistocles had alleged. Behind him stood one of the last people I should have expected to see at that moment – his children's tutor, Sicinnos. His mild, scholarly face could never have seemed more incongruous than against that background of armed men, flushed faces, voices upraised in argument, the air seeming to vibrate with anger.

'I thought you were in Aegina with the children!' I exclaimed.

'He was,' said Themistocles, 'but I've a fond wife, so he volunteered to come to find out what was happening to me. And he's the reason why you're going to be blind tonight.' He was now speaking in a low voice, and lowered it still further as he continued, 'And here the need for real security starts.'

We sat on his flagship. The guards who sprawled about in the sun seemed negligent enough, but no one would have been permitted to get within earshot. From appearances Themistocles, maddeningly unconventional as usual, was taking time off to give his children's tutor instructions concerning their education, ended with writing a letter to be taken to his wife. But the instructions were nothing to do with education, and the letter was addressed to the last recipient in the world you might expect. It was a letter to Xerxes.

'We've two problems needing solution,' he said to us. 'I think I've found the answer to both. We have to stop a mass retreat to the Peloponnese, and we have to find a way of making sure that Xerxes attacks us where we want him to. And Sicinnos is going to do the job for us.'

'Sicinnos!' Sicinnos, like any god or goddess at Troy, restraining Adeimantos, inspiring Eurybiades, Sicinnos putting into Xerxes' mind what we wanted him to do – we gaped at his unassuming figure.

'Perhaps I haven't put it very well,' said Themistocles. 'God knows I'll never underestimate what Sicinnos is going to do, but what's really going to crack this nut for us is Xerxes' own vanity.'

He outlined his plan. 'There is to be another council this evening. We can guess what's going to happen. I shall openly display disgust as I make my way there. I have no doubt that news of this will be carried to Xerxes. And so, when a few hours

238

later my children's tutor comes over carrying a letter from me – guard your expressions! – intimating complete disillusion with our allies, and belated recognition of the fact that on the whole I hate the guts of Sparta and Corinth more than I hate the guts of Persia –'

'He'll never fall for it!' I whispered.

'I think he will. Thank God in this case for the Thebans and other collaborators – how's he to know we're any different from them? Remember the man's colossal vanity – it will never occur to him that anyone would ever try to fool him. And remember something else. He'll *want* to believe it. He wants to finish the whole business off quickly – he's been out of Persia too long, delay, frustration are things he can't endure. *And remember that his mind's been prepared for this by what happened at Thermopylae.* There, too, an impossible situation – the same frustration, delay – was solved by the opportune arrival of a traitor. *We'd* call it a miracle; *he* thinks it the kind of thing to be expected by a Great King. The gods look after their own.'

'But there's all the difference in the world between a disgruntled peasant and you!'

'Not in Xerxes' eyes! My dear fellow – what kind of idea do you think he has of us Greeks? Think of the exiles who've cluttered his court and his father's court as long as he can remember! Think of the collaborators he's found in Thessaly and Thebes! Why should I be any different? And haven't I had to take orders from a blockhead of a Spartan and swallow insults from a swine of a Corinthian?'

'Right,' said Habronichos after a moment, 'he'll accept the fact that you've turned traitor. But he's hardly likely to hand over to you the conduct of his campaign.'

'Granted. But if I know anything of the man I expect only one reaction to the news I shall be sending him.'

'What news?'

'That we're disunited, demoralised, defeatist – so much so that the decision taken at the council this evening is to break out while we can, and go hell for leather for the Peloponnese. It being too late to start the operation tonight, we'll do it under cover of darkness tomorrow. The aim will be to link up with the land forces south of the Isthmus. By the time we get there, some kind of order and discipline may be restored, but at present we're a panicky lot, and the predominating idea is every man for himself.'

'So it will be up to him to stop us as soon as possible?'

'I shall make no suggestions; who am I to offer ideas to the Great King? But I think the notion may occur to him – or to his staff.'

'And he'll try to stop us – here?'

'Theron, you've *spoken* with the man. He'll never let us get away – and, by God, he'll want to see it all happening. So it'll happen here – in Salamis Strait. He'll block the two exits overnight.'

'He could try to starve us out,' said Habronichos, but without conviction, as Themistocles remarked.

'He wants a quick kill. He'll block both channels, which will give even the Corinthians no option but to stand and fight. After which perhaps they'll listen to what I suggest – a feigned breakout northwards towards the Bay of Eleusis. Panic when we find the Megara Channel blocked, and feigned retreat. And *they* won't be able to resist the temptation. They'll come in after us – from that exit and from the other. And then we shall have them just where we want 'em.'

We sat silent. Then Habronichos said, 'It should work.' He turned to Sicinnos. 'You're a very brave man.'

Sicinnos said in his precise, elderly voice, 'I am an Ionian Greek. My own people were once free.'

'And you'll be free again,' said Themistocles. 'Have no fear. Go and get some sleep now; you've a long night ahead of you.'

I began to argue as soon as Sicinnos had gone. 'Can't someone else go? To row across – to row back, let's face it, Sicinnos, though brave as a lion, could be younger. Let me go! It would be plausible enough – I had that invitation from Xerxes himself, didn't I?'

'No,' said Themistocles. 'You'd have no chance of coming away safely. You'd be taken straight to Xerxes, and he'd keep you by him, and I hate to think what would happen to you when he realised he'd been fooled. Sicinnos' great chance of safety lies in the fact that he's a slave. They're not to know he's a highly intelligent man, treated as one of the family. He's going to act the part of a two-legged animal, trained to obey orders, not to think. Fairly easy for him to slip away after giving the message; impossible, I think, for anyone else. Now, this is what I've planned. He'll take a boat . . .'

It was a very long night. We had passed word to our men, who ignored the dim figure taking a boat, rowing slowly but steadily away into the darkness. There was another conference; Themistocles and Habronichos were attending it, I remained on the beach straining eyes and ears long before it was humanly possible for Sicinnos to get back, seeing the black outline of the little boat, hearing the faint splash of the oars a score of times.

It all depended on three factors.

Xerxes' vanity – who would dare to fool him?

Xerxes' liking for quick results – delay, frustration, maddened him.

Xerxes' belief in his conquering destiny – a disgruntled peasant had shown him the track over the mountains at Thermopylae. Now again a disgruntled Greek offered him the chance of greater victory. And this was the proper nature of things.

And we were such a jealous, disorganised rabble, always at each other's throats, with no loyalty but to self-interest.

It was a long night.

Twice Habronichos left the conference, came down to the beach, whispered, 'No news?'

'Not a sign of him. How are things going?'

'We've a breathing space. About twenty-four hours, I'd say. Themistocles is outdoing even the Spartans in simple piety. Now that we've sent for the images of the tutelary heroes of

Salamis we can't clear out before they've been brought here. Aristeides should get back after dark. Eurybiades is taking it all very seriously. If we snub the heroes, there may be a nasty storm on the way back to the Peloponnese.'

The chain of the Persian Higher Command was a lengthy one. How long would it be before the news was given to Xerxes? Would they dare rouse him with the news? How long before Sicinnos could slip away? He'd have to escape in darkness; dawn wasn't so far off now. And even if – when – he came back with the news that the letter had been safely delivered, we shouldn't know until tomorrow night if the bait had been taken.

Another twenty-four hours.

Could Themistocles hold them?

Would Xerxes take the bait?

Sicinnos came back just before dawn. A whisper of oars, a solid blur in the dimness – I sprinted down the beach like an Olympic champion, grabbed the boat, hauled it in.

'Done?' I whispered.

'Done,' came a tired, elderly, triumphant voice. 'After I'd seen it passed to a cousin of Xerxes – and had observed the general reaction – I thought it safe to slip away.'

'And the general reaction?'

'Exultation is almost an understatement. An immense amount of shrieking, waving of arms, high-pitched laughter.'

'So they think they've got us!'

'Yes. And, judging from their reactions, so will their master.'

I gave him my arm, and took him to Themistocles' ship, made my own way to Eurybiades' headquarters. I found that Themistocles had taken up a position so that he faced the door. I did my best to make my expression non-committal but his eyes, meeting mine the moment I entered, read their message clearly enough. He gave a little sigh.

'It is agreed then,' Eurybiades was saying, 'we'll wait only for the return of the images, then, after paying them proper reverence, we decide whether we stay or go south.'

242

'It must be decided finally tomorrow night,' said Adeimantos. 'We must have cover of darkness for the evacuation. And to stay for more than twenty-four hours will be suicide.'

Themistocles began to remonstrate angrily – then started to yawn, great, cracking yawns, apologised. The general reaction was relief. If he were so fatigued, there'd be no more argument. And so the meeting broke up, and the moment we were outside, he whispered to me, as I had whispered to Sicinnos, 'Done?' and, as Sicinnos had replied, I answered in my turn, 'Done.'

19

So now all that we could do was wait. Eurybiades called another conference in the late morning to appoint a committee to establish, as he put it, the amount of foodstuffs remaining on Salamis. Adeimantos, who had probably prompted the idea, grinned happily when the project received general approval, although he seemed taken aback when Themistocles raised no opposition. Themistocles, in fact, was delighted that Eurybiades had discovered something to keep everybody occupied during the hours of daylight. By the time they'd discovered how little food there was, indeed, on the island, the choice of fighting or fleeing would be out of their hands.

As we came away from the meeting, a hand touched my arm. Hormos, commander of the trireme Cleandros had once sailed in. 'I hoped I'd catch you. Cleandros died some hours ago. They've burned his body.'

Themistocles was a few paces ahead of me. I overtook him; 'I want just a little time off – Cleandros is dead.'

'A little time, yes. But send word to your ship.'

I sent word.

There is a bay so small, so strewn with rocks that even the most desperate evacuee had not thought of pitching a tent there. She was sitting on one of the rocks. The look in her eyes was the look I had seen before; she was seeing things over and done with and past all help now.

I briefly spoke to her averted face. 'I've heard. I can't offer to do, or even say much, because I'm needed back at the ships, but whatever I can –'

Had she heard me? She had not turned to look at me. It

seemed as if I had always known the precise, graceful way the small dark head balanced on the slight shoulders.

The sun beat down and here in crowded Salamis we were quite alone in the tiny bay and seemingly surrounded by silence except for the sound of the waves breaking at our feet.

And I must go back to the ships.

'What can I do for you?' I asked.

She turned to me then with a sudden violence that was almost shocking. 'If we are defeated, I can't expect a miracle to happen again. Give me a knife, and show me how to use it. I won't be captured alive.'

Sense enough. I gave her my dagger. 'Put the point here. Aim upwards a little. If you've courage enough, lean forward on the blade.'

'I shan't be afraid.'

'When you're wounded, you feel the steel cold at first, then the hurt comes; if you're resolute, there should be little pain.'

'I am not afraid of the pain.'

There was life enough in her now.

A wave slapped at our feet, the sun beat down, we were alone in the little bay, but it was a double isolation, of time as well as of space. We should have been alone if we had stood in a crowded market place, and this moment was quite isolated in time too, quite apart from my old life. It might be the beginning of a new life, but whatever happened it would always remain quite separate, like the pass through a mountain joining two deep valleys. My heart thudded, the blood rushed through my veins as if I were charging with the phalanx, standing in the prow of my ship with the crew bending to their oars to send the trireme racing forward, it was as glorious and alarming as all this, but there was one great difference. The other excitements were productive of death; this might be productive of the opposite.

I took the dagger from her. 'I stand here showing you how to kill yourself, teaching you death. If we win, let me come back and show you life.'

I wanted to touch her more than anything else in the world –

245

but then I remembered our first meeting, her passionate outburst when we had talked of *The Suppliant Women*. My hands dropped to my side, and I stepped backward. I said, 'I'm sorry. I had forgotten how you feel about women defenceless against man's greater strength — ' I turned to go.

I thought I heard her sob, and swung round to apologise again.

She was laughing. She quoted — from *The Suppliant Women* — '*Doth woman dread the yoke of one she loves?*' And: 'I should never be afraid of your greater strength,' said Cleisidice.

I was laughing, too, and moving forward.

'I should glory in it!' she whispered, and came to me.

The kiss was an unqualified success. An embrace in full armour, however, leaves little mental impression on the man, encased like a human lobster, and probably too much physical impression on the girl, leaving her black and blue. I took her face between my hands.

'When we marry,' I said, 'I shan't always be in armour.'

That was all the time I had. I must go back to the ships.

As I came up out of the little bay I looked back.

She was kneeling, and was raising her hand, half-wonderingly, to her lips.

It was then for the first time I experienced something I have experienced with increasing frequency ever since — the ability to know exactly what she is thinking.

I called to her. 'Cleisidice! It *did* happen!'

She sprang up. A little gust of wind, allied with her rapid movement, caught her dress straining behind her in tempestuous folds. She looked like a statue of Victory alighting on earth.

Her voice came clearly.

'I am glad you told me, for ever since you came striding across the meadow with the sun on your face I began to dream of it, and even more so since I saw you again with the sun on your face, and I ran to you. So I could not believe it was true now!'

Salamis

'Well,' said Themistocles, looking up, 'obviously it's happened.'

'What do you mean?'

'Equally obviously,' he continued, ignoring my question, 'it's been going to happen ever since you came back from that crazy trip of yours.'

I said in that case it had been more obvious to him than it had been to me.

'Of course. You weren't able to see the change in yourself. You were a walking mental casualty after Thermopylae; I didn't think you'd be much use to yourself or anyone else — otherwise I shouldn't have spared you to go galloping off as you did. And luckily for all concerned you were given the opportunity to play Perseus, since when you haven't looked back. Well, I'm damned glad for a variety of reasons, having said

247

which, let me invite you to put yourself in Xerxes' royal shoes and have a guess at what he's planning now.'

I tried to put myself in Xerxes' royal shoes. It should have been difficult; it wasn't. I had wits enough to appreciate that if we couldn't put ourselves in Xerxes' shoes, Cleisidice would have little opportunity of donning a saffron marriage veil.

So we scrutinised the contents of Themistocles' letter as we hoped the Persians were doing. And what he had written must surely stand up to scrutiny.

How would it read to them? That the Greeks were in no mood to fight. They had offered no challenge to the Persian squadrons ever since they had come down to Phaleron. If cornered, they would surrender. And if they planned to leave Salamis, obviously the withdrawal would be made at night, when the Persian squadrons gave up their patrol and put in to harbour. And the direction of the break-out was equally obvious. Up to this moment the Greeks had been able to keep in touch with Aegina and the Isthmus from the Western Bay through the western channel. It was the only way they could go.

The other question was timing. The previous night had been unexpectedly dark, because of clouds, but tonight there should be a full moon. If the fugitives hoped to avoid pursuit, they must be well into the Saronic Gulf before their escape was detected – six hours' hard rowing at least. If the break-out were to remain a secret, it could not commence before dusk; midnight would be the crucial time because then the fleeing vessels might barely have passed the southernmost point of Salamis itself – and by this time the moon might be at its full.

But long before this, the Persian squadrons would have sealed off the western channel.

'Can't you imagine,' said Themistocles, 'the King of All Men saying as only He Who Must Be Obeyed can say it, "And remember! The whole success of the operation depends on complete secrecy!" And a courtier will leap up and say, "But that will be no problem, Majesty! Those Greeks – always ready to betray each other. But *your* ever-loyal subjects –" '

248

'No doubt,' said Habronichos, 'but I'm also imagining a scene not so far away as that. I've a feeling that, as we're visualising a hypothetical break-out — as seen through Persian eyes — Adeimantos has worked out precisely the same details in grim earnest, and as oldest ally is probably arguing the case before Eurybiades at this very moment.'

'And I'm relying on my ally Xerxes to see to it that the plan never develops beyond the hypothetical,' said Themistocles calmly.

And indeed it all depended on Xerxes now. There was nothing we could do but wait until nightfall, when we might find out whether he was prepared to win our fight for us. As soon as it was dusk, Habronichos and I would take our ships very cautiously and quietly, the one to the east, the other to the west, to find out if indeed he were playing our game for us. Themistocles by this time would be attending what we prayed would be the last conference — at which Adeimantos would report triumphantly that stocks of food were running low and reproach Eurybiades for unSpartan activities in defying the orders of the Panhellenic Congress. But if Xerxes played his part, it would not matter in the least even if Eurybiades lost his nerve and ordered immediate withdrawal.

It all depended on Xerxes. Would he remember how another traitor had enabled him to attack another Greek force at both front and rear soon after another dawn?

20

It was a very long, a very hot afternoon, as blistering as it seemed endless. The pitch ran between the planks, but oddly enough I kept thinking of other scents, fresh, young scents. I remembered – and this was something I had not remembered from childhood – the smell of a woman's hair, it must have been my mother's, newly washed. Thyme-scented. And other scents, and this again must have been recollection of my mother. Jasmine and whitethorn. I remembered then that you put wreaths of these along the lintels of a door for a marriage. God only knew under what circumstances my own – no, our own marriage would take place.

I remembered the words of the wedding hymn; '*Bad have I fled, better have I found . . .*'

'Share the joke,' said Habronichos.

'Not a joke. Appreciation of the truth would be nearer to it.'

The sun was still high in the sky.

'God,' I said, 'how this afternoon drags.'

'Spoken like a true prospective bridegroom,' said Habronichos, his mouth twitching. 'Nervous waiting for the night.'

'Themistocles,' I said without resentment, 'must have talked.'

'Themistocles didn't have to talk. I've never seen a fellow return from a visit of condolence with *that* look in his eyes before.'

But at last it was dusk. Themistocles had gone off to his conference; I wondered enviously if the man had a single nerve in his body. Habronichos had gone aboard his ship; I was stepping aboard mine. We had warned our own crews what we were looking for, hoping for. Their faces had lit up. An end to waiting. A prospect of getting to grips with the enemy who had burned the Acropolis, driven their families into terrified exile,

ravaged Attica. There was a kind of murderous exultation in us
as we swung carefully, quietly along the narrow channel towards
the still-luminous west. And there they were, just rounding
Cape Petritis. They could not see us, but for one brief moment
we saw them outlined against the western sky, and then the last
glow of light had gone, the sea before us was completely dark,
but a blind man would have known that a great fleet was there
in the distance. We heard the splash of oars, the hum of voices;
once a gong boomed.

The phosphorescent water was patterned by their oar-strokes.
So it would go on all night. 'Well, boys,' I said in a low voice,
'we've seen what we've come to see. We'll go back now to report,
and get some sleep while those silly bastards take up their
positions, then patrol up and down all night. They'll be feeling
like hell in the morning.'

Habronichos was waiting for me; we had thought it best to
make a joint entry with our momentous news. He grinned at me
with savage cheerfulness. 'Sealed off!' he said. 'Masts thick as a
wood. The same with you?'

'They were just beginning to come into Western Bay, should
be in the Megara Channel now. Dozens of them.'

We found we were gripping each other's hands, stammering
in ecstasy, 'He's *fallen* for it! *Fallen* for it!'

'I've told my people no need to ration the supper tonight,' I
said.

'Quite right. It'll all be over and done with by this time
tomorrow. Do you know, when I actually *saw* them there –'

'Like a dream coming true? I know. I could have yelled my
head off with delight.'

'Same here. And do you know what I remembered? You and
me at Delphi – and the second prophecy, Salamis and the
wooden wall. By God, it's been a long trip and a rough trip
since we were there, but I think we've finally made it.'

Adeimantos had proved conclusively that, since the food

251

supply on the island was to all intents and purposes non-existent, we had only two alternatives before us – to make for safety or to stay and be starved into surrender.

Eurybiades had declared that while we could still communicate with Corinth, he intended to send off a swift galley that night to get definite orders. If those orders were for evacuation, they would be carried out regardless –

'Sorry,' said Habronichos, entering with me at his heels, 'they can't. You can't even send for them.'

'Who says I can't send for them?' said Eurybiades, puffing up like a bullfrog.

'Xerxes,' said Habronichos, dropping into the vacant seat by Themistocles. 'He's blocked both of the channels.'

But they would not believe us. No doubt the fact that we were close to Themistocles had much to do with it. They refused to accept that the western exit had been blocked. In fact, although my furious repetitions that I had seen a large part of Xerxes' fleet rounding Cape Petritis left them partially convinced, it was not in our favour. I might have seen the enemy ships, but I'd seen them at the most deceptive time of all, between dusk and darkness, and I'd mistaken their direction. 'They're not bearing north!' blared Adeimantos. 'They're running west – to Corinth as I've always said they would! Why in the hell should they do otherwise?'

I looked at Themistocles, wondering if he would tell them of his ruse. He gave a slight, almost imperceptible shake of the head. Sense enough. They'd never believe a word of it.

'Send your own ships to see, then!' I flared.

And suddenly Eurybiades launched into a speech. Nothing was to be done until he'd received fresh instructions. He should never have disobeyed instructions in the first place and come to Salamis. Disobedience to orders – that was not the Spartan way of doing things.

'Even if they're the wrong orders,' I shouted. 'Yes, I've seen something of that!'

In the ensuing uproar, Themistocles dragged me out of the

hubbub of furious men. He clapped me on the shoulder, and said under his breath, 'Burn with rage if you like – I can't afford to be angry. Anger kills judgment.'

'It's not only the Corinthian bastard – Eurybiades gave tongue too, didn't he? An eye-opener. Wonderful how a little stomach-churning fear can help eloquence.'

'You're unfair to him. He isn't a coward, and he isn't a villain. Being a Spartan, he's simply cautious.'

'Cautious? As if anyone can afford to be cautious now!'

'Oh, of course, of course,' he said half-absently. 'This has gone on long enough – too long. But you'd better get a breath of fresh air, and cool down in every sense. I tell you, anger won't help.'

Outside, I walked up and down – endlessly, it seemed. The stars were pale; dawn was not far off. A man came hurrying out of the darkness, recognised me in the little pool of light in which I stood, gripped my arm.

'Theron! Where's Themistocles? I must see Themistocles!'

Aristeides, whom I had never thought to hear expressing any desire for meeting Themistocles – whom I had never thought to see in that particular state of mind. A kind of mental dishevelment.

'He's trying to convince Eurybiades –' I began, and he interrupted me with, 'However much he and the Corinthians want to retreat, the decision's no longer theirs. The enemy are drawn up outside the western entrance to the Straits. You know I was sent to Aegina –'

I could not help saying, 'That didn't involve reconnoitring the enemy fleet.'

'No risk,' he said. 'I sailed up past Cape Petritis, turned into Western Bay, came across by foot. They were outlined against the moon; we were invisible under the coast of the island.'

'I still think it showed nerve.'

He considered, then said, 'I don't think anyone could have felt brave at the sight of what seemed the greater part of the Persian navy. But I must see Themistocles – the sight of our people *sleeping* –'

'It's all right,' I said, 'we've not been caught unprepared. Themistocles said that our men might as well have the advantage of a few hours' sleep, while the Persians were wakeful throughout the night.'

'Oh!' said Aristeides flatly. 'I hadn't realised. In that case, there's no point in my —'

'Indeed there is,' I said. 'I'll get Themistocles now!'

They were going at it hammer and tongs when I went back inside, just in time to hear Adeimantos, scarlet-faced with rage, spitting at Themistocles, 'You're no longer a man with a country, so keep your mouth shut, refugee!'

'I am the commander of the Athenian fleet,' Themistocles said evenly, 'and so I can find a city wherever I choose. Before God, if you're not prepared to defend our families, I'll embark them tomorrow, and sail for Italy. Why in the hell should Athenian ships be prepared to defend you, when neither your armies nor your fleets — such as they are — will do anything to defend us? Xerxes will be only too pleased to see the back of us — he knows, if you don't, that you're finished without our ships. He'll grant us an armistice for the asking if it'll get us out of the way.'

There was dead silence.

He sat down. 'So now perhaps you understand the position — at last,' he said to no one in particular.

Adeimantos found his voice. 'You're not asking us, you're *ordering* us now.'

'Not quite accurate — demanding is the better word. For let it be clearly understood — the moment for Athenian *requests* is over.'

I caught a mutter, 'He has us by the throat.'

Eurybiades had heard it too. 'And he's capable of shaking you by the throat until he gets what he wants,' he said grimly. So Themistocles had finally won him over.

'We must have time to discuss this new development,' said Adeimantos.

I plucked at Themistocles' arm. 'Come outside.'

'*Now?*'

'It's important – may make all the difference.'

'What?' he grumbled. 'Is Xerxes out there offering me the entrée to his harem?'

'No, Aristeides –'

'Aristeides? The last man to have a harem –'

'He's seen the enemy ships at the western entrance –'

'Ah!' said Themistocles. 'I see. Yes, by all means let's see him.'

I had almost liked Aristeides at the end of our first conversation. The sight of Themistocles, however, seemed to transport him from the darkness of Salamis back to noonday on the speaker's platform. I found myself, half incredulously, listening to oratory.

'. . . as we have been rivals in the past,' Aristeides concluded, 'now let us be rivals – especially now! – as to which of us can best serve his country!'

After Corinthian malice, and Spartan incomprehension, Aristeidean rhetoric might well have been the last straw as far as Themistocles was concerned. Instead, I think it came as welcome light relief. I, who knew him, could interpret the signs – nothing so overt as a hastily suppressed grin, but the wry lifting of an eyebrow in my direction, the unThemistoclean pompousness with which he prefixed his reply when Aristeides eventually reported what he had seen. 'I would not have chosen to be outdone by you –' he commenced, but after a few more sentences in this vein he got down to business. 'This bottling up is what I wanted – in fact, I had something to do with bringing it about. But thank God you've come – I still can't be sure that the fellows inside will listen to me when I say Xerxes has solved our problem for us, but you'll carry weight, they won't doubt what you say, because even Adeimantos can't think I've put you up to it.'

He and Aristeides went in hurriedly. I remained outside, not wishing to be exposed to a fresh blast of oratory. I was thinking of the commanders of the Persian fleet, growing hourly wearier

—and surely hourly more uneasily aware that they had been fooled? But they could do nothing about it—even if they had been Greeks, they could not get messages through to scattered squadrons in the darkness in time to get eighty thousand tired men ashore to snatch food, a little sleep, re-embark them before we had streamed off in God knew what direction. But above all, these were the subjects of the Great King. It was not for them to make decisions; above all, it was not for them to disobey orders issued by the royal Commander-in-Chief. That would be literally as much as their lives were worth. I suppose that any intelligent Persian commander soon realised that really he had no choice, he could obey orders and commit suicide, or he could disobey orders and have his head lopped off.

So they were getting progressively more tired, and more depressed. The crucial period would come with the dawn, when spirits are always at their lowest. *Then*—if Themistocles could win this preliminary battle in the council of war—we must attack.

If he could win this first battle.

For the second time that night I was hailed from the darkness. Tyrrhastiadas. He said with an odd catch of his breath, 'No need to cram me into your ship—I've been offered a place in another one,' and drew forward a dark-haired man on whose face weariness vied with excitement. 'Panaetios of Tenos,' said Tyrrhastiadas. 'He's made a better job of it than I did—he's brought his galley over with him. And he's fresh from a top-level Persian conference.'

I could have hugged the pair of them. In fact, I think I actually did hug the pair of them, but the next five excited minutes were blurred as I dragged them both into the conference.

I don't know whether Themistocles would have won without Panaetios' entrance; he might have managed it, because the first thing I can clearly remember of that lamplit scene was Adeimantos' face—hard black eyes now less inexorable, the facial muscles seeming looser. I could have sworn that his heavy fist had not thudded on the table since I had last been there. I think he was beginning to realise that the feeling of the meeting was against him, and was not liking it.

I believe, from Aristeides' high, indignant stare, that Adeimantos had indeed professed to detect some collusion between him and Themistocles, but the Corinthian had not been able to carry his colleagues with him.

And then I ushered in an honest-to-God patriot who had come over to us. Even Adeimantos could not profess to see an Athenian agent in Panaetios.

But, listening to Panaetios, I soon forgot Adeimantos. Xerxes had made up his mind by mid-morning. He had completely accepted that we would attempt to slip away by night. We were cowards, who'd done the same thing at Artemision. But this time we would sail into a death-trap.

The council of war working out the details of the death-trap had gone on until late in the afternoon. Then the orders had come thick and fast. The Egyptian squadron, one of the four already cruising off the eastern channel, had been ordered to sail westwards round Cape Petritis to block the Megara Channel. Two more squadrons were to close up on either side of the little island of Psyttalia, another to patrol off the southern coast. Four hundred troops had been landed just before dusk on Psyttalia to deal with the crews from our wrecked ships who would be carried on to it.

This brought the first interruption. And it was Themistocles' fist that crashed on to the table. 'Got them, by God! He's going to force a battle in the narrows!'

There was a sudden frenzy of excitement. I remember that the Aeginetan admiral hit Themistocles on the back, the commander of the squadron from Megara was wringing his hand. Someone – whom I don't know, could it have been *Aristeides?* – hurled a honey cake into the air above his head. Finally Eurybiades came to his senses and bawled a Spartan order for quiet.

Xerxes' only fear was that his superb planning might not be

equally superbly carried out. He therefore followed his usual tactics. If the Greeks got away, every captain would lose his head.

By midnight each squadron was to be in position. They were sealing off the western entrance to the Bay of Eleusis, patrolling the Saronic Gulf, and blocking the whole channel as far as Munychia. Now it was only a question of waiting for the demoralised, squabbling enemy to come trailing out in complete confusion.

'They'll be straining their eyes in the darkness throughout the night, bearing in mind his threat.'

'What were they planning to do – simply to wait for us to come straggling out, then finish us off piecemeal?'

'At first. Then of course, your ships bringing up the rear would realise what was happening, and would crowd back. You would be finished off when it was light – not before, because Xerxes wants to see it happening. In fact, the kill won't begin until the signal has been given that he's comfortably on his throne, watching.'

'*Watching*!' blared Eurybiades, every Spartan instinct bawling out in revolt.

'From his gold and ivory throne on – what is it? – Mount Aegaleos.'

For a moment I was miles away to the north. He had watched another battle from that gold and ivory throne.

Then I was back in the present. Eurybiades sat brooding, his lower lip thrust forward. After a moment he said, 'One thing we'll have to bear in mind. They'll fight better than they did at Artemision now that their king's watching them.'

And Themistocles allowed himself the luxury of good, clean anger at last. 'And how in the hell do you think the Athenians will fight, with their wives and children watching *them*?' he blazed.

Wives and children, I thought. That might reduce our motives for fighting well to nothing more than the mere instinct of any beast fighting for his mate and whelps, but I did not think so. I still do not think so. In fact, I believe it added a further dimension to what we could and would endure, what we could and would accomplish. Until a short time before I had been prepared to die for the freedom of the City, and before dying I should have fought as well as I was able. But now I knew that when the clash came I should have another picture very clear in my mind. A girl with a dagger in her hand. Every Persian confronting me I should see as bringing that dagger inching closer and closer to her breast. So any Persian before me this day would need all the help his barbaric gods could give him if he hoped to be still alive at nightfall.

Perhaps no better than the instinctive feeling of the male animal after all. But nothing can be more formidable than the male animal fighting in defence of his mate.

Now it was all enormously simple. There they were, most of them, with their prows pointed towards the southern entrance to the Straits. We must suck them in to destruction. And to an overweeningly confident enemy, as the Spartans had proved in that first day at Thermopylae, there is nothing more alluring than apparent flight. For the last time Themistocles went over the details.

21

We went outside into the greyness of early dawn, and then each commander went to his squadron; Adeimantos and the Corinthian ships were to hold a detached position towards the northern end of the narrows, the Megarians and Aeginetans the right of the line, the Athenians and the Spartans the left. But first each commander spoke to his own men, briefly, for there was not much time now. Themistocles said that we Athenians had a greater incentive to fight to conquer than any others in the fleet; we had seen the Acropolis alive with flames, our temples and sanctuaries desecrated. We had seen all Attica under a pall of smoke as the enemy fired our houses and fields. And those of us who did not have women and children praying and waiting, watching us here on Salamis, had them waiting and praying for us in Troezen or Aegina. We alone, and our ships, stood between them and worse than death at barbarian hands. He quoted what Tyrrhastiadas had said to me once, which I had related to him – and which he had never forgotten. 'Do you wish to curse the gods because your wife or daughter or little son has beauty?'

'Cleisidice,' I thought. 'My dear one. Maiden of Athens, protect my Cleisidice. I've never given her one word of endearment –'

'Men of Athens! The barbarian king has set up his throne overlooking the straits to encourage his hordes to attack us with more fierceness than they've ever shown before! Men of Athens, with our wives and children watching us here from Salamis, with our gods watching us from their desecrated temples, shall we not fight as no men have ever fought in the whole history of this world?'

There was a great shout in reply.

'Go quickly,' said Themistocles. 'They've profaned our land too long.'

The rowers got the ships afloat, took their places. The marines embarked. No one talked more than was necessary, but it was not the silence of fear. If we were to make a speedy end of the barbarians, we needed to keep our breath for essential business. We rowed gently to the places assigned to us.

I was no longer thinking of Cleisidice. I was thinking of defiled bodies in a muddy pass, a head struck off and impaled on a post. I thought of a faceless crying thing that had taken so long to die outside the gate in Sardis. Dear gods, let these — and countless like them — be avenged today. Dear gods, prevent our beloved land from becoming a permanent setting for such obscene horrors.

The dawn haze was beginning to lift. Within minutes the sky was like an opal. To the east the sun was coming up; the mountain crests were tipped with it. The air was still morning-fresh. The sea was like glass except where it shivered under the rhythmic beat of the oars.

And you could hear the thunder of your heart!

Suck them in. Stream away to the north, to Eleusis, as if in abject panic.

Watch for the breeze —

Cleisidice, can you hear my heart beating? Cleisidice, never one word of endearment. You know I'd even forgotten your name —

'Time to go, comrade.'

Now, comrade, it's the time to stand and fight and finish them. Friend of my soul, pray God I don't let you down. *'Athens needs her captains,'* you said. I have forgotten nothing, you see.

'One day you may marry and have a son, and you will tell him —'

Yes, one day I will, please God, but today —

The sun was higher, the surface of the sea splintered into flying silver under the beat of thousand upon thousand of oars, oars driving forward ships attempting to fly in disorder, confusion —

'This is the most difficult part of it all,' Themistocles had said. *'Only expert crews can make it look convincing enough.'*

Convincing enough for the monarch sitting on his gold and ivory throne to think, 'They're running for the Megara Channel — which they don't know is blocked!'

When would he leap from his throne shrieking, 'We've got them'? I thought that moment would come when he saw Adeimantos' squadron hoisting sail — sure indication of flight.

What was the etiquette for the phalanx of servile courtiers when the monarch went hysterical with glee?

And, more important, how long would the royal order to move in to the kill take to pass down the Persian line of command?

Wait for the breeze.

Wait for the trumpets.

Cleisidice. Once I had forgotten your name.

Suck them in.

Wait for the breeze — that southern breeze so well known to us that we could foretell its coming from the clouds, the morning breeze that even now should be raising a swell out at sea that would soon come up the Straits, breaking up the waves, throwing them back on each other from the opposing coasts, broken water, the last straw for a great fleet trying to reform its front after crowding into the narrows, crowding in so fast on each other's heels that there would be no chance of an organised withdrawal. But withdrawal was the last thing they were contemplating; they were chasing a beaten, fleeing enemy.

Was that a breath of wind in my face?

You sent me away because you said Athens needed expert captains. Let me justify my leaving you now!

There they are*!*

Back, lads, back! Suck 'em in!

Our own Athenian line was sagging, wavering beautifully, beaten before we had even started to fight.

Suck 'em in! Further in!

Back, lads!

'They're coming, captain?' from one of the rowers.

'In a hell of a mess already – ships out of line, supports pressing forward – twenty in a line – they've brought the boat poles out to stop fouling each other – they'll never keep their prows towards us!'

Yes, it was wind on my cheek, strong, sharp – and the ripples in the sea surrounding them were more than the ripples made by their oars – it was a choppy sea, they were beginning to roll already –

Let me justify my leaving you now!

Trumpets.

And, at that signal, in every ship we began to sing.

We sang the paean, *O, Saving Lord*. I can never adequately describe that moment. Aeschylus did, years later:

> '. . . then was borne
> A sound across the sea, a voice, a strong
> Clamour exultant like a leaping song,
> And Echo answering from the island rock
> Cried battle.'

I only knew that when I heard, clear in the morning air, that sudden singing, that great burst of voices in song, strong voices exultant in the assurance of victory, tears ran down my face, even as I sang too, and laughed. I could not weep after Thermopylae, but I wept before Salamis. And I was not the only one.

To the end of my life, when I feel that south wind on my face in the morning, I shall feel also those tears of gladness wet on my cheek, and I shall hear those exultant voices.

One of the first casualties of the battle must have been Xerxes' complacency. When he heard that singing, even before he saw us abandon the pretence at flight and re-deploy he must have realised he had been completely fooled. But, being Xerxes, it would take longer for him to realise that he was being as completely beaten.

Realisation would have come much more quickly to the captains of his ships. Nothing can be more shocking than the discovery that a runaway – and therefore defeated – enemy is suddenly launching into a furious attack, bearing down on you, great bronze rams gleaming. You are utterly unprepared for it in every way.

We had Phoenicians opposite us – high decks, stern-castles, crowded with archers and marines, thirty to our eighteen. Pressing forward into that narrowing space, they had been forced to contract their line, which would have led to confusion in any case. Then with the swelling sea they began to roll. Their high superstructures, the number of men they carried, made them yaw wildly. Even before our trumpets sounded, they were in difficulties because of the confined space, the choppy seas, fouling each other, swinging broadside to us.

('You bastards,' I thought, 'nothing like jostling together to get to the fun, is there? *Did you jostle in the same haste to get across those straits to see the dead at Thermopylae?*')

Then our trumpets sounded, and we swung over into the attack, singing. No wavering in our line now. And their first ships, on seeing it, checked. But the support vessels behind them, not knowing what had happened, rowing hard to get into the action, did not check in time, and crashed into their rear.

It was into this utter confusion that we charged. People told me later I was shouting, 'Boys, we've sucked 'em in. Now all we have to do is chew 'em up and spit 'em out!' I don't remember this. I went first for a monster of a ship rolling broadside on, perfect position for a ramming attack, struck her square amidships, in a glorious splintering crash, then drove on at the vessel just astern of her, sliced off her oarbanks.

Other sounds began to mingle with the noise of our cheering, our exultant shouting. The noise of the enemy. Screams of fear – unmistakable. Curses – equally unmistakable. Desperate cries that may have been prayers to the gods who had betrayed and forsaken them. And then, with the destruction of enemy ships, another sound, scarcely human, more like the bleating of terrified goats. The cries of the drowning seemed almost to grow as the strength of the criers weakened. But even the most shrill and desperate calls had to end eventually in coughing, retching, in the vain attempt to rid lungs of the salt water that was choking them, and, after that, silence.

And over us, all the while, great flocks of sea-birds wheeling and shrieking.

Archers from more than one ship shot at us so that we achieved a kind of plumage of arrows; two of our marines were wounded, but not seriously, and the rowers, of course, were well below the line of the deck, so completely protected. Twice a sinking enemy tried to board us, leaping from their higher, tilting decks on to ours. The first incident was over quickly, only a dozen sprang aboard, and we used our spears to deal with them, running them through and tossing them overboard as if we were pitch-forking hay in a field.

The second boarding attempt was different; it seemed as if their full complement of marines was hurtling down on us, headed by a swarthy, hooknosed fellow I recognised. I had seen him in Sardis. He was one of Xerxes' kinsmen; I had seen him at the gate of Sardis, laughing at the thing that lay there. He came running at me screeching and waving a scimitar, and just before we met, a grinding crash as our ram slammed into the vessel next to his caught me for the moment off balance, fumbl-ing for my sword. His own whistled over my head like a scythe. But he didn't manage to lop it off, for I dodged in time, and the next blow, that would have taken my left arm off if it had connected, only ploughed a gash down the flesh of the upper part. Then my sword was out, and I was at him. He was scream-ing curses at me; I launched a stroke that cut him on the thigh, and whispered 'For you, whose name I don't know', as I grazed his head, and then, streaming with blood and almost, but not quite, blinded with sweat, I lunged forward with all my strength. 'A slave for you, Leonidas,' I said, and drove my sword clean through him. A scream, and he was lying glassy-eyed but quite dead at my feet. Luckier than his source of entertainment in Sardis. I pulled out my sword, kicked him overboard, turned to deal with the next one. My left arm was useless, but the sickness and giddiness didn't hit me until we'd cleared our deck of them. They bobbed butting against the sides of the galley as if they were still trying to board her.

It was odd, that encounter. In the brief moments when it was taking place, I had been quite deaf to the other noises surrounding us – the shouts, the crashing of masts and spars, the gigantic thuds as ship hit ship. The only sounds were our voices, the whistling of our breath, the clang when our swords met. Hatred in its way can encapsulate two people, isolating them, as much as love can do.

They had been trying to back off for some time, and now they were beginning to break and run for it, turning armoured prows on each other in the mad haste to get away, smashing the oar-banks of the vessels next to them, charging the vessels astern of them as if they, not we, were the enemy, ploughing wildly through floating spars, cordage, men drowned, men drowning, rending crashes, rending screams, bloodied sea – the spray that flew up from our oars was red, it settled on the decks like crimson dew. And they went on trying to tear, to gore their way through like frenzied beasts in stampede. Some of their own vessels that barred the way they rammed, others they forced ashore. And we hunted them through the narrows.

To the enemy dead already piled thick along the reefs and beaches, floating in the sea, Xerxes added his own contribution. The Phoenician support vessels on their right had been forced aground by their own fleeing front line. Some of the crews had managed to struggle ashore, but did not survive for long. The right should have been the safe shore for them, Persian held – unlike the shore to the left of their line where any enemy who crawled up on the beach was soon despatched by those Greeks awaiting them. But the Phoenician survivors, by Xerxes' order, were immediately beheaded for cowardice.

It was hot, God knew how many hours had passed, my mouth was parched, my eyes smarted from the sun and sea water, someone had roughly tied up my left arm, hanging useless at my side.

266

The seaworthy Phoenician vessels had clawed their way out of the narrows; the enemy ships in the centre, dismayed at the rout of the best squadrons in the Persian fleet, faltered; trumpets sounded from Themistocles' flagship calling us back from the pursuit of the flying enemy. He had trained us so that our galleys could spin round almost within their own lengths. We halted, on one side the rowers back-watered, on the other they pulled their hardest, we were round, launching into fresh furious attack on the rear of the enemies still stubbornly resisting. Behind us the fleeing enemy ships were hoisting sail; a western breeze had sprung up to help them in their flight, but from the look of many of them, they would not get far.

Back into the attack, the same old story of close in and crush, but the details becoming more and more blurred as the blood trickled down through my fingers. All that kept me on my feet was the smarting of the sea water caked on my arm. Vessels still locked together, but fewer now, wreckage of ships and their crews clogging the straits more and more so that it was hard to advance, and the rowers, after hours of fighting, almost fainting at their oars.

And then the last resistance broke. I have seen a stream in spate in spring bringing down branches of trees, soil, stones, other débris, building up a dam against itself. Our attack had been like this. We had forced the foremost ships back and back, crushing them up against their rear until finally the pressure became irresistible, and the great mass of ships broke, disintegrating into as much wild, swirling chaos as the shattered hillside dam had done. And it was every man for himself. Each enemy captain was ready to sink any allied vessel that seemed to hinder his own break for safety.

Nothing but the chase now for us. No more fighting. I was wet through, right down my left side, not so much from sea water as blood. No more fighting. I began to slide down on to the deck. I was slipping in my own blood. I was a revolting mess. No more fighting — for a little while.

They had put in briefly to carry me ashore, then had carried on with the chase. I came to myself lying among black rocks at no great distance from the shallows, where swarthy bodies rolled in and out as the waves swirled them idly to and fro. The water was veined with bloodstains growing thinner. The arm of one dead thing was stretched out vainly to the land, a dark, limp hand that, when a sudden surge of water bore it up, seemed to have life in it, clutching at the land in menace or despair. But then a strong eddy carried it away from the shore, into deeper and deeper water until it was only a shadow without shape, and then nothing.

I was glad of that. I had been afraid to slip back into unconsciousness while that dead hand seemed to threaten.

I was roused later by the sound of voices.

'A pity.'

'Yes, he did well —'

'If there had been more like him, there would have been more of us alive now.'

They were placing someone beside me. The sun was beginning to set; that was why his face seemed less bloodless than it must have been. Tyrrhastiadas. Dead. Tyrrhastiadas, who had steadied my elbow when I was taken before Xerxes, Tyrrhastiadas, who had come over to us in the dreadful dawn before Thermopylae, dead in the glorious sunset of Salamis. I reached feebly out with my good hand and took his as if I in my turn might help him on the journey on which he had now embarked.

'Are they finished?' I whispered to the men bending over me.

'Finished,' one of them replied. 'Those still afloat have made for Phaleron, where their army can protect 'em, but they can't stay there for long. They'll start running again soon enough. So will Xerxes. Can you hang on?'

I nodded, went on grasping Tyrrhastiadas' hand as if by touch I could inform his spirit that what remained of the enemy ships would be limping back to the Ionian ports they had left so vaingloriously in the spring, sails stained, faded, timbers fouled, crews in worse shape than the vessels. 'Comrade, we've won, comrade, it's only the beginning — we've saved ourselves, but we must go on to free Ionia —' While I remained conscious, I went on talking to him.

It was quite dark when I opened my eyes again; already the stars were growing bright. I lay with my head in someone's lap. Warm tears splashed down on my face.

'Cleisidice?'

She bent to press her lips to my cheek.

'I shan't die.'

She put her own cheek to mine, and her arms about me.

'I can't talk much now — but I shan't die. If you could see my face, you would see me smiling at you.'

Smiling with happiness, and also remembering an old story. There had once been a man, a wanderer, who had been told that he would find his home where rain fell from a clear sky. One day when he was in despair his wife took him into her arms, and wept. Her name was Aethra* — and so rain fell from a clear sky, and he had found his home. I tried to tell her this.

'I'm home,' I said, feeling her heart beating beneath my cheek. And for the first time I used a term of endearment to her. 'Cleisidice, my darling, I'm home.'

* Literally 'Bright sky'.

BOOKS FOR FURTHER READING

Edited by Higham, T. F., and Bowra, C. M., *The Oxford Book of Greek Verse in Translation* (Oxford University Press 1938)

Aeschylus, translated by Gilbert Murray, *The Persians* (Allen and Unwin, London 1939)

The Seven against Thebes (Allen & Unwin, London 1935)

The Suppliant Women (Allen & Unwin, London 1930)

Herodotus, translated by Aubrey de Selincourt, *The Histories* (Penguin Books, Harmondsworth 1971)

Burn, A. R., *Persia and the Greeks* (Edward Arnold, London 1962)

Casson, Lionel, *Ancient Mariners* (Victor Gollancz, London 1959)

Green, Peter, *The Year of Salamis* (Weidenfeld & Nicholson, London 1970)

Hignett, C., *Xerxes' Invasion of Greece* (Oxford University Press 1963)

Olmstead, Albert Ten Eyck, *History of the Persian Empire* (University of Chicago Press 1948)